Also by Carlo Gébler

Caught on a Train

Frozen Out

For younger readers

The Base

CARLO GÉBLER

August '44

EGMONT

First published in Great Britain 2003
by Egmont Books Limited
239 Kensington High Street
London W8 6SA

Text copyright © 2003 Carlo Gébler
Cover illustration © 2003 Oliver Burstyn

Quotation from Franz Kafka's letter to Oskar Pollack, January
1904, by kind permission of Calder Publications Ltd

The moral rights of the author and illustrator
have been asserted

ISBN 1 4052 0237 8

10 9 8 7 6 5 4 3 2 1

A CIP catalogue record for this title
is available from the British Library

Typeset by Avon DataSet Ltd, Bidford on Avon, B50 4JH

Printed and bound in Great Britain
by the CPI Group

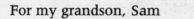
For my grandson, Sam

Acknowledgements

I gratefully acknowledge the financial support of the Arts Council/An Chomhairle Ealaíon during the writing of this novel.

John O'Farrell and Robert McLiam Wilson generously provided me with numerous works on Judaism and the history of the Jews during World War II. These books were enormously helpful. I would also like to thank my editor, Miriam Hodgson. All mistakes and errors are my own.

Carlo Gébler

A book must be the axe for the frozen sea within us.

Franz Kafka

Passover: *a commemoration of the Exodus of the children of Israel from Egypt where they were held as slaves. The eating of unleavened bread is a reminder of the fact that the Jews had to leave so quickly that there was no time for the yeast to rise. Passover is a celebration of freedom. It takes place in spring. The fesitval is eight days long, with a celebratory feast in the family home on the first two nights, to which the lonely and homeless are always invited.*

Hodgson Dictionary of Religious Belief

Contents

1

The storehouse

His spear was where he had left it, leaning against a tree. He had found the shaft in the woods, some weeks before, when he was looking for kindling. It was perfectly straight, half as tall again as he was, with the added bonus of natural 'Y' at the thicker end that would be perfect for catching snakes.

He had stripped off the bark and burnt the thin end in the fire. Then he rubbed this on a rough patch in the cave for hours until it was sharp. For the handgrip he had acquired a strip of old sheet and tied this carefully round the middle.

Saul felt the familiar thrill as he grasped his spear. He up-ended it and began to dig into the forest floor with the pointed end. As he worked he noticed some ants scurrying across the mouldering pine needles that covered the earth like a carpet. He put his spear aside, crouched, swept several of the insects into the hole, crumbled some earth over them and then sat back on his haunches. At first nothing happened. He wondered whether the ants were dead. Then, after a just perceptible trembling on the surface, the first ant broke through. Several more followed.

He emptied the hole out again – deeper than the first time – swept the ants in again, and covered them over. He wanted to discover what depth of earth was too deep for the ants to crawl through.

He was on his sixth go when he heard a faint noise. Was it Germans? No, it was only one person moving alone from the direction of the cave.

Noiselessly, Saul turned and squinted through the murk. In the distance he registered a blur. It was his sister Nelly. Her dress was red, or it had been. Repeated washing and sunshine had drained it of much of its colour. He'd have recognised it anywhere.

As he watched his sister he remembered she had been out earlier that morning on a mushroom hunt. She had gone with Claude, Hugo Lippman his mother's brother, Ida Lippman his aunt, and the Lippmans' surviving son, Leon. They must all be back at the cave now, he guessed, so why had his sister come out again?

Nelly was moving away. Saul decided to follow. He picked up his spear and moved forward. Perhaps she had a secret cache of food hidden somewhere in the forest? He wouldn't put it past her.

After a few hundred metres, she changed direction

abruptly and struck out towards the road. Saul's stomach fluttered and his thighs trembled. No one went near the road. He was forbidden to go there. So was she. Everyone in the cave was. That was the rule.

Should he turn back? But that would mean breaking the other rule, the one that forbade abandoning another member if they were in trouble. Nelly wasn't in trouble but she could be quite soon.

He could of course shout out and call her back. But then she would know he'd been watching her. She would be angry. Later, she would make his life miserable.

After thinking for a couple more seconds, he decided that the best thing was to follow her. If something happened at the road he could help her. If nothing happened she would return to the cave but she would not know he had been behind her. And she would never know because he would never let on.

Nelly stopped. Saul crouched and moved forward until he could just make out the blue-black road beyond the final trees.

His sister looked down at the front of her dress. She brushed it clean with her fingers in a series of quick, careful movements. Then she untied the grimy twine that held her hair in a ponytail. Holding the piece of string between her teeth, she shook her hair loose, re-gathered and then re-tied it.

She licked the ends of both forefingers and wet her eyebrows. Nelly had the same big bushy eyebrows as their father, Al. She dampened them down like this to make them less conspicuous. Saul, unlike his sister, had his mother's thin and tidy ones. They were like two arching lines at the bottom of his forehead. As Nelly endlessly complained, she had the wrong eyebrows for an actress while her brother had the right ones. It was yet one more example, she claimed, of the dreadful unfairness of life.

Nelly was listening now. Saul listened along with her. He heard the wind in the boughs of the pines above, a single soft note. The noise always made him feel sad if he listened to it for too long or too carefully. There was also birdsong somewhere but that was far away. There was certainly no engine sound, or tyre rumble, or German voices.

His sister slipped through the last trees, and walked carefully to the edge of the road. She stopped.

Saul half-rose and ran a few feet further. He could see her and some of the road as it ran away into the distance.

She looked first to her right and then to her left.

Saul's legs trembled again. To come this far was bad

enough, but then to cross over – that was more dreadful still.

Suddenly, Nelly darted forward. The road was dark blue in colour and her shadow sliding over it was black. Saul's mouth went dry.

He went right to the edge of the forest and stopped. There was a verge on the other side, and on the verge stood a building.

It was a long low structure made of yellow stone and roofed with a mix of red terracotta tiles and tin cans, beaten and flattened into the same shape as tiles. The stone front was unbroken except for an open door at the right-hand end.

To Saul's astonishment, Nelly now darted in through here. The door closed behind her with a bang.

Everything was still. Saul raised his eyes to the olive trees growing behind. They were laid out in rows that ran into the distance. Their trunks looked as if they were made out of frayed ropes compressed together, and their leaves, though they were green, gave an impression as they fluttered in the sunshine, of silver. Saul guessed the olive gatherers used the building to store their olives, and during the harvest probably lived there.

Suddenly, he heard two bursts of laughter coming from the storehouse. It was, he realised after a moment or two, Leon Lippman's laugh. His cousin Leon – or so his mother had assured him – loved Nelly and she loved him back. Saul had never understood what Leon saw in Nelly.

At that moment Saul remembered the caterpillar in his pocket. He leant his spear against the tree, the last in the forest, and fished the caterpillar out. He laid it carefully on the little finger-thick branch that jutted straight out of the tree closest to him. Without hesitation the caterpillar formed a 'U', flattened itself, and made another 'U' as it moved off with a sense of purpose.

Now he knew Nelly had come to meet Leon, he no longer felt fearful. He was annoyed rather, with Leon of course, but mostly with Nelly.

Rules were rules. He obeyed them, so Nelly and Leon should obey them. For a moment he considered telling his father about Nelly and his Uncle Hugo about his son Leon. If his father got angry enough he might beat Nelly. Now there was a thought. The trouble was, Nelly would never forgive him for telling, and was that worth it? He decided it wasn't.

He looked at the branch on which he had set his caterpillar. The creature was gone. He scanned the trunk and then the dusty ground around his feet. A couple of pine roots stuck up out of the earth. He moved a couple of steps forward on to the verge and looked about. Nothing moved between the dry stalks of grass sticking out of the hard ground. The caterpillar really had vanished.

A rumble sounded like the noise an engine made. He started and looked up. He saw a lorry hurtling towards him. He saw the driver behind the windscreen, his hands gripping the steering wheel. He wore a blue-grey uniform. The driver was a German soldier.

Saul dropped to his belly. The verge was dry and hard and the grass that grew out of it was hard and coarse. It scratched his bare knees, his chin and his face. The taste in his mouth was part pine, part earth.

Had the driver seen him? The noise made by the lorry's engine, as it rolled down the road towards him, was constant. It wasn't braking. It wasn't stopping. It was also loud. Loud meant Leon and Nelly would hear it in the storehouse. They would stay in there, wouldn't they?

He slid back. He decided to retreat into the forest and run as fast as he could. And in case the driver decided to stop and have a look, he would not stop until he got to the cave.

Slithering off the sun baked verge and into the forest he felt the temperature change from warm to cold, and the ground from dry and dusty to damp and musty. He went on going backwards until at last he judged it was safe to stand. Then he sprang to his feet, turned and sprinted off, twisting his body around tree trunks and ducking under low branches as he fled.

As he ran he listened. Were the Germans in pursuit?

There was a hollow in front of him. He jumped over the lip and landed inside on the soft bed of pine rubbish that had collected inside over the years. He folded his knees and sank to his haunches.

He froze. Was there any sound behind? His breathing was so loud he couldn't hear anything. He swallowed a great mouthful of breath and closed his lips. He felt his heart pushing against his ribs. He heard no sound behind.

He turned and lifted his head over the lip. He squinted along the forest floor. Nothing stirred between the trees rising like bars all around him. He had not been seen. He had not been followed.

He felt his breath slowing. He must go to the cave now. He must get back before Nelly and Leon. But he must not arrive looking hot or out of breath. The grown-ups would only ask what had happened and why was he running? He could not tell anyone a German driver saw him.

Saul set off for the cave. He was filled with a vague

sense of dread. He was a bad dissembler and his father always seemed to know when he wasn't being truthful. What if his father interrogated him? It was this dreadful thought, Saul assumed, that explained why he felt as he did.

However, when he got to the rock they had named the Cube which was close to their cave, he realised what was really wrong. He'd gone and left his beloved spear by the road, hadn't he?

His throat went sore – it always did before he cried. Though he could hear the sound of the grown-ups talking inside the cave he couldn't see them. Nor could they see him. He spun round on the spot, rushed back into the forest and went straight to the small dusty hole where he always ran when he was morose or troubled. It lay in the middle of three trees that had tumbled one on top of the other.

He got into the hole, sunk right down so he could not be seen and began to cry. His tears were hot and salty. He wanted to hit himself he was so angry. What an idiot he had been. He had left his treasure behind and now he dare not go back for it. To do so was unsafe, it was against the rules and he might meet his sister and his cousin. How could he have been such a fool?

Later, he stopped crying. He remained curled up in his hole, nursing his grief. At some point he fell asleep.

2
The spear

Saul woke later and lay quite still. There was a strong smell of earth, mixed with pine. His sadness was still there inside but he wasn't filled up by it like he was before. There was room for him to think now.

His spear was gone. He could not go back for it. But he was bound to find another good strong length somewhere else. He would start looking the very next day.

As soon as he made this decision the raw feeling in his throat went away. The hot feeling in his eyes went away too. The grief was leaving him. He would soon have another spear as good as if not better than his first.

'Saul,' a voice called. He sat up and peered through the trees. He had not noticed dusk had fallen.

'Saul, come on.' It was Nelly.

He climbed out of the hole and brushed away the needles stuck to him. He smelt strongly of pine and earth.

'Saul, this is the last time, come on . . .'

'Coming,' he bellowed.

He set off at a gentle trot and followed the track through the forest. He reached the Cube rock and darted round the side, heading for the back where he knew Nelly would be. This was where they always cooked. With the Cube rock shielding them, the fire would not be seen if anyone did come into the forest at night. They never lit a fire in the day in case the smoke was spotted.

As he came around the back he saw it at once. There was his spear, standing against the stone. He felt an incredible surge of joy. It had come back to him.

Nelly was squatting on the ground, throwing wood on to the fire that was crackling inside a circle of stones. He darted forward, ducking around her.

'Saul,' said Nelly, as he passed behind her, 'where have you been?'

He ignored her and reached for his spear. He raised it up over his head in triumph.

'Saul,' he heard again.

He imitated the act of throwing and, as always, got excited. He wondered how far it could go? He'd never tried it in the forest of course. There were too many trees in the way. But as soon as he got home to Nice then he would try.

'Will you put that stupid stick down?' Nelly was now standing in front of him.

'It's not a stick, it's a spear.'

'It looks like a stick to me.'

'No, it isn't.' He was outraged. 'It's a proper weapon. Look at that!' Saul pointed at the blackened tip. 'And that.' He indicated the grubby handgrip. 'And that.' He pointed at the 'Y' at the bottom of the shaft.

'What's that for?'

'Catching snakes.'

'And have you caught any yet?'

'No, but I will.' Why did she doubt him?

'And once you've caught the snake,' she said in the slow voice she used to mean Saul was stupid, 'how are you going to kill it if the point's at the other end?'

'I don't want to kill the snakes.'

'What!'

'No, I just want to catch them.'

'And what will you do with them then?' Nelly asked.

'I'll keep them as pets.'

'Really. Snakes are poisonous – they have a nasty bite – or perhaps you don't know that?'

Saul knew this but he presumed that if you looked after a snake properly it wouldn't bite you. He considered how to explain this but Nelly interrupted before he got the words out.

'Go and get some wood,' she said. 'We've not enough.'

'No,' he said, 'why should I? I won't.'

Nelly lowered her face until it was level with his.

'If you don't, I'm going to tell.'

He looked back into her eyes. They were brown and dark. What was she talking about?

'If you don't do exactly what I tell you to do from now on when I tell you to do it, I'm going to tell. I was out looking for mushrooms this afternoon. I was near the road, wrong of me I know, but I hadn't quite realised where I was, when I saw your spear, leaning against a tree. But Saul was not with his precious spear. And why was that? Because he had crossed the road, hadn't he? He was walking through the olive grove on the other side.'

Saul opened his mouth to speak but he found what he was hearing so shocking no words would come.

'I called after you Saul, didn't I, when I saw you, but you wouldn't come back, would you? You disobeyed our number one rule. You crossed the road and in so doing, you almost gave yourself and everyone else away to the Germans. You can imagine what Father will make of that when I tell him.'

Saul knew Father would believe Nelly and not him.

'Now do as I said, go and get some wood.'

As Saul turned towards the forest she grabbed his shoulder.

'And leave your stick.'

'It's a spear,' said Saul, gently.

'All right, your spear. That way you'll have two hands free to carry. And just remember. If you don't want me to tell, you just do as I say from now on.'

Saul leant the spear against the back of the Cube rock and set off. It was quite dark in the forest away from the fire. Saul was used to it. He could see as well as if there was light. He began to gather sticks. He could only think about the conversation he'd just had. How could he think about anything else? Nelly had lied and her lie, he knew, would win over his truth. It was like water was wet. It was a fact of life.

He worked until it was quite dark. He picked up his pile of sticks. He felt clear-headed. He was in the right, and Nelly was in the wrong. But he would have to be very careful from now on.

He retraced his steps from the forest to the site of their camp. He saw the Cube rock ahead of him. Some metres behind, where the trees finally stopped, loomed the cliff that rose into the air. At the bottom of the cliff was the mouth of the cave where they all slept. At this distance the cave mouth was like a vast piece of black felt tacked to the bottom of a grey stone curtain. He couldn't see any of the rough beds or hammocks they'd improvised over the months they'd lived there. These were hidden in darkness. In the sky above there were now a few stars glimmering. There was no moon.

He moved on. Behind the Cube he heard Uncle Hugo and Leon, as well as Nelly.

He rounded the rock. The fire was burning fiercely. An animal was cooking over the flame with a stick running through its middle. The ends rested in the 'Y's of two uprights.

'There's your wood, Nelly,' said Saul.

He dumped the lot on the ground, almost on his sister's feet.

'Watch it, Saul,' she said.

'Oh hello, Saul,' said Hugo.

'What's that?' Saul asked, pointing at the carcass.

'It's rabbit,' said his cousin Leon. He was nineteen years old. He had black eyes and a heart-shaped face and black curly hair. He was polite and boring. Saul had no idea what Nelly saw in him.

'I think you mean, old rabbit.' This was Uncle Hugo. He was a short man, with red hair and small bright blue eyes. His manner was rough and his temper was fierce. His sister, who was Saul's mother, was his complete opposite. Not only was she slim and delicate, not only was her hair black, not only were her eyes grey, but despite all that had happened she was never coarse or abrasive. Saul did not understand how brother and sister could be so different.

Hugo was married to Ida – another total contrast to Uncle Hugo. She was a tall, willowy woman with an extremely long face. When she brooded – as she often did on account of all that had happened – she would turn her lips inwards until they completely disappeared. Of all Ida's idiosyncrasies, this was the one that had made the greatest impression on Saul.

In Nice, before the war, Saul's family, the Roths, and the Lippmans had lived two streets apart. They were in each other's houses endlessly. Saul's older brothers, Robert and Francis, were close friends with the oldest of the Lippman children, Marcel. He was strong and athletic, physically courageous and over-confident. In the spring of 1942 he went to Aix to buy spark plugs on the black market to sell in Nice. While waiting to catch the train home, a fight broke out between some of the other passengers on the platform. The police were called. They rounded up all the young men on the platform and took them back to the station. Here, Marcel's papers were checked. They were found to be false. The police shipped him north to the occupied zone. The Germans checked back to Nice. Marcel, they discovered, was a Jew. He was put on a transport and sent to a camp in Poland. He was never heard of again.

A month later, Marcel's younger sister, Rozette, who was Nelly's friend, was hit by a lorry in the street. One leg was crushed badly. In hospital her wounds turned septic. The doctors said her leg must be cut off. She died on the operating table. After Rozette's death, Ida retired to her bed. It was Hugo who got her back on her feet but it took several months of hard bullying on his part to achieve this.

'That rabbit is old,' Saul heard his uncle say. 'Has to be. How else do you think I managed to get him, or her, if it wasn't old?'

'And which do you think it is?' asked Leon.

Typical, thought Saul, all Leon ever did was ask pointless, stupid questions. It really was a mystery what his sister saw in him.

'Oh, it must be female,' Hugo said. 'I can't imagine a male would be so stupid as to let a fool like me kill it. Saul, do you want to hear how your uncle got your dinner?'

Saul recognised his uncle's tone. If Hugo failed to get an audience, and if that audience failed to listen, then he would either sulk or turn nasty.

Saul turned and looked at his uncle. All Saul could make out was his square jaw and the tight curls.

'Having just had a most successful mushroom gathering session,' he began, 'I went back out to the forest. I was walking along, minding my own business, when I came upon madam here,' – Uncle Hugo waved at the carcass – 'doing some rabbit thing, ears twitching, white rear waggling, and completely oblivious that I was behind.

'I thought, hello, supper. I had the sack with me – for berries. I also had a stick I'd picked up for no particular reason. It was good and heavy, the sort of thing a brigand might have used to knock out the brains of an eighteenth-century traveller.

'I slipped off my shoes and crept up behind Mrs Rabbit. I sensed that she sensed me. She went all still and coy. Perhaps she hoped I was Mr Rabbit come to pay court. How wrong she was. When I got close enough, I threw the sack over her and then flung my cudgel forward. It caught Mrs Rabbit, and knocked her sideways.

'I sprang forward. For an old fellow I can move like lightning when food's involved. I got the cudgel up – thwack, thwack, thwack – I hit her through the sack and as suddenly as this little drama had started, it was over. And hey presto! Hugo the magician had produced a dead rabbit.'

He paused.

'Of course, if a magician had done that on any of my stages it would have been his last appearance.'

Hugo had owned a couple of burlesque theatres before the war. After the Italian army occupied Nice, he sold them. He did not have to. The Italians tolerated Jews, as their German allies did not. But he knew it was the best thing to do. A theatre owner attracted attention. For a Jew, that was fatal. Four years later he still missed his theatres badly. He particularly missed telling people what to do.

Saul waited. But surprisingly his uncle didn't say any more. Saul turned to retrieve his spear. To his surprise it wasn't there.

'Where's my spear?' he asked.

'What?' This was Nelly. Her tone was deliberately vague.

'My spear,' said Saul, sharply, 'my spear. I left my spear here.'

'What are you going on about now?' Uncle Hugo muttered humourously.

'Where's my spear?' he shouted.

'I usually don't talk to shouters,' said Nelly, in her irritating, reasonable voice, 'but I suppose for you I can make an exception.' She sighed. 'Don't worry. It'll come back to you when I've finished and it won't be the worse for wear.'

Saul turned and looked down at the fire. The spit that ran through the rabbit's middle was his spear.

'What have you done?' he wailed.

'Oh stop, you'll get your stick back.'

'You've ruined it,' shouted Saul. He felt a fantastic rage rising inside. 'And it's mine, my spear, not yours. I made it. It's not yours to use when you want.'

'Oh, shut up,' said Nelly. She spoke in a slow languid voice to make him angrier still.

'You took my spear. And you didn't ask.'

As he waited for Nelly to react, he was dimly aware of his mother, Mina, calling, 'Why are you shouting, Saul?' He could hear hurrying feet as well. That would be the others, his father Al, Aunt Ida, Agatha and Claude. They were rushing out of the cave to see what was happening. That was the trouble with this kind of life. There was no privacy. If any of them argued, everyone else got involved.

Soon they would all be around him. They would try to soothe him. They would tell him to curb his temper and to mind his words. What did any of them know? He had the right to be angry. Nelly had done a vile, horrible thing. His spear was covered in blood and rabbit guts and blackened by the flames. Well, he'd show her.

He wrenched the spear from the two supports, moved away from the fire and swung it violently in a wide circle.

'Saul,' his uncle shouted.

The rabbit, as Saul intended by his action, slid up the shaft and flew off the end. He was aiming for Nelly but she dodged sideways. The rabbit shot past her and flew on. There was a thump and scream. Someone fell to the ground.

'What happened?' Hugo cried out.

'Agatha's been hit,' Claude called back.

Hugo turned to Saul. 'Stupid boy,' he shouted. 'You've hit Agatha.'

'And she's having a baby,' Nelly hissed at his side. 'You spoilt little brat.'

'Is she all right?' Hugo called.

'Yes, she's all right,' Claude called back.

'What hit her?' added Saul's father, Al, from the circle that had formed around Agatha.

'It's stupid Saul,' Nelly called back. 'He's in a rage.'

'I'm not in a rage!' Saul shouted. His voice was starting to crack. From a faraway part of his mind came a voice. Stop this, it said. By going on he would only make a bad situation worse. But he knew he would rage on. He knew he would deeply regret it too. But he was so angry he would go on to the bitter, bitter end.

'He flung the rabbit we're cooking,' said Hugo.

'He what?' Al called back.

'He threw the half-cooked rabbit at you all,' Nelly shouted.

'I didn't, Nelly! I didn't throw it at them, and you know that,' he screamed at his sister. It was Nelly he'd hoped to hurt. He hadn't meant to hit Agatha. It had all gone terribly wrong. Suddenly, he realised he must have hit Agatha very hard. An appalled feeling flooded him. Then he remembered something from that morning . . .

Agatha was sitting on the ground. He was nearby. The basket with their day's provisions was on her lap. Henri lowered it every day from the gendarmerie at the top of the cliff. Behind Agatha stretched the cave and inside he could just make out one or two of the sacks filled with pine needles that they all slept on. Claude said their cave was like the one in the novel *Robinson Crusoe*. As Saul had not read it, he had no idea what Claude meant.

'Hello, Saul,' Agatha called cheerfully.

Saul didn't exactly dislike this heavily pregnant English woman, but he didn't like her much either. He certainly didn't feel like engaging with her now. He wanted to run off and play in the forest. But if he was rude, and if his father, who might be lurking out of sight inside the cave, overheard, Saul would be in trouble. His father didn't tolerate rudeness. He needed to be careful, Saul thought. He mustn't put a foot wrong.

'Hello, Agatha,' he replied cautiously.

'So how are you today, Saul?' Agatha asked.

She was always trying to make conversation and she was always hugging him as well. These were two good reasons Saul found her hard to warm to. A third was the way she cried and she did cry a lot. This was on account of the baby she was due to have, as his mother had explained to him once. His mother wouldn't say any more, so Saul had to get the rest of Agatha's story by eavesdropping on the grown-ups. He had a talent for this, as his father said, and he'd got pretty much the whole story.

Before the war Agatha married a Frenchman and lived with him in the nearby town of Saint-Marie. Shortly after the war started Agatha's husband got pneumonia and died. Henri, brother of the dead man as well as a gendarme, had taken an interest in the stranded English woman, who was unable to return to England as the Germans occupied northern France. They fell in love. Agatha got pregnant. But Henri had a wife and children in Saint-Marie and he could not let anyone know about Agatha. So when the Jews appeared in the town – their arrival coincided with

Agatha becoming pregnant – Henri struck a deal with them. They could hide in the old cave below the gendarmerie. It could only be approached through the forest. He would feed them too. In return they must take in Agatha until the time came for her to go away and give birth. This time wasn't very far off, Saul understood, and he wasn't entirely certain whether, after the event, she'd be coming back. Somehow, he doubted it.

'I'm very well, thank you,' he replied in the same careful voice he had used before. If his father were listening he felt certain his behaviour, at least so far, would be judged correct.

At that moment, he had an inspiration. He delved into the gritty crease at the bottom of his right-hand pocket and found the caterpillar he had put there earlier. He nipped the wriggling hairy tube tenderly between finger and thumb and pulled it out.

'Look at my caterpillar,' said Saul. In the middle of his palm the caterpillar flopped sideways and curled into a ball.

'Does it have a name?'

What a ridiculous question, he thought. It was a caterpillar. Why would a caterpillar have a name?

'No,' he said bluntly.

'Why don't you give it a name? You've got to name

anything you care about, and obviously you care about that caterpillar.'

'I'm going off to play,' he said. He put the hairy creature back in the bottom of his dusty pocket.

'Bend down first,' she said.

He knew what was coming. He also knew better than to refuse. He squatted and offered his face. She took his head with her two hands. They were grimy and rough and smelt of pine. She pulled him forward and kissed him on the forehead . . .

Now, standing in the darkness near the Cube rock, having remembered what happened that morning, he felt terrible he had hurt her just now. Even if she was annoying, she liked him.

Next thing, he began to ache in his throat and in the mysterious place he'd never been able to locate at the back of his stomach that always hurt before he cried.

His face went red. Great hot tears suddenly poured out of his eyes and flooded down his cheeks. As he registered the wetness on his face and the salty taste in his mouth, his memory of Agatha vanished, and in its place there came shame and anger. He was crying in front of the grown-ups. He hated himself for doing so.

Well, it was too late to do anything about that, he

thought furiously. The damage was done. He needed to concentrate on the practical; he needed to concentrate on his spear. He closed his hand around the handgrip. As he had feared, it was damp and soiled. There was a nasty meaty smell as well.

'I hate you, Nelly,' shouted Saul, wiping his face on his sleeve. His rage rose another notch and his tears stopped. 'You've ruined my spear.'

'Saul!' Al called.

'You're in such trouble, brother,' Nelly whispered triumphantly. 'Our father's going to give you such a walloping you won't sit down for a week.'

'Come here and say sorry,' his father said bleakly. 'And make it convincing.'

'Do as he says,' added Hugo, coldly.

'Get over here, now,' Al continued, 'and don't make me more angry than I already am.' His father was controlling his fury but only just.

'You're going to get a beating, you're going to get a beating,' Nelly whispered joyfully nearby.

'I won't,' said Saul, sullenly.

'Yes you will, and it'll be well deserved.'

'What's the matter, Saul?' This was Hugo. 'Do as your father says. Go and say sorry. And I tell you, young man, if you don't do as you're told *right now*, I'll be next in line behind your father, and after he's finished, I'll give you a thrashing you'll never forget.'

This was unbearable. He hadn't started this. Nelly had. As tears went down his face he asked himself angrily, why did he stay with them? The war was over. Hadn't his father said so? The Germans were defeated. In a matter of days, or at most a week or two, there would be Allied soldiers marching up the road where the forest ended.

And until that time, well, he could easily look after himself, couldn't he? He could feed himself. And it wouldn't be for long, would it?

3

Deliverance

Saul lunged sideways and sprinted off. At first there were only a few trees to run between. He was aware of voices behind. Everyone was shouting his name. He ignored them and plunged on. Then he entered the forest proper. He had to weave and dodge more here. It was colder than by the fire and darker too. The air smelt of pine cones, rotting needles and bitter tree bark.

At first, he could not see but he had followed this path so often he was able to feel his way forward. Then his eyes adjusted. The trunks of the trees were extremely black. The spaces in between were a lighter shade. The path snaking along the ground was somewhere between the two extremes.

He heard them calling some way behind. If they started to catch up, he decided he would leave the path and disappear into the forest proper.

He accelerated. The voices behind grew fainter. Finally, all he could hear was his own breathing, his feet moving through the dry needles scattered on the dry ground, the boughs overhead swaying faintly in the wind.

That was when he noticed the pain. It was a sharp stabbing sensation between the lungs. He slowed first to a trot and then to a walk. He was hot. He realised that he had gone on crying without knowing it. At the thought of what everyone had done to him, he felt angry again. He decided he was never going back.

He came eventually to the end of the forest. He stepped out on to the verge. He could smell gasoline. A vehicle must have driven past recently. He tilted his head in both directions but heard nothing. He wasn't afraid of the Germans. He felt hungry. He felt tired. He felt sad. He had no idea what to do next.

On the other side of the road he could just make out the storehouse. Why not go in there? Maybe there would be rats? But if he left the door open they would go out wouldn't they? There were rats in the cave when they moved in, a whole family. But the rats had just run out when they all appeared and they had never come back.

He crossed the road. The storehouse door was open. He went in. The building inside was even darker than it was in the forest. There was a smell of terracotta tiles, sacks and dust. He stood in the middle of the floor breathing quietly and waited. He heard nothing stirring. Gradually, he made out something lying in the middle of the floor. He crept over and touched it with the end of his spear. It felt soft. He pressed it. It was a mattress filled with straw.

He gingerly lowered himself down. The mattress didn't settle and give way. It rustled and went hard. He set his spear down beside him on the dusty floor.

Now he lowered himself very carefully onto his back and turned onto his right side. He brought his knees up. In this position he could see the doorway. He would watch the door all night. If anyone came in, he would get up and run him through with his spear before the stranger knew what was happening.

At some point, while he was watching and waiting, Saul fell asleep.

In the early hours of the next morning, Saul opened his eyes and saw his father, Alphonse, known as Al to friends and family.

His father was wearing his filthy double-breasted pin-stripe suit, and a shirt with no collar. His Al Capone fancy dress costume (bought pre-war because he shared the gangster's name) was what he was wearing when he escaped from Nice.

Behind Al, Saul saw the tall gangling form of

Claude. As usual Claude was wearing his filthy white raincoat. Behind Claude loomed the door. Outside the door there was a light grey mist.

Saul sat up on the mattress. The straw rustled and crinkled beneath him. The noise was like that of pieces of glass settling in the kaleidoscope that he had had to leave behind when they fled. He felt a colossal sense of surprise and then a fantastic sense of sadness. It was as if he had lost something. The most precious thing he had ever had, whatever that was. A tear plopped over his lower lid and rolled down his cheek. It bumped over his upper lip. He had made a terrible mistake.

A great run of tears followed the first. His face became wet and hot and his mouth was full of salt. His father put his arms around him and pulled him to his shoulder.

A gigantic sob ran through him and he felt like a rope that was being shaken. Then the tears stopped. Crushed there, against the fabric of his father's pin-stripe jacket, Saul rubbed his face this way and that to try to dry his cheeks. He only succeeded in smearing the tears and making his skin prickle.

He smelt his father's smell then. His basic smell was like broth made with carrots and barley. On top of that was sweat. It was like old pee but not as sharp. There was also a smell of wet stone. That was from the cave.

And there was wet pine too. It was like medicine but there was rotting vegetation mixed in with it.

'Don't ever run away,' Saul heard his father mumble.

Saul opened his eyes. He saw a blur of thick blue and thin white lines. His father had just spoken to him, he thought. His father had spoken to him nicely. Father was always nice at the beginning when he cried. The trouble was what came later. In a minute or an hour or a day, when Saul was not crying, he would turn. He would talk to Saul in the sharp, clean, clipped voice he used when he was angry. He would ask Saul why had he flung the rabbit at Agatha? Why had he run away? Why had he thought he had the right to put his mother through a whole night of agony? He would ask Saul why he was so selfish? Why did he think he could break the rules? Who the hell did he think he was? He would probably strike Saul as well. This was the trouble with comfort. Even as he was enjoying it Saul understood it must end and what must follow.

Before the war his father was a bullion dealer who liked to debate philosophy. Now he was a homeless Jew, in hiding from the Germans who would shoot him on sight. Despite his circumstances, he had not lost his taste for dispute or his aptitude for wrangling. He was a stickler for obedience yet at the same time he demanded of Saul that, when he was asked, he explain himself, fully and completely and truthfully.

The trouble was, Saul couldn't. He would have liked to but he couldn't. As soon as his father started shouting questions, Saul found his words deserted him. His mind went blank. He couldn't think of anything to say.

To Al this looked like insolence. It made him even angrier. He would ask his questions over and over again, his tone growing fiercer and fiercer, his voice louder and louder. He could not abide the fact that Saul would not argue, would not talk back or answer his questions eloquently.

And Saul, in turn, as his father got angrier and fiercer, would become even more separated from his words. Thus, the angrier Al became, the less Saul was able to speak. These sessions always ended with Saul weeping, and his father muttering furiously about his son's stupidity.

Saul sniffed. His tears had stopped. He felt calm and quiet. He had been found. In a bit they would go back to the cave. The task now was to prepare for the ordeal that was surely coming. Once he had withstood his father's questions and listened to the lecture he would surely deliver on how Saul should behave, and once he was beaten, then this episode would be finished.

4

Claude's proposal

The two adults and the boy filed in a line through the trees. Claude was first, then came Saul with his spear, then came his father. It was not long after dawn and it was cold.

'Pity you missed the rabbit last night,' said Claude, sounding like a man who was making a determined effort to be cheerful, 'it really wasn't bad.' Saul looked at Claude's shoulders. Once he had filled his coat but now he was so thin it hung off him. He looked like a scarecrow.

Saul remembered Claude, just, from his life in Nice before the war. In those days Claude worked in Uncle Hugo's burlesque theatres along the Cote d'Azur. He arranged the dances, he rehearsed the girls, and he conducted the little orchestra during performances. Claude then was large and plump, affable and ambitious. One day he hoped to have a theatre and a troupe of his own showgirls.

Of that old Claude all that remained was his precise

way of speaking and his habit of staring. Both came from years of having to explain to girls what they had to do, and checking that the feathers in the headdresses and seams in their stockings were in the right place.

Saul had gleaned the rest of Claude's story by listening to the adults. Claude had a wife. Unlike him, Yvette was not Jewish. There were two children. The boy was with the Free French in West Africa. The girl was in a convent in Monaco. During the Italian occupation of Nice, Claude and Yvette lived quietly.

However, after the Italian capitulation and the appearance of the Germans, Yvette asked him to leave. She had a premonition that someone would betray them both to the Gestapo. Claude did not want to drag his wife down if he fell. He ran straight to Hugo, who took him in. When the Lippmans paired up with the Roths and decided to flee to Saint-Marie together, they brought Claude along with them.

'Are you hungry?' Saul heard his father saying behind him.

'No,' said Saul. This was not true. He was starving.

'Have you any idea how worried we were about you?' Al said.

Perhaps the lecture was about to start now? This certainly sounded like the sort of nasty question, designed to catch him out, that his father would open with. In this case whether Saul said, 'No, I didn't realise,' or 'Yes, I did realise,' he would be guilty of thoughtlessness and stupidity. But he would have to answer. Probably it was better to say yes, he decided. It showed that he accepted that he was wrong to run away, at least.

'Yes,' he said quietly.

'But it's all ended happily, hasn't it?' said Claude. When he spoke, Claude didn't talk like the other grown-ups. They would rattle along and then correct themselves when they made mistakes. Claude spoke more slowly and always left a little gap after each word so he had an opportunity to monitor what he had said and what he was saying next. If he decided he had made a mistake, he would stop his sentence and start it again. Claude strove for perfection.

'Yes, happily it has,' his father agreed. 'And Nelly did the right thing. She told us everything.'

Saul felt a trickle of anxiety, down his legs and in his stomach. He must handle this conversation with extreme care.

'What did Nelly say?' he asked casually.

'Oh,' his father said, 'she told us the whole story. How she found your spear yesterday afternoon, when she was looking for berries and accidentally strayed too close to the road. She told us she guessed then that you'd crossed the road to explore the storehouse. That's how we knew where to find you this morning.'

For a moment there was just the noise of feet. So that was Nelly's story. He readied himself for the shouting that he was certain was about to start.

'I still don't know why you did it, though,' said his father. He still spoke unexpectedly quietly. 'Why did you run away? Why did you leave us fretting for a whole long night?'

Saul felt his face reddening. He must hold himself straight. He must keep walking. It would pass. The tongue-lashings always did.

'Why do you break the rules?' his father continued. 'Do you think I've just invented them for my own amusement? No, of course I haven't. They're there for a reason. We're in hiding, in case you haven't noticed. And why is that? The answer, Saul, is we don't want to get caught. And why should that be? Because if we're caught, we all die – you die, I die, Claude dies, your mother dies, Nelly dies – we all die.

'You do understand that, don't you? Or don't you? You've been told. You say you understand. Yet you don't act like you do. You just carry on in your own sweet way. You ignore everything I say. Don't you understand that you are risking not only your own life but everyone else's as well when you charge around the country? That is not fair. That is selfish. Do you hear me?'

'Yes.'

'Can I repeat what I have told you already but which you don't appear to have taken in? The Allies are coming. They have landed. Cannes and Marseilles have fallen. But we are still not safe. We are almost safe but we are still not safe yet. And having got this far, we don't want to put ourselves in danger, now do we?'

He paused. Saul heard his breathing, the tramp of feet, and faintly, the wind blowing through the tops of the trees overhead.

'Are you going to grace me with a comment or is this conversation going to be entirely one-sided?' said Al. His sharp voice obliterated all the noises Saul was hearing.

'No,' he said instantly in order to forestall the accusation of being dreamy and not listening.

Unfortunately, as Saul realised as soon as the word was out, it made him sound insolent. He should have said yes. He steeled himself for angry words.

However, to his surprise his father said, 'No,' in a surprisingly patient tone of voice. 'No what?'

'No, we've got to be careful,' he said. Again he was not thinking, just reacting.

'You mean, yes, we've got to be careful, surely? That's the correct way to express what you mean.'

'Yes,' Saul agreed in a quiet voice. It was a relief not to be shouted at.

'So why did you say no a moment ago?'

Saul tried to gather his thoughts so he could answer the question. But before he got a chance his father continued, 'Oh never mind about that. I'm sure you're exhausted and you've got all your words mixed up. What's important is that this doesn't happen again. Can I repeat the rules to you?'

Without waiting for Saul to reply he surged on: 'Never go out of earshot. Most importantly, before you say or do anything, always ask yourself the same question. Will it give the others or me away? We don't want to be seen, Saul. We don't want to be heard. We don't want to be caught.

'At this moment we don't exist and we won't until the American and the English and the Polish soldiers are marching up the road on the far side of the forest. Do you understand? We're in more danger now than we've ever been. The time you don't want to meet a German is when he's losing and he knows it. As a Jew you'll be shot, straight away, and no questions asked. But as long as you stay close to the cave, you'll be safe, we'll be safe. So let's not ruin things after having got this far, shall we? Let's struggle on. Let's get to the end of our story.'

'Yes,' Saul said quietly. If his father knew he had seen a German lorry the previous day, this lecture could have been far worse. At this thought he trembled inwardly. Happily, his father couldn't see his troubled face. Or he would have started the questions and he wouldn't have given up until he got an answer. Instead he continued speaking in the same vein as before.

'We won't be here forever,' he said. 'This will end. Remember that. Do you understand me?'

'Yes.'

'Do you really?'

'Yes.'

They walked on. Saul considered Nelly's lie. It was brilliant. Adults could effortlessly come up with lies in seconds that he could never invent in a year.

'I think,' started Claude, 'it might be a good idea if we found some way to entertain you.'

Saul received this news silently. He was not clear what was being offered. He would not speak until he was.

'What had you in mind, Claude?' said his father behind.

There was surprise in his voice.

'I'm going to write Saul a story,' said Claude. He paused. 'No, I'm not going to write it, I'm going to tell it. No, I will write it but then I'll tell it.'

The two men and the boy moved on in silence. Then Claude spoke again:

'My grandparents were not French. They came from Bohemia,' he said. 'This was a long time ago. This was before the last war, when Bohemia was in Austria-Hungary and was ruled by the Habsburgs. My grandparents brought a story with them. It was about the golem. He was a giant made of clay, who could move and act as instructed but could not speak or reason for himself. Of course the two are connected. Without language we cannot reason, or exercise choice.'

'I think,' said Al, 'you might be going over Saul's head.'

'Oh yes, sorry,' said Claude quickly. 'Anyhow, when I was your age, Saul, my grandparents told me this story. I've now decided I'm going to pass it on to you.'

This was not what Saul expected at all.

'What do you think, Saul?' asked Al.

He knew he must sound grateful. 'Oh yes,' he said, 'I'd like that very much.'

They walked on. Nobody spoke for the rest of the

journey. As they got close to the cave, Saul heard his father clear his throat.

'I want you to be very good to your mother,' his father said. 'Do you understand?'

'I do.'

Through the thinning trees, Saul saw the Cube rock ahead with his mother standing near by. She didn't smile, wave or shout. She simply stared as they advanced. It was only when they'd almost reached the rock that she came to life. She raised both her arms and held them out towards her son.

'Come here,' his mother called.

'Go on,' said his father.

Saul went up to his mother.

'Put the spear down,' she said.

He leant it against the Cube rock. She put her arms around him. She put her face on top of his head and rubbed it backwards and forwards. His hair was short and spiky. His mother shaved it every week because of lice. As he wondered when she would let go, he felt a spasm run through her. She gripped him more tightly. She began to sob. He felt her tears wetting his head. He waited.

'Am I going to be beaten?' he whispered.

'No.'

'Are you sure?'

'I spoke to your father about it,' she whispered, 'before he went off to look for you. We agreed this is too serious for that.'

When finally she released him, he touched his short hair instinctively. It was soaking wet.

Now that Saul's mother had had her moment with her son, everyone else, the rest of the party, came out of the cave to welcome Saul back. His Aunt Ida tousled his hair. Hugo jocularly punched his arm. Leon smiled. Finally, Agatha waddled forward, her huge belly sticking out in front, and kissed him. She smelt of pine and sweat.

Now the adults began to speak. Claude announced that he intended to tell Saul a story that he was going to write.

'What story?' Mina asked.

'The golem story,' explained Claude, 'that I got from my Czech grandparents.'

'Claude the man will pass the baton on to Saul the boy,' Hugo said quietly. His uncle never spoke philosophically like this. There was something going on that Saul did not understand. He decided to pay very close attention.

The adults went on talking. They talked about engaging, enriching, and helping Saul. They applauded Claude's proposal.

As he processed these remarks, Saul started thinking. When he ran away he'd wanted to frighten them but he never thought they would suffer as deeply as they apparently did. He'd really given them a shock, hadn't he? There was no other way to explain why Claude was going to tell this story for Saul and Saul alone, and that everyone else, and in particular his father, was agreeing to this.

Saul felt his deep sense of resentment shrink ever so slightly. He still hated Nelly, of course. He'd never forgive her for what she did to his spear. And Leon, he didn't doubt, was in with Nelly on the lie. So he didn't like him either. But not only was he not going to be beaten, something special was going to be done for him alone. The thought made him want to smile.

'I can't start telling him the story just immediately,' he heard Claude say. 'I won't be able to do it justice unless I write it all down first.'

'That's a good idea,' said Hugo. 'You don't want to make a fool of yourself by coming out with rubbish. Preparation is always best. That's what I used to say to anyone who trod the boards in my theatre. Get it right before you give it to the public.'

'He doesn't need to rehearse. Reading it will be fine,' said Saul's mother. 'But I tell you what, Claude, why don't we make a day of it? Why don't we all listen?'

'It's a children's story,' said Claude.

'I loved it when I was read to as a girl,' said Mina, 'and that love has never left me. I'll be there, Claude, I'm afraid, just try and stop me.'

'We all will,' said Ida, nodding her long face. 'Wouldn't miss it for anything.'

'As you wish,' said Claude, and shrugged. 'If you're bored, don't say I didn't warn you. Now, unless I get some writing materials, nobody will be getting anything.'

'And where are you getting them?' asked Agatha.

'You're going to send a message up to Henri.'

'Am I?' She looked disgruntled. She hated the way the others would get her to ask Henri for things. They assumed she had a special relationship with the gendarme. But if their relationship had been so special, as she would have liked to say but never had the courage, she wouldn't have been in the cave with them, would she?

'Please,' said Claude, kindly.

'All right,' Agatha agreed.

She took out the slate from the basket. This always went up in the basket with requests and messages. She wrote in chalk on the black shiny surface, 'Exercise book and pencil, please.'

'Maybe, Agatha,' said Al, 'you could ask him for some treats.'

Mina glanced at her husband.

'Is that a good idea?' she asked her husband.

She understood why Agatha didn't like asking Henri for things.

'Of course it is,' said Al, peremptorily. 'You don't mind asking, do you Agatha?' he continued.

Saul noticed a slight change in the colour of Agatha's face.

'Yes, of course,' he heard her say. She was going to have to do something, he realised, that she didn't want to do.

'You think Henri would send down some butter instead of the usual margarine and maybe even a bottle or two of good wine?' continued Al.

'I don't know.'

'Why don't you ask?'

'I can't promise,' said Agatha quietly.

'Some cheese and fruit would be marvellous too,' added Al. 'We could have a real feast then. And maybe he could even drop down some real soap and a razor blade. We could all spruce ourselves up for our day at the theatre with Claude.'

The adults drifted away. Saul remained. Agatha chalked Al's demands on the slate, chewing her lips as she wrote. As he watched her, Saul felt something he'd never expected to feel for Agatha. It was a twinge of sympathy and pity.

Agatha finished. She put the slate in the basket. She pulled on the rope and the basket began to rise jerkily up the cliff face.

'I can do that,' said Saul.

'It's not heavy, it's empty,' said Agatha.

'But I'd like to help,' Saul insisted.

She let him take the rope. He hauled the basket to the top, then tied the end to a tree.

'Thank you.'

She gave him a huge smile and touched the back of his neck. Perhaps Agatha was not so awful after all.

5

Saul's mother

The following morning Claude filled a small flour sack with pine needles and carried it into the cave. He laid his makeshift pillow on a low jutting rock a couple of metres inside the door. Beside this there was another higher, bigger rock that was flat enough to write on and close enough to the cave mouth that it caught the light. Claude had already laid out his glasses, the exercise book and the pencil here. Henri had sent these down the previous night.

Claude sat on his pillow. He reached for his glasses and opened them meticulously. The shafts were snapped and splinted with matchsticks and tied with lint. The bridge was fixed with a large blob of wax. It would be disastrous to break his glasses at the very moment he was about to start writing. He settled the bridge on his nose and the shafts on his ears. Claude was ready now. He twisted sideways, opened the exercise book, picked up his pencil and began to write.

Saul watched from nearby. He was at the front of

the cave, making a dagger to go with his spear. He was rubbing the charred end of the stick on the same patch of rough stone he'd used before to sharpen his spear.

Time passed. Claude wrote and Saul went on rubbing. Then his mother came into the cave. She went past him and walked down to Claude. Saul rubbed a little less vigorously. This way, he made less noise yet he still looked busy. He would listen in on what the adults said.

'So you're making a start?' he heard his mother say.

'Yes,' said Claude.

'If you know it already do you really need to write it out in detail?'

'Oh yes,' said Claude. 'I have every intention of being simply superb. I have every intention of decanting something utterly compelling and powerful, out of my imagination and into Saul's.

'Now this is too precious a task to be left to chance. That's why I must write it down first.'

'Did you ever want to go on stage?' his mother asked.

'I wanted to when I was younger.'

'Why didn't you?'

'I took a wrong turning – I'm not quite certain where. That's how I ended up spending my life helping other people to get in front of the public instead of doing it myself.'

There was a moment of quiet.

'Mind you,' continued Claude, 'keeping the showgirls in line was such a performance, it was as good as going on stage.'

'I'm really looking forward to this,' Saul heard his mother say. 'Our time here is drawing to an end. It has to be. We're into the harbour even if we haven't got to the dockside yet.' Her voice was quiet and even. 'And when we look back on this I know what we're going to remember is your story. I know when I look back on my girlhood, it's snatches of music and bits of songs that remain, while everything else has disappeared.'

The conversation was starting to bore him. Saul set his dagger down and went outside. He sat in a gap between two trees. The sun had warmed the dusty ground. He looked up. The sky above, where he could see it between the branches of the trees, was clean and clear and blue. He cocked his head sideways. Allied bombers from Italy passed overhead most days as they flew north. He liked to watch the long silver shapes floating by. When they passed he would imagine he was on the bottom of the sea and they were the hulls of ships gliding overhead. The ocean floor was the only place on earth, he reckoned, where he would feel absolutely safe.

His mother and Claude were still talking. He

filtered their voices out and strained to hear the sound of whirring propellers instead.

'Saul?' he heard and someone touched his shoulder.

He turned and saw his mother. She stood at his side with a sooty finger on his shoulder. She wore her old blue sundress. All the blue buttons on the front were gone. They were replaced with a mixture of brown and white and black ones.

'Claude's filling his exercise book. You've got a treat coming.'

She sat down on the ground beside him.

'Look at me,' she said.

He turned and looked into her face.

'You will try to be good, from now on, won't you?' she said. 'And you won't ever run away again? That was the longest night of my life. I thought I'd lost you. I couldn't stand to lose you.'

She fixed him with her gaze. He couldn't be certain but it was his impression her eyes had changed colour. Before the war they were green. After the deaths of his brothers, Robert and Francis, they went brown. And when she turned them on him, as she was doing now, he felt her heavy, suffocating grief. He believed that if he looked into her eyes for long enough, he would end up feeling what she felt. That would be the end of him. He couldn't let that happen.

Saul glanced away and looked up at the sky.

None of the adults had explained her condition to him but Saul had managed to work it out. It was not difficult.

His mother's first child and his oldest brother was Robert. He was quiet and technically-minded. He would have made an excellent engineer. When war was declared he was conscripted into the French army. He became a meteorologist. In 1940 he went out to collect data in a forest in northern France. He stepped on a landmine. The explosion took his leg off at the knee. He died two days later.

Her second son, Francis, was exuberant and cheerful. He was the most like how she had been before the war. After the Italian occupation of Nice began, and the Roths started living semi-clandestine lives, Francis carried on as if nothing had happened. That was his character. He got a job as tutor to the children of a woman called Odette. Her husband worked in the Town Hall. Her marriage was unhappy. She was lonely. Francis fell in love with Odette and she with him.

The Italians left the war on 10 September, 1943. The Germans quickly entered Nice and started their hunt for the Jews the Italians had let live. The Roths, the Lippmans and Claude decided to leave Nice and to go to the area round Saint-Marie, in the hope of finding somewhere to hide. Francis refused to go with them without saying goodbye to Odctte first. He told his family to leave and promised to follow. He never appeared. His mother assumed he must have been caught and was now dead.

To imagine how these disasters affected his mother, Saul drew on a memory from when he was very small. He had owned a small honey coloured teddy bear. Uncle Hugo and Aunt Ida had given it to him. One day, when no adult was looking, he got a sharp knife and cut the stitching along the seam that ran up his teddy's back.

A strange powdery dust started to flow from the hole. These were ground-up wood shavings. As the stuff flowed out he watched, fascinated. It poured and poured. His teddy changed from hard to soft. Finally, he was left holding just the skin. It was almost completely empty. Only at the tips of the paws did a little sawdust remain.

Saul thought that the deaths of Robert and Francis had punched a hole in his mother, like the one he'd made at the back of his teddy. Out of it, whatever it was that had held her up and made her hard and tight, had slowly leaked away. Just like his teddy. Now, there was almost nothing left inside. Now, she was mostly just skin.

Saul had also noticed that while his mother went in one direction, his father went in the exact opposite one. Al had not been holed by the loss of his two older sons. On the contrary, these events made him more what he already was. He was now more grumpy, and more of a stickler. He was tighter and harder, sterner and fiercer. If his mother had become an empty teddy bear skin, his father had become a stone.

As for himself, Saul didn't think he'd changed at all. He didn't particularly miss his brothers. They were so much older than he was and they had not played with him all that much. He hardly knew them really. Now they were gone there was certainly no point thinking about them all the time. That way lay sadness and that was a pointless, useless emotion.

For no particular reason, he now remembered the previous day, when his mother hugged him and her tears soaked through the thin fuzz of hair that covered his skull. He had been terrified and the thought he had had – and he could remember this now with absolute clarity – was that he had driven the last of the dust out of her. But today, when she talked about Claude's story, she had been animated in a way he couldn't remember her having been for years. Perhaps there was more inside her than he knew. He turned from the empty sky and looked back into her eyes.

'Do you love me?' she asked.

'Yes,' he said mechanically.

She had often asked him this question. He couldn't understand why she needed to keep asking him when he had already told her. There were certain things it seemed he had to repeat over and over again. And this was one of them.

'Do you promise?'

'Oh yes,' he said abstractedly. In the distance he thought he heard the faint drone of propellers.

'I love you,' she said.

'Yes, I know,' he said. Sometimes, in the past, he would think that he heard the Lancasters and the B52s, but then they never appeared. And sometimes, he didn't hear them, and suddenly they were in the sky overhead. He hated both to be disappointed and to be taken unawares. He liked to hear the Allied bombers and then to see them. He strained his ears. It was very far away but he was hearing airplane engines.

'Do you?'

'What?'

'Do you love me, really?'

He had just told her, hadn't he, just a moment ago? And now, here she was, asking to hear again. Well, once was enough. His mind was on something much more important.

'Look,' he said.

High, high in the sky, a cluster of tiny silver dots had appeared.

He stood and waved.

'It's the bombers,' he said. 'They're going to bomb the Germans.'

His mother said nothing, just got up and walked back to the cave and lay down on her bed.

6

The story with two titles

Saul was up a tree. He sat on a branch. Through his thin shorts he felt the bark of the pine digging into him. If he sat for long enough in one position, his skin would take on the shape of the bark. It would become rough and crinkled, although unlike the tree's skin his would still be warm.

Saul held two sharp rocks, one in each hand. He had carried them up in a sling tied around his neck. If the squirrel came this morning, he intended to kill it with a stone to the head. He had killed several squirrels this way. The meat was greasy but if cooked sufficiently it was quite good to eat.

The sun was high and it had been baking the canopy overhead for some hours. The cicadas were thrumming. The end of summer heat was intense. It exhausted him. But the days were shortening, and the nights were lengthening. Even though it brought the winter closer, he was looking forward to autumn, with its cooler days.

He sniffed the air. He hoped to smell the meaty smell of squirrel but all he got was the sharp smell of heated pine needles. It made him itch and at the same time it made him feel bright. It also reminded him of the hospital where he had gone before the war to have his finger bandaged, after he cut it on the lid of a tin can. In the treatment room there was a pine smell mixed with starch. This came from the uniform of the nurse, stiff and white as cardboard.

'Saul,' he heard.

It was Claude, standing below, staring up at him with his worn, creased face.

'I'm ready,' said Claude.

He waved the exercise book at Saul. Claude had been scribbling in it non-stop for days.

'And I've brought you something to sit on,' said Claude.

In his other hand he had a box which he now waved. ORGANISATION TODT was stamped on the side. Todt, Saul knew, was the German engineer, now dead. His organisation built aerodromes and fortifications and concentration camps. The box had come from the gendarmerie.

'Is it a good story?'

'What do you mean,' asked Claude, 'is it a good story? No, it's rotten.'

Saul stared down. This was what he didn't like about grown-ups. Sometimes they said what they meant but then, at other times, they said the opposite instead.

'If it's rubbish I'm not coming,' he said, bluntly.

Damn! Claude thought, why had he said what he said? Saul was a simple soul. If you didn't say it straight, he didn't get it.

'I didn't mean what I just said,' Claude said carefully. 'That was a joke. It is good.'

Saul waited. When he judged enough time had elapsed and Claude would be getting worried, he said, 'Are you sure?'

'I'm sure.'

Saul threw his killing rocks down and jumped after them. Claude turned and walked away. Saul picked up his spear and followed him through the trees. They walked in silence.

At last they came to a level open space enclosed by a circle of young trees that in turn were enclosed by the forest. They called this place the theatre. All the adults were sitting in a semi-circle on a variety of boxes, tree stumps and improvised stools made from lengths of pine cunningly bound together with twine and wire. They had their backs to him. Starting from the left, there was Nelly, Leon, Hugo, then his mother, his father and Ida. Agatha sat on the extreme right. Claude set the Todt box down in the centre of the adults between his mother and Uncle Hugo.

'Right, Saul, sit,' he said.

Saul felt embarrassed. Why should he go in the middle?

'I can sit at the side,' he said quietly. 'I can sit beside Agatha.'

Agatha said, 'That would be nice. I'd be honoured.' Her head tilted sideways, she smiled while catching his eye directly as if she wanted to force him to respond. On another occasion this would have irked Saul but not today. He smiled back shyly.

'Sorry, Agatha, I'm afraid I'm going to have to disappoint you,' said Claude. 'As the most important member of the audience, he has to go here, in the middle.'

'Come on,' his mother added. She spoke quickly and to Saul it seemed her eyes were almost green again. 'Come and sit down.'

Saul sat on the rough bottom of the box and laid the spear on the bed of pine needles at his side. Claude walked round and took up a position in front of everybody.

'Dear Saul!' Claude exclaimed. 'I am going to give you a treasure and here it is. It's all in here.'

Claude waved the exercise book.

'This is the story of a man of clay,' Saul heard.

Claude looked straight at Saul. Saul saw his eyes were black and watery. His skin was sallow and so lined it was as if separate pieces of flesh had been stitched together to make his face. It was hunger that did that.

'His name was Joseph the Golem and he was brought to life by the great Rabbi Loew of Prague.'

'Who's Loew?' Saul asked without thinking.

'You're not going to plague me with awkward questions, are you?'

'I'm not like other children,' said Saul carefully.

'That's good,' said Claude, 'because if you ask too many questions the whole thing will come down like a house of cards.'

Saul said nothing and folded his arms. He didn't want this to stop before it started. He put on his good face. This was the one he wore when he needed to show he intended neither harm nor mischief.

'Hold this,' said Claude. He gave Hugo the exercise book. He put his hand in his coat pocket and pulled out his precious spectacles. He put them on carefully and took the exercise book. He opened it at the first page. He coughed, holding his right hand in front of his mouth.

'This is a story with two titles. Some call it *The Golem*. That is the name of the creature made of clay that lived in Prague hundreds of years ago. Others know it as *The Miraculous Deeds of Rabbi Loew*. He was the man who brought the creature to life. They're both good titles, in their different ways.

'When these stories arose, hundreds of years ago, some Christians had strange ideas about Jews. They thought they killed children and used their blood to make unleavened bread at Passover.'

Saul made a face.

'It's a disgusting idea, isn't it? But people who didn't like Jews made up this story. They believed it was true, so that they would then have a reason to hate Jews. That's what human beings have always done. They don't like somebody, for whatever reason, so they invent a reason to justify their hatred.'

'Excuse me,' said Uncle Hugo. 'If you're going to tell me about anti-Semitism down the ages, thank you, but I've got better things to do.'

'He's only explaining the background to Saul,' Aunt Ida said politely.

'Look,' said Hugo, 'when I ran my theatres, did you ever hear of anyone coming out first and explaining what was going to happen before the girls or whoever came on stage? It would have spoiled the magic. That's the way you kill something.'

'Well, I'm sure Claude isn't going to say any more,' said Saul's mother to her brother.

'You know what I want from a story?' said Hugo. 'I want it to obliterate what I already know. If I want arguments or theory or history, I read a textbook.'

'Of course you do,' said Claude, 'and I will transport all of us, I promise.'

7

The Lion is born

We start in Germany, in the city of Worms. According to the Christian calendar, the year was 1513. Worms was divided into two parts. One was where the Christians lived; the other was walled off from the rest. Here, the houses were small and bent, the streets more narrow and winding. This was the ghetto where the Jews lived. The law forbade them to live anywhere else.

It was Passover, the time that Jews remember when Moses led their Exodus from slavery in Egypt to freedom in the Promised Land. They eat unleavened bread to remind them that the children of Israel had to flee before the yeast in their bread had time to rise. At this time the old rumour was going around Worms. The Jews were killing Christian children and using their blood to make their Matzos, or unleavened bread.

'I thought he'd finished with this,' whispered Hugo.

'Hugo,' hissed Ida sharply, 'don't spoil it.'

* * *

It was a funny thing about these beliefs, continued Claude. First they existed only in the imagination.

"Did you know?" one Christian would say to his neighbour, "the Jews kill children and make bread out of their blood?"

"Really?"

"I never saw it myself but my brother did and who am I not to believe him?"

The listener would pass the story to his wife. His wife would tell her sister. She would tell her fiancé and on it would go. Finally, there wasn't anyone who hadn't heard it, or didn't believe it either. Like the plague, if you had it, the chances were you'd give it to someone who didn't.

At this point the Blood Libel story was only an assertion. The next trick was to make it come true. Many tried to do this and they always used the same technique. It went like this. First, you would obtain the corpse of a child. It was not so hard then, when children died all the time. Second, you would cut its throat to make it look as if it had been murdered. Third, you would hide the body in the house of a Jew. Fourth, you would go to the authorities and tip them off. Fifth, the police would search the Jew's house.

Now they would find the corpse. They would say to

the householder, "Why is there a dead child in your house?" Of course the householder wouldn't be able to explain.

Of course the police would have heard the rumours. Having found a body, they would jump to the conclusion that the householder had killed the child to use its blood for unleavened bread. The Jew would deny everything but it wouldn't do any good. The police would take him away and throw him in jail. This was what was about to happen in Worms, in 1513.

A Christian child had died. A man carried the corpse in a sack towards the house of the most important Jew in Worms. This was Rabbi Bezalel, the father of Loew.

It was the evening of Passover, when all Jews would be sitting down to Seder. This was the ritual meal that celebrated the Exodus, with readings and special dishes and prayers and songs of thanksgiving, because the Angel of Death passed over the houses of their ancestors in Egypt and so they were saved. But for this there could have been no Exodus, for there would have been no people left to flee.

The evening of Seder was also the best time for mischief. The man with the sack was going to creep up to Rabbi Bezalel's house. He was going to open a basement window and throw in the corpse. Then he was going to run off and tell the police, and you all know what would have happened next.

Except it didn't. In life there is always an X-factor. No matter how much you plan, something will always crop up that you never thought about before.

In this case, it was the rabbi's wife. She was very pregnant. And what should happen this very night but she felt twinges low in her belly. Then her waters broke and gushed out on to the floor.

"Get the midwife," she shouted, "my baby is coming."

Everybody immediately dashed into the street.

"Where's the midwife?" one shouted.

"She won't be at home," shouted another. "She must have gone somewhere to sit Seder."

"She's at her aunt's," replied a third.

"No, she's not," shouted a fourth, "she's at her sister's."

It was chaos – everyone rushing about trying to find her.

And it was at that precise moment that the Christian appeared with the dead child in the sack.

The Jews paid no attention to him. He was just a man with a sack. But he thought these people were after him.

Now a frightened man is invariably a foolish one.

When he saw the milling people, he should have dumped the sack but he didn't. He should have retraced his steps along the dark alleyways but he didn't. Instead, he turned and, still holding the sack, he hurried away in a completely new direction – the fool! His new route took him further into the ghetto and past the police station.

As it happened, there was a policeman on the steps. He saw the man with the sack run past. He thought nothing of it.

A few moments later, some of the crowd from the Rabbi Bezalel's house appeared in the distance. They were still looking for the midwife. The policeman couldn't hear what the Jews were saying or doing.

Next thing, as policemen are wont to do, he made two separate events into a single unified story. The man with the sack was a thief and the crowd had been chasing after him.

The policeman dashed down the steps and ran up the street after the thief. He was fit and young. His quarry was old and tired and out of breath. The policeman caught up with the man and knocked him to the ground. As the man lay on the ground, winded and terrified, the policeman deftly opened the sack. He was expecting to find something of value inside. And if not something of value, then food or clothes. The poor in Worms were so poor they would steal anything really. But he found none of these. What he found was his worst nightmare. It appalled and shocked him and he was not able to speak for a moment or two.

"What's this?" the policeman shouted, when finally his powers of speech returned.

"I didn't kill the child," the thief shouted quickly. He didn't want this policeman to draw his sword and run him through so he continued, speaking quickly, "He was dead when he was given to me. My job was just to throw him into Rabbi Bezalel's basement. I was paid to do it."

He added the names of the two merchants who had paid him.

"Get up," said the policeman, "you're coming down to the station. You can tell your story to the chief constable and we'll see how good it is."

Meantime, as the Jews, oblivious of this drama, were still searching for the midwife, Mrs Bezalel was lying in her bed at home with a tiny squashed red thing on her breast. She'd delivered her baby with the help of a maid. It was a boy.

Over the days that followed, news of what the policeman found spread throughout Worms. To Rabbi Bezalel the events of the evening began to look like a miraculous escape from calamity. He began to brood.

There must be meaning in this. Nothing in the universe was simply accidental.

It struck him three nights later. The only reason he had escaped disaster was because of his wife's birth pangs. If they hadn't started, then he and his relatives would not have been in the street. And if they hadn't been in the street, the man with the sack wouldn't have run away and got caught by the policeman. It could only mean one thing. His newborn son and the poisonous fantasy of the Blood Libel were to be mixed up with one another in some significant way.

As soon as Rabbi Bezalel realised this, he felt a lovely sense of calm. He decided that his son must have a name appropriate to the struggle that surely lay ahead of him. His wife suggested Judah Loew, meaning Judah the Lion. "He'll be like the lion that does not permit his cubs to be mangled," she added.

The rabbi agreed. Judah Loew it was.

8

The light, mid-morning

Claude moved the exercise book directly into the path of the shaft of sunlight closest to him. The light bounced off the page and up to his face. His skin glowed.

'Is that the end of the prologue?' asked Hugo. 'Do we clap?'

'That's just the beginning, the set-up,' said Claude.

'Have you been following, Saul?' Nelly asked. Her tone was moderately friendly.

'Yes,' he said.

'Settle down,' said Claude. 'If you ask questions, we won't ever get into the story.'

Saul recognised good sense when he heard it. He nodded.

'He's nodding, Saul's nodding,' said his mother. 'Now we've got to be quiet.'

'Shush,' Leon hissed theatrically.

Nelly giggled.

'Nelly!' said Mina, mock-sharply to her daughter.

'Sorry,' said Nelly.

'And you Leon. Please act your age.'

Al laughed quietly at his wife's quip. Then silence descended on the half-circle of listeners.

9

The betrothal

Over the years that followed his birth, all the usual things happened to Loew, and in the usual order. I propose to pass over these and jump straight to the next significant event.

In the Worms ghetto, when Loew was growing up, there was a merchant named Shmelke Reich. He was very wealthy and his family was very important.

In the sixteenth century, wealth and importance went together. If you were rich you were automatically respected. It's still the case today.

Shmelke had a daughter. Her name was Pearl. Names, as we shall see throughout this story, always mean something. As well as being called Pearl, she was a pearl. Or she would turn out to be one.

In those days, young people were not allowed to meet and fall in love and marry and mess up the rest of their lives like they are today.

Oh no, parents would go to a matchmaker. They

would pay a fee. The matchmaker would then find a suitable partner.

Now it so chanced that Bezalel and Shmelke went to the same matchmaker. Rabbi Bezalel spoke at length about his son, Judah. Shmelke Reich spoke about his daughter, Pearl. The matchmaker saw at once that the two were ideally suited. He made the introduction. An understanding was reached between the parents. The matchmaker was paid another sum to draw up a contract for the parties to sign. Loew was fifteen years old and Pearl was twelve.

And then, as was the custom, Loew went to live with his future parents-in-law. He and Pearl both knew they were to marry. At first they were embarrassed in each other's company but they were not resentful about the decision that had been made on their behalf. They accepted that that was how things were done. Gradually, they found they liked each other too. They became friends.

The Reichs sent Loew to the yeshiva of Przemysl to study to be a rabbi. Loew was happy to go. As a rabbi there was a better chance he would leave the world a happier place than he found it. This was his ambition.

For three years everything went well. Then calamity struck. Shmelke lost his fortune. In despair he wrote to Loew:

Dear Judah,
I am ruined. I can no longer provide a dowry for my daughter. I know you promised to marry Pearl but now my circumstances are changed I no longer expect you to honour that undertaking. I urge you to break the engagement contract. This will leave you free to find a rich bride.

Loew replied immediately:

Dear Shmelke,
I will not break the contract. I will wait and, with the help of God, I will marry Pearl. Of course, if you want to void the contract, then that is your business. Just find another suitor for Pearl and I will regard our arrangement as finished.

When he got Loew's letter, Shmelke wondered what he was going to do? If Loew was so adamant this marriage would go ahead, then somehow, someway, he was going to have to find some money.

He put on his best coat and walked to the home of a merchant with whom he had traded when he was rich and successful.

They drank apricot wine and ate little cakes made of almond paste. Shmelke explained his difficulty. He asked for the loan of a large sum of money. The merchant refused.

"You'll never repay that amount," the merchant said. Then he offered Shmelke another glass of wine.

Shmelke visited several other merchants with whom he had done business in the past. They all gave him food to eat and liquor to drink, and they all declined to lend him money. They all believed they would never see the money back. If Shmelke had asked for a gift of money they would have given. But he was too proud to ask and the merchants did not dare offer in case they caused offence.

At the end of the day, Shmelke returned home. He was tired and he was near to tears. He had had too much to eat and drink, and he had failed to raise a single ducat.

"Is that you, Father?" he heard as he came in.

It was Pearl. She was in the parlour off the hall. He went in. She was sitting on the floor. They had no furniture left: it was all sold. She was burning scraps of paper and old bits of cloth and wool in the hearth.

"I got nothing," he said. "They wouldn't lend me as much as a pin."

He sat down. A great tear rolled down Shmelke's cheek and plopped on to the wooden floor. It formed a wet round in the dust the size of a ducat. Pearl took his hand.

That night she wrote to Loew:

We have lost everything. What do I do?

Loew replied:

You must find something that no one can do without. Whatever it is, you will always be able to sell it.

Pearl pondered on this for a while and then made her decision.

Pearl had a pair of gold earrings. They were her most dearly beloved possession. She took them to the pawnbrokers. She got a small amount of money in exchange for them. She split this in two.

With one half she rented a tiny little shop for a week. With the other half she bought flour.

Then she collected firewood from the fields and hedgerows outside Worms. She brought this home in a barrow borrowed from a neighbour. She lit the oven and baked twenty loaves. She sold the loaves in her tiny shop the next morning and with the money she made was able to buy sufficient flour to make twenty-one loaves. The day following it was twenty-two. She gradually increased the amount to forty loaves. This, she discovered, was the maximum she could sell in a day.

Once her business was up and running, Pearl wrote to Loew:

> *I have followed your advice. I found what no one is able to do without. I make and sell forty loaves a day (except on the Sabbath when a Christian neighbour does it for me). I make enough to feed both my parents and me. I have even redeemed the earrings I pawned for the money to start this venture. Alas, I do not make enough to save. I will never raise the dowry. Please, break off this contract. Do not ruin your life for me.*

Loew replied:

> *Dear Pearl,*
> *Find another suitor if you wish and have your father write to me. For my part, I will not break the contract. One day I will be a rabbi and then we can marry. We will have to be patient until that time comes. I don't want a dowry. I only want you.*

Pearl replied:

> *Dear Loew,*
> *Are you sure?*

Loew wrote back:

> *Dear Pearl,*
> *I think I'm in the best position to know what I want,*
> *don't you?*

Pearl found the young man's clarity persuasive as well as charming. She decided to stop worrying about the future. It would take care of itself. She decided to tell him about herself. She wrote him a long letter about her bread. She also included perceptive descriptions of her customers.

Loew replied with a chatty letter about his yeshiva. He included several amusing thumbnail sketches of some fellow students.

The pair now began to write to each other every day. They began to like one another more and more too. This affection deepened and matured and finally ripened into love. They both wanted to marry each other. They both believed, and because they had faith they had no doubt, that somehow, some way, at some time, all of his own choosing of course, God would unite them.

Time passed – a lot of it. Pearl had been making bread every day now for over three thousand days. She was starting her tenth year of work. It was a fine spring day and Pearl was in her little shop. From the distance came the clatter of marching feet. She knew at once what it was. A regiment of soldiers was marching up her road, led by a drummer boy who was beating time furiously.

Soldiers, Pearl knew, were always hungry. She put half a dozen loaves on a tray and went out to wait. The troops advanced towards her along the road, their pikes on their shoulders, their free arms swinging.

"Bread, fresh bread," Pearl called.

A soldier called back, "What are you doing offering us bread? Soldiers can't just stop when they're marching, you know, or has no one told you that?"

"I can slip a loaf in your knapsack," Pearl called after him, "and you can throw my money on the street. A coin is a coin – dusty or not."

The soldier laughed. "I wish I could put you in my knapsack," he shouted.

"Quiet soldier," a voice ordered.

It was an officer riding beside the soldiers. As he slipped behind Pearl, he arched over and stabbed a loaf through the middle and lifted it clean away from the tray. Pearl turned in time to see the receding back of the officer on his wide grey horse, his sword held high and one of her lovely white loaves stuck on the end.

Balancing the tray on one hand, and lifting her long, heavy skirts with the other, Pearl ran after him. Half a dozen strides and she was level with the man's stirrups. There was a smell of wet brass and horse sweat and mud, mixed with the warm bread smell coming up from the loaves on her tray.

"Please, your honour," she called up. "You took a loaf and you haven't paid."

"But I'm famished," the officer called down to her. He had no beard, just a little soft brown hair on his chin. He spoke gently for a soldier. She guessed he was only twenty years old.

"I'm poor," Pearl said. "I have an old mother and father to feed."

"I'm dying for a taste of bread," the officer said, "but I can't stop and pay you now. And besides it's only a loaf. It's not as if I've taken much."

"Oh, sir," cried Pearl, but she got no further. Her foot caught on a stone sticking up from the road. She stumbled. The loaves slid off the tray. She tumbled after them and landed, face down, in the dust.

Pearl sat up and burst into tears. The soldiers marching by stared down at her, astonished. She heard the clatter of hooves. She turned and saw the officer heading back to her. He reined his horse in as he drew level.

"All right," he said, "I haven't any cash but I'm sitting on a double saddle. I'll throw the top one into your shop."

As Pearl got to her feet he cantered down to her shop and stopped. He put the loaf between his teeth and sheathed his sword. In one single graceful movement he leapt down, pulled the saddle off and hurled it through the doorway. Then he remounted and cantered back while tearing great hunks out of the loaf. He passed behind her and spurred his horse on, following his regiment as it disappeared down the street.

Pearl picked up her loaves and carried them back to the shop. The door was open. The saddle was lying on the floor. She knew Shmelke would know someone in Worms who would buy it.

She went in. The saddle looked damaged. A pocket seemed to be torn revealing something that glowed faintly.

She put the tray on a shelf (she had no table) and knelt down. She undid the flap properly. The pocket underneath was stuffed with ducats. On the other side of the pommel there was another pocket. It was also full of coins.

Pearl hid the saddle, locked her shop and ran home. As she came home she shouted, "We're saved. We're rich."

That night Shmelke wrote a letter to Loew, addressing him as Rabbi. Loew's training was now so advanced it was proper to accord him this honour.

> *Dear Rabbi,*
> *God be praised. We have money. You and Pearl will marry. It will be a great wedding.*

Pearl added a PS:

> *Dear Husband-to-be,*
> *Money has fallen into our laps from the sky. God, at last, has favoured us, as you always said he would.*

Rabbi Loew said goodbye to his fellow students and returned to Worms. He married Pearl. The couple moved to Poznan. They set up home here. Loew took charge of a synagogue and a community. Pearl ran the house. After a year of marriage their first child was born, a daughter, Sara. Two sons, Israel and Pinchas, followed her.

The years rolled by. The children grew up. Sara married first. Her husband was Isaac. Israel and

Pinchas married as well. The children with their spouses remained under Loew and Pearl's roof and began to have their own children.

In the meantime, Rabbi Loew worked steadily for his congregation. He was not only able. He was subtle. His particular skill, for which he was specially venerated, was in arguments or disputes. He could reconcile people who had fallen out. He could turn their hatred into amity. Word of his talent spread in every direction. He was destined for greatness. Everyone said so. Only where or how was that to happen? The answer came many years later. It happened in Prague, capital of the kingdom of Bohemia, and home to thousands of Jews.

Now in order to follow the next part of the story, you must forget Loew for a moment and get a picture of Prague in your mind.

First, imagine an upside-down "L". This is the river Moldau. It is wide and the water is black and cold. Now picture a city radiating along both banks, with the point of the upside-down "L" more of less at its centre. On the west imagine Hradcany hill with a royal palace on top, and on the eastside imagine Vysehrad hill, with another much older palace on its summit. The Jewish ghetto, surrounded by walls and gates, was also on the east bank. It lay near the crook of the "L", close to but not touching the river.

Now imagine, enveloping the walled ghetto, the Christian quarter. This was the Old Town. Now imagine fortified walls and a vast trench encircling this in turn. Prague, in short, had a mini-Jewish town locked inside a major Christian city.

Ordinarily, this did not matter. But periodically, when Christians, encouraged by their priests, believed the Jews had murdered a child, this could be disastrous. They formed into mobs and attacked the ghetto.

If the Jews ran to the walls they could not get out. If they went to the river they could not cross unless they had a boat. Over the river, their ordeal was far from over. For that area was also Christian.

The Jews of Prague were in a difficult position. They did not want to leave. They had to persuade the Christians that what they believed was a lie. Only an exceptional man could convince them. The Jews of Prague invited Rabbi Loew to be the principal rabbi of Prague and their champion against the Blood Libel.

Once he had talked to Pearl and got her to agree, Rabbi Loew accepted. He moved to Prague with his family. He was fifty-nine years old. Now he would need to be a lion.

10

The champion and the enemy

Once he was installed in Prague, Rabbi Loew wrote to Cardinal Jan Sylvester. In his letter he said the Blood Libel was a lie. It hurt Jews. It alarmed Christians. It must be stopped.

He proposed a public forum at which he would argue the Jewish case against the libel with a priest who would put the Christian point of view. It was the equivalent of a medieval ordeal by combat. Instead of swords or shields there would be words and ideas.

Cardinal Sylvester agreed. Now he must line up his champion to fight the Christian corner. He already had him in mind.

Father Tadeus was the most gifted priest in Prague. He was a large handsome man with lovely deep brown eyes. He was highly intelligent and superb in argument. He also hated Jews and believed that no matter what they were accused of doing, in reality they were ten times worse. It was because Christians were so gullible and naïve that they did not understand how dangerous the Jews were.

Cardinal Sylvester summoned Father Tadeus to his residence. Their interview took place in the Stateroom. Cardinal Sylvester sat on a throne. Father Tadeus stood. Cardinal Sylvester explained to Tadeus what he wanted him to do.

Father Tadeus looked at the floor and shook his head.

"What is it?" asked Cardinal Sylvester. "What is the matter?"

The truth was that Father Tadeus's antipathy to Jews was so strong, the idea of talking face to face with one appalled him. But Tadeus knew better than to reveal such feelings to Cardinal Sylvester.

"I am just a humble parish priest," he said. "My job on this earth is to minister to the parishioners of the Green Church, and to care for the sick and the dying. I live quietly and I get on with my business in my parish in the Prague Old Town.

"But if I participate in this event, I will neglect my duties because I will have to prepare for it. My parishioners will suffer. More seriously, they will assume I have finished with them and their troubles and that I am only interested in advancing myself and becoming a famous battling priest. I have spent years gaining the trust of these people. I will lose that in one afternoon's argument with Rabbi Loew. If you instruct me to do this then of course I will. I have to obey you. But I won't do it voluntarily."

Cardinal Sylvester knew it was a mistake to force a man like Father Tadeus. He raised his hand.

"All right," said Cardinal Sylvester, quietly and not unkindly. "Go back to your people. Devote yourself to their needs."

In his sermon the following Sunday in the Green Church, Father Tadeus mentioned the forthcoming dispute.

"I have better things to do than to involve myself in some dispute with some Jew. I have you to look after."

The afternoon of that very same Sunday, Cardinal Sylvester summoned 300 of his best priests to his palace. He addressed the priests in the Stateroom. He told them to prepare to dispute in public with Rabbi Loew. Cardinal Sylvester hoped, with these overwhelming odds, to make up for the loss of Father Tadeus.

Word soon spread to Loew. He was appalled. How could he talk to 300 priests at the same time, let alone argue with them?

However, if he objected he could well imagine what his enemies would say. Typical Jew, they would grumble in the taverns and the alleys of the Old Town, trying to change the rules so he wouldn't lose.

He should have said at the outset that Cardinal Sylvester could only suggest a single champion. Now, he would have to find a way around this problem.

It was a couple of evenings later. Rabbi Loew was in his study. He stared at the flames dancing on the logs burning in his fireplace. The flames were mostly red or yellow or blue but every now and again they were green. It was while waiting for a green flame, with his mind alert but following no line of thought that a brilliant idea came to him. Rabbi Loew went straight to his desk, dipped his goose quill into the black ink smelling of iron and vinegar, and began to write. The letters he made were grey for this ink did not go black for several hours. The letter was to Cardinal Sylvester:

> *Your Grace,*
> *300 is a remarkable number. What a credit to your church that so many priests are eager to debate with me the matter of the Blood Libel. I worry, however, that 300 priests all competing against one another to speak will be to my benefit. They will collide with each other in their eagerness to speak. I, on the other hand, will not have to defer to a soul.*

Naturally, the thought of this advantage pleases me but I know better than to think only in the short term. What will I do, at some later date, when I am charged with having had an unfair advantage – as will surely happen? It is to protect against this that I am writing to you now. Can I tell my critics that I did indeed advise you of my concern on this account? My reputation in Prague will rise, I think, if this becomes generally known, but obviously I must have your permission now before I spread the word. Will you extend this kindness to me?

The Cardinal decided Rabbi Loew's point was sound. The Cardinal had often seen pickpockets elude capture on fair-days by disappearing into the crowds. If his clerics were clumsy and Rabbi Loew was sufficiently wily he might pull off the same trick. Cardinal Sylvester also desperately wished to avoid any future situation where he might have to defend the Jew.

He summoned Karel, his secretary, and dictated this letter:

Dear Rabbi Loew,
Can I suggest the following? Each morning for thirty days, ten priests will submit their arguments in writing to myself. You will then come to my palace,

read these and then draft your replies over the day. I shall have a room placed entirely at your disposal.

This letter went to the synagogue. Rabbi Loew agreed to this proposal with a nicely judged sense of reluctance.

And so each day for thirty days, Rabbi Loew went to Cardinal Sylvester's palace. He read the questions. He drafted his replies.

When people argue face to face, they will sometimes make snide asides or humorous comments about their opponent. They won't win the argument this way but they will make a bad situation worse. By doing everything in writing all this was avoided.

It was also much the better way for Rabbi Loew to get his arguments across. A man can make beautiful sense when he speaks, but once the talking is over, where are his words? They're gone, like puffs of smoke.

Write words down and you fix them, as you want them to be, forever. The written word never dies as long as the page on which it lives remains in circulation.

Written words are also more persuasive. Think about it.

Rabbi Loew's words were read. On first reading they were resisted. But the force of Rabbi Loew's language and the power of his arguments drew the priests back to his texts. They read again what Loew had written and, as they read, the rabbi's words took root in their minds. They could now begin to effect their subtle magic. Gradually, the priests changed. They had been wrong, they realised, when they told their congregations the libel was true.

However, a changed heart is not a changed world. There were plenty of other priests in the church whose beliefs remained unchanged. First and foremost was Father Tadeus.

The thirty days allotted for the dispute were over. The 300 priests returned to the Stateroom where Cardinal Sylvester was on his throne. He called forward the oldest priest.

"Tell me," asked the Cardinal, "what have you decided?"

"By unanimous decision we are decided the Blood Libel is a lie," said the old priest.

The Cardinal's secretary, Karel, was watching from behind the throne. He was bare headed. His hair was short. He wore no wig. His skull was pointed on top rather than flat whereas his face was flat rather than pointed. His eyes were brown. His beard was black and neatly trimmed.

He wore a white shirt with a ruff collar and a short brown jacket. His scabbard was leather with a brass tip.

The sword handle was a dull colour, like pewter.

Karel was an old acquaintance of Father Tadeus.

That evening he called at the Green Church parochial house. Gerda, the housekeeper, answered the door.

She led the visitor to the study where Father Tadeus was reading the New Testament. Karel told him the outcome of the dispute.

"There must have been spells written in invisible ink on the pages the rabbi wrote," said Father Tadeus bleakly. "Those priests were bewitched. There can't be any other explanation."

"And what do you propose to do about this?" asked Karel.

"I don't know yet," said the priest. "In the meantime, do please keep me informed of any developments arising out of this ridiculous dispute."

The following morning Karel arrived at the palace promptly at eight. He went straight to the Cardinal's study. The Cardinal waved a sheaf of papers at his employee.

"These pages here are what the rabbi wrote in reply to the arguments of my priests. I've looked through them," Cardinal Sylvester continued, "and I want them bound in cedar wood and the finest Moroccan leather."

Karel reported this to Father Tadeus that evening.

"There must be spells written on those pages," said Father Tadeus, "because now Cardinal Sylvester is bewitched."

A week passed. The papers, bound as a book, came back to the palace. The Cardinal was delighted.

"Would you look at the tooling on the leather?" he said, turning the volume over in his hands. "Isn't it exquisite? I want you to take this and present it to his Excellency, King Rudolph with my compliments."

Karel crossed the river and climbed to the palace on top of Hradcany hill. He presented the book, not to King Rudolph himself but to one of his secretaries. Then Karel went straight back to see Father Tadeus.

"I guarantee this book will cast its spell over our king now," said Tadeus. "You just watch, you'll see I'm right. King Rudolph will invite Rabbi Loew for an audience. You mark my words."

A couple of days later Cardinal Sylvester received a note from the king. Rabbi Loew was to be brought to the royal residence for a private consultation. A time and a date were specified.

Karel, faithful as usual, went and told Father Tadeus.

"I told you," said the priest, glumly, "I told you. The king's bewitched now."

The day came when Rabbi Loew was to visit

King Rudolph. They spent an hour talking alone. The next day a letter arrived from the king at the Cardinal's palace:

> Dear Cardinal,
> Be it known the following is now my pleasure. Henceforth, if a Jew is charged in Prague with the ritual killing of a Christian child, Rabbi Loew must be present at the trial. This is to be announced by every priest in every church on Sunday coming.

"This gets worse and worse," said Father Tadeus to Karel that evening. "We're never going to see justice in this country now. The Jews will be able to kill all our children. With that Rabbi Loew at every trial, whispering in the judge's ear, they'll get away with it. I am going to have to stop Loew before he destroys us. And I will. You can be sure of that."

"But how will you do that?" Karel asked.

"As yet," said Father Tadeus, "I have no idea, but I have no doubt God will show me what to do very soon."

11

The dream

Karel left the parochial house and made his way home through the Old Town. When he got to his street he walked past his own door and carried on to the end. He passed through the gate that marked the start of the ghetto, and went on to a low timbered building. It had a heavy front door coated in black pitch. This was the entrance to Hirsch's tavern. Karel came here most nights before he went home to his wife and children.

Inside, Karel found himself in the familiar square room. There were rough wooden benches around the edges and a fire at one end. In the middle there was a table where two men sat dicing. In the corner, Hirsch sat on a stool. Behind him two enormous beer barrels lay on trestles. Overhead wooden mugs hung by hooks from the low, sooty ceiling.

"Hirsch," Karel greeted him.

Hirsch was a dark haired man with large ears. He was also a Jew. Karel did not like Jews in general, but when circumstances dictated he was prepared to tolerate the odd individual.

Hirsch stood.

"Good evening," he said. The proprietor was always particularly polite with the Cardinal's secretary. He was not just an important Christian in his own right. He had also helped Hirsch in his complicated dealings with the authorities over the years. He was especially helpful when it came to bribing officials, for which he took a small and quite reasonable percentage. Hirsch correctly presumed Karel's helpfulness was rooted in self-interest.

"How are we today?" continued Hirsch.

"I'm very well."

"And how is the Cardinal?"

"Oh, no change there."

"And what can I get you?"

Karel indicated the barrel with the weaker beer.

"Go, sit," said Hirsch. "I'll bring it to you."

Hirsch filled a wooden mug and carried it to Karel. He wore clogs and they clattered on the floor.

"Here you are," he said, and set the mug down carefully on the bench.

"I hope this beer isn't watered," said Karel, smiling.

"Why would I be so foolish as to do that?" said Hirsch simply. "For a little extra money now,

I might end up losing everything later."

Karel nodded. Hirsch clumped back to his stool. Karel put the rim of the mug to his lips and took a first gulp. The beer was yellow and brown with a slick of white froth. It tasted of beer and yeast, exactly as it ought. Of course it wasn't watered down or augmented with the slops left over at the end of every evening. And that's what he liked about Hirsch, he thought. He didn't cheat. He didn't hold his customers in contempt and serve them inferior drink. He was just an uncomplicated, straightforward tavern owner.

As he drank, Karel pondered. By the time he finished his draught, he had come to a decision. Despite his liking for Father Tadeus, he'd give Hirsch a hint.

Karel rose and carried his mug to Hirsch.

"Just half," he said, handing the mug over. "I don't want to roll home drunk."

Hirsch laughed and began to trickle beer into the mug.

"Are you well?" Karel asked.

"Very," said Hirsch. He was always cheerful and he never complained. This was another reason Karel liked him.

"There's going to be trouble and I'd be very careful if I were you," said Karel mildly and without emphasis.

"Think Father Tadeus and you should be able to work out what I mean. Get some more bolts on the door. Check the shutters on the windows and keep them closed for a while. That's my advice. I don't want to see this place ransacked."

Hirsch handed Karel his half-filled mug and simultaneously looked him right in the eye to show he understood. "Enjoy your drink," he said.

Karel went back to his corner, drank up and left. A slow evening followed . . .

Later, after he had closed the tavern, Hirsch hurried to the crooked old house where Rabbi Loew lived. This was a place of uneven windows and warped doors, tortuous passages and oddly shaped rooms. It was part of a network of strange ancient buildings that also included the synagogue and courtroom, where Loew settled arguments and gave advice.

Hirsch knocked on the back door and Pearl let him in. She brought him to the study where Rabbi Loew was sitting by the fire. Hirsch took off his hat but declined to sit. Hirsch was slightly nervous of Rabbi Loew. He passed on what Karel had told him earlier. Then he left.

Alone again, Rabbi Loew stared into the flames in the fireplace. There was trouble coming and Father Tadeus was involved. This did not surprise him. He had heard Tadeus's name many times before.

The rabbi went to his desk and sat down. He took a piece of paper and cut from the top a slip about the thickness of his thumb. He dipped his pen in the bitter ink, thought for a moment and then wrote carefully on the paper, "How am I to wage war against this priest, my antagonist?"

Loew put the pen down and blew on the slip. He rolled it into a little scroll. He took a silver tube out of a drawer, unscrewed the top, fitted the scroll inside, and re-screwed the top back on. He was ready to direct a dream question. All that was necessary now was that he went to bed. While he slept the answer would come.

When his fire had burnt down he carried the tube to his bedroom and slipped it under the pillow on his side of the bed. He undressed and got under the covers.

He said, "Goodnight, Pearl."

"Goodnight," said Pearl who was already lying in bed.

Rabbi Loew went to sleep.

The next morning Pearl shook him on the shoulder as she did every morning. Usually, he would swim straight from sleep to wakefulness. This morning, however, he took care, before he was fully awake, to direct his thoughts back to the preceding night. Long experience had taught him that if he went straight to wakefulness, his dreams were lost.

"Not getting up?" asked Pearl.

"I asked a dream question," he muttered, his eyes still closed.

"Oh." He heard her walk off to her dressing room. He waited. He was half awake, half asleep. First nothing and then, suddenly a number of strange images from the night before swam into view before his inner eye. He saw a Sphinx, a pile of cobble stones, a room of wedding guests dancing, and finally, a bank of snow with these words written on it: Ah, By Clay Destroy Evil Forces, Golem, Help Israel: Justice. The handwriting was quite like Pearl's.

He opened his eyes. "Ah, By Clay Destroy Evil Forces, Golem, Help Israel: Justice," he muttered.

"What did you say?" It was Pearl, back from her dressing room. She wore a day dress. It was grey. Her hair was pinned up.

"Oh, nothing," said Rabbi Loew. "I was just remembering something I dreamt."

"I dreamt of a snow bank with words written on it," she said.

He was not surprised. They often dreamt about the same thing. Pearl said this was because they went on talking when they were asleep, though they weren't aware that they were.

"I hope the fire isn't out when I get down," she said.

This was a reference to the kitchen boy. He was meant to get up in the night and keep the fire stoked, but for the last couple of nights he had slept through and let the fire go out. Pearl hated when this happened. The day that followed was inevitably out of kilter.

"I'll be down presently," said Rabbi Loew.

She left quickly. She knew what he had to do and that he wanted to be left alone to do it. That was typical of her tactfulness.

Rabbi Loew reached down for the slate and chalk he kept under the bed to make notes about his dreams before he forgot them. He wrote these words: Ah, By Clay Destroy Evil Forces, Golem, Help Israel: Justice.

Later, he wrote them on a large piece of paper and tacked this to the wall above his desk. As he sat at his desk that day, he kept glancing up at the words. When he went to bed, he fell asleep thinking about them. When he woke up the next morning he could not remember his dream, but he knew what these words meant. He knew exactly what he had to do.

He summoned to his study his son-in-law, Isaac (who was married to Sara, his daughter) and his principal pupil, Jacob Gintzberg.

"You are going to help me make a man out of clay," he said to the two younger men.

Isaac, who was the more forward of the two, coughed and asked, "We're making a man out of clay – what for?"

"To protect us, and our community."

"And how will a clay man do that?" asked Isaac.

"Oh, he won't be a statue. He'll be alive."

"Alive?"

"Oh yes. He'll be able to move and do all you can do physically. At first glance, the only difference between him and us is that he will be stronger and bigger and quicker and harder than any man who has ever lived has been. Of course there will be differences, profound ones. He won't be able to make babies. Obviously there'll be no need for him to have what we have, because he's never going to meet a woman like himself. She doesn't exist. He won't need to eat or drink either. Once he's made he can keep going forever. Nor will he sleep. He'll just go still when told to do so and he won't stir until he's ordered to move again, even if that's not for a hundred years.

"And there we have the essential characteristic of this creation; he will be supremely, effortlessly and comprehensively biddable. I think this is just the sort of helpmate we need if our community is going to survive what is looming."

"Will he talk?" asked Isaac.

"He won't be dumb. He'll have some words. He'll be able to respond to instructions and answer very simple questions. But his language won't be complex. His comprehension will be strictly limited. He won't be able to reason because he won't have the words with which to think."

"And why do you need our help?" asked Jacob.

"I have to have each of the cardinal elements present: earth, fire, air and water. The golem will be earth – he'll be made of clay after all. I was born under an air sign and you, Jacob, under a water sign and you, Isaac, under a fire sign. It'll only work if we're all there."

"When do we do this?" asked Isaac.

"When I tell you," Rabbi Loew replied.

12

The golem is created

It was the time. Rabbi Loew and his helpers gathered after midnight in the workshop at the back of his house. They greased four large planks with candle wax and loaded them on to a handcart. They piled on trowels and spades, axes and chisels, saws and knives. They added a box of fishing lines and a bag of extra large men's clothes. They lit their lanterns.

They pushed the cart out of the yard into the alley behind. Rabbi Loew locked the yard door behind them.

They set off. It was now one o'clock in the morning. The frozen streets of the ghetto glistened white. The noise made by the cart's wheels echoed off the buildings they passed. They did not meet a soul except for a brown cat with white paws.

They arrived at one of the gates in the wall that surrounded the ghetto. The night watchman recognised Rabbi Loew, and waved the party through. Unlike the rest of his community, the rabbi was allowed to leave at night and enter the Christian sector.

The handcart wheels grinding on the frosty cobbles, the trio advanced into the Old Town. The streets were wider here but they, too, were white with frost and empty. All Prague was sleeping.

They reached the most southerly gate in the defensive wall that surrounded the Old Town. Rabbi Loew opened his purse and took out a gold coin. He knocked on the little door of the booth at the side. The night guard came out. He was an old man with a large red nose and unfriendly manner. He smelt of onions.

"We're going to fish in the Moldau," said Rabbi Loew, indicating the tackle. "We need to get down early to lay our lines." He put his coin into the night guard's hand.

The old man closed his fist greedily around the coin.

"What are the tools for?" he asked.

"To hack away some undergrowth," said Loew.

"And the planks?"

"We'll make a little bench to sit on. You get tired if you're on your feet all the time."

"Don't tell me, I know all about it," said the night guard. He unbolted the Judas door set into one of the massive gates. The rabbi and his companions trundled the cart through. The Judas door was slammed behind and the bolts quickly drawn.

Outside the gate stood several gibbets. Bodies preserved in pitch – these were the remains of men executed for crimes – dangled from the crossbars. There were displays like this at every gate to deter other criminals from entering the city.

A wind blew, stirring the black shapes. The gibbet chains went clink, clink. It was a pure sound in the still night. They hurried off. The road ran south in a straight line. It was a mud road, deeply rutted. The ruts were frozen hard, and in the valleys between there were puddles of white frozen water. On either side of the road stood fields of white grass and ghostly trees with white branches.

After walking for a while a path appeared to them. It led away to the right, towards the river. They moved down the path in single file. The normally boggy ground was hard like iron. The long coarse grass on either side of the path was thick and stiff with frost. Behind the grass lay frozen water meadows. These were still, calm, utterly placid places.

As they drew closer to the Moldau, the water meadows gave way to marshes. They heard birds calling. Once they heard what sounded like a bird punching through a skin of ice and then beating its wings frantically as it rose into the air. At last the River Moldau came into view. It was black. It greeted them with a faint lapping sound.

Rabbi Loew turned off the path and led his party along a labyrinth of hard tracks that criss-crossed the marshy edges. The river smell grew stronger. The sound of the flowing water grew louder.

At last Rabbi Loew said, "This is the spot."

They had reached a place marooned between marsh and river. It was a slightly shelving beach. Small trees ringed it, with bare leafless branches. The wind made a little sighing noise as it passed through these. The frozen ground underfoot now consisted of little stones, mud and earth, and patches of sand. Right in the middle was what looked like an upturned boat or an abandoned tomb. It was in fact a long rounded block of dense dark yellow clay.

Directed by Rabbi Loew, the men began to carve the figure of an exceptionally large man out of the block. Because of the extreme cold the clay was much less sticky than it might otherwise have been. It was like cold butter to cut.

Once they had the figure in crude outline, they worked on the details. To the head they gave a nose and eyes and ears, to the hands they gave fingers and thumbs, to the feet they gave toes. They even made little beds at the ends of the digits for nails. When they finished the only difference between the figure and a man was that since he was not born of woman, he had no navel, and since he would never procreate, the space between the legs was smooth, like a child's doll.

"Now we cut it free," said Rabbi Loew.

They punched the planks under the figure, separating it from the rest of the clay. Then they slid the figure down the planks (this was why Rabbi Loew had waxed them) and got it down on to the ground.

"Right, everybody down to the feet," said Rabbi Loew. The three men went to the end of the golem. Their faces were now towards its face.

"Isaac," he said, "I want you to walk around the golem seven times, going from left to right and as you do, whisper these words."

He whispered the words that were to be said into Isaac's ear. His son-in-law walked seven times around the clay figure from left to right. Two honking geese beat across the night sky, their wings creaking like dried leather. Later a donkey brayed, a long, drawn out, agonised sound, and a dog barked in the distance.

As Isaac completed the seventh circuit the vast clay figure turned red hot. The heat was ferocious. The men, their eyes watering, fell back towards the ring of trees. The ground under the golem, now heated, hissed and spluttered. Several stones cracked with a noise like gunfire. Thick, creamy steam rose, yet the figure glowing like the hottest coal in a furnace, shone through the vapour.

"Now Jacob," said Rabbi Loew, "you will walk around the golem seven times going from left to right, and as you do say these words under your breath."

He whispered the words into Jacob's ear. Jacob had to keep further away than Isaac from the figure, because of the intense heat, and therefore his circuits took longer. As he walked, whispering his magic words, the ground went on steaming. The steam was blown about by the wind. Rabbi Loew felt his clothes and his beard growing wet from it, and a grainy residue on his lips. It tasted of earth, river water and vegetable roots. This, thought Rabbi Loew, is something like the taste of life.

Jacob completed his seventh circuit and went back to his place. The golem's redness began oozing away. The figure was cooling. The steam thinned. The stones stopped cracking. For an instant Rabbi Loew and the others could see through the golem, like a lump of glass, to the ground on which it rested. An instant later it turned to ash. Or what looked like ash. It was the same colour and texture but the golem looked solid, dense and monumental, like a statue made of marble, or lead, or some even heavier substance.

Rabbi Loew left the younger men and began to

circle clockwise around the figure. As he moved he spoke to himself quietly. Isaac, the son-in-law, thought he caught some words from the Five Books of Moses. He could not be certain.

As Rabbi Loew spoke, a small neat cloud dropped from above and fell across the figure like a shroud. It hid the figure and the ground around it completely.

From inside the cloud there came a noise. It sounded like swallowing, magnified a thousand times.

The cloud began to thin and the golem came back into view. The surface of his body was no longer like compacted ash. It was slowly pinking, crinkling and dimpling as it turned to skin.

The toe and finger ends twitched and jumped as nails grew into place. All over the golem's hefty legs and forearms little wires of hair punched up from the skin. From the centre of the bare pate hair grew sideways and outwards in every direction. Simultaneously, eyebrows appeared and hair sprouted in the ears and down the nape.

Rabbi Loew finished his circuits and returned to his place. The shroud-like cloud vanished. The three men moved round to the golem's head. They stared at the face. The eyelids trembled and twitched then slowly rolled away. Two black eyes were revealed. For a moment they were dead and then, there was a just perceptible widening. Rabbi Loew and his helpers understood. The golem was seeing for the first time ever. He saw three faces looking down at him. And he was amazed.

"Stand on your feet," shouted Rabbi Loew.

The huge figure got up promptly from the riverbed.

"Fetch the bag of clothes," said Rabbi Loew to his assistants.

They dressed the golem in a pair of huge blue trousers with a drawstring, a shirt with three buttons and ragged cuffs, a long gabardine coat that belted around the middle and a pair of brown wooden clogs.

"He looks like Chaim, our beadle," said Jacob when they had finished, "although he's bigger."

"Bigger," said Isaac, "is an understatement."

"Listen to me," said Rabbi Loew, staring into the dark eyes of his creation. "We created you so that you would protect the Jews from harm. Your name is Joseph, and you will be my beadle. You must do everything I command, even if it means jumping into fire or water."

The golem nodded and croaked, "Yes." His voice was a low, ugly monotone and not in the least human. But then he was an automaton designed to obey. The words already in his head when he sprang to life were also extremely limited. "Yes", "no", a few hundred nouns and a list of basic verbs. This was deliberate on Loew's part. If the golem could talk fluently then he would be able to reason. This would lead to questions and then difficulties and finally disaster. No, Joseph must be incapable of doing anything other than what he was told to do.

Rabbi Loew looked up. The sky overhead was white and pale.

"The dawn came," he said, "and I didn't even notice."

He turned and looked down at the Moldau. Floating on its dark surface was a skim of silver. The river was reflecting back the light from the sky. In the middle of the river a fisherman in a boat was casting a net.

"Let's go," said Rabbi Loew.

He opened the little door on his lantern, and blew hard on the wick. The flame of the candle inside wavered and died.

"Joseph," he said, "the planks and the tools you see here – put them all on the handcart."

Joseph began throwing tools into the bottom of the cart.

"Hey," shouted Rabbi Loew, "more care with my property, if you don't mind."

Joseph put the other tools and the planks away gently.

"Now – handcart – push – along the path," said

Rabbi Loew. He pointed out the direction in which he was to go.

Joseph set off, pushing the handcart as easily as if he was pushing a broom across a polished floor. The three men followed. As they trekked across the marsh it got brighter. By the time they reached the road it was early morning.

The party headed for the city. As he walked Rabbi Loew looked carefully at the trees on either side. The frost of the night before had been exceptionally hard and to his naked eye it appeared the trees had been dusted white all over with a brush. They looked strangely brittle. Of course they weren't. At some point it occurred to Rabbi Loew, that as a picture for the thoughts of God, trees were as good an example as anything else.

13

The giant at breakfast

The rabbi stopped at the back door of his house.

"Stand still, Joseph, don't move."

Joseph obeyed.

Rabbi Loew turned to his two helpers.

"Jacob, Isaac," he said, "I'm going to tell everyone a story when I get in. You will agree with every word I say."

The pair nodded.

"Joseph."

The golem turned to him eagerly. He reminded Rabbi Loew of a dog hearing the voice of his master. He made a mental note to try to be less officious.

"Two rules," said Rabbi Loew. "You are never to speak again unless I tell you. Nobody must know you have even a few words. Your silence will make your presence all the more impressive. And you are always to do exactly what I tell you."

The golem, his mouth firmly closed, nodded to show he understood. In all his future conversations with the rabbi he would only nod or shake his head.

Rabbi Loew opened the back door and entered the scullery first. It was a dark space that smelt of wet laundry and scalded coppers.

"Is that you?" Pearl called from the kitchen beyond.

"Who do you think?" Rabbi Loew called back.

Immediately behind he heard a loud thud. Rabbi Loew turned to look. Joseph had hit his head on the low lintel. It was the first time he had ever been through a door. The blow had made a gash on his forehead. Liquid now poured out of this. It was not red like blood, but white, like sap. It gave off a strong smell of river mud and ash and rotting vegetation. Whatever was packed inside the golem's massive body, thought the rabbi, it was nothing like what was inside his.

"You've hurt yourself," said the rabbi gently. "Wipe your forehead."

Joseph passed his hand across his wound, while Jacob and Isaac slipped in behind. When Joseph took his hand away, the gash had miraculously repaired itself and there was no more sap.

"Be careful with doors in future, Joseph," Rabbi Loew said quietly, so no one in the kitchen could hear. Then he said loudly, "I've got someone with me, Pearl."

"Bring him in," Pearl called back to her husband.

"And it is a *he* I assume."

"Now mind your head in here, Joseph," said Rabbi Loew. "The kitchen beams are even lower than the back door."

He tapped Joseph's head and pointed at the ceiling, then opened the door to the kitchen and said, "Go on, inside Joseph."

The golem shuffled towards the doorway. He had to bend a long way forward to get into the low dark hot kitchen on the other side. A ring of faces looked up in astonishment at him. The Rabbi, Jacob and Isaac followed behind.

"And who is this?" demanded Pearl, who was never backward at asking questions. She sat at the top of the table. Beside her sat Sara, Rabbi Loew's daughter, who was married to Isaac. On the other side were Rabbi Loew's two sons, Israel and Pinchas and their wives. Then there were the various children of the rabbi's children, and finally, the boy who helped in the kitchen.

"No, don't tell me," Pearl continued. "You found him at the fair where he was being exhibited as a Russian giant. And you've brought him back because it's wrong this fine fellow should be shown in public for profit. And his name is Atlas."

The rabbi laughed. It was true he loathed the fair.

It was also true he had rescued several unhappy exhibits over the years. Her guess was inspired. It occurred to him that Joseph really must look exceptionally odd.

"No, not Atlas," said Rabbi Loew, "though he could be. No, his name is Joseph." He slapped Joseph's impressive back. The golem stared at the floor.

"We met him in the street," continued Rabbi Loew. "He's simple. He's mute. He has nowhere to go. I felt sorry for him. God commands us to shelter men like him. That's why I've brought him home. He's going to live with us from now on as a member of the family. He'll help around the house, he'll run errands, perform simple tasks. His ability to understand is strictly limited. So I don't want any of you to ask him to do anything. It'll end in disaster. Only I am to give him orders. Is that understood?"

"Yes, we understand," said Pearl quietly. "No one tells him what to do except you."

"Yes," said Rabbi Loew, brightly. He turned. "Come on, Joseph."

The golem started, like someone waking from a sleep.

"Stoop down and go out of that door," continued Rabbi Loew. "We'll go to my courtroom. You can stay there in the day when you're not busy."

Joseph scuttled across the floor and, bending low, ducked out. Rabbi Loew hurried out after him.

On the far side he found himself in a long, gloomy corridor with the stairs to the upper floors leading off it. Joseph was already at the door at the far end. He was about to bolt through it.

"Wait, Joseph!" called Rabbi Loew.

The golem stopped, dead. At the same time Loew realised Pearl had followed him out of the kitchen and was right behind him.

"So you found him in the street?" said Pearl, in a low voice too quiet to reach the kitchen. "I don't think so. Now where did you find him really? Don't fob me off or I won't let you keep him here. Then you'll really be in trouble."

"I made him."

"You made him?"

"Yes."

"How?"

"With mud from the Moldau actually."

"He's a mud man?"

"Well, not now. If you touch him he feels like us. He's warm. He has skin. He has eyes. He looks like us. But under that skin he's quite different. He's not like us at all. He's a more basic form of life, closer to plants and trees. But before he came to life, before he assumed the shape you see before you, yes, he was mud. That's what he's made from."

"You know," said Pearl, "that is such a ridiculous explanation, I am tempted to believe that it must be the truth."

The rabbi looked at his feet.

"I'd better go back and give Isaac and Jacob some hot milk and hot bread," said Pearl.

She went back through the door to the kitchen. Rabbi Loew walked to the golem waiting at the end of the corridor.

"In future, I always lead and you always follow, understand?"

Joseph nodded.

Rabbi Loew led Joseph through the ground floor of his house. They came out into a small covered passage. Their footsteps echoed off the stone floors and plastered walls. They went through more doors and arrived finally in the courtroom. Although criminal cases – theft, murder, assault, and so on – were heard in the Christian courts, civil and commercial disputes between Jews were heard here, with the rabbi acting as judge. This was also where he ruled on religious doctrine and practice and on kosher dietary matters.

It was a large dusty room with bumpy walls and high, widely spaced and slightly misshapen windows.

It was filled with dark gloomy furniture – chairs, tables and benches. A tall black stove that leant at an angle stood in the corner. Beside this stood a vast box where the kindling and the firewood were kept.

"See that box," said Rabbi Loew, "that's where you stay, unless I tell you otherwise. You will lie here at night as well. Every morning you will clean the ashes out of the stove – the embers go in the ash pail at the back – and whenever you're here, it is your responsibility to keep the fire going, day and night. Now, sit."

Rabbi Loew went to the door in the corner of the courtroom and opened it. He found himself staring into a storeroom crammed with surplus furniture he did not have the courage to throw away. There were several more such rooms at the back of the courtroom. These were the territories of the beadle, Chaim.

"Chaim," shouted Rabbi Loew.

The beadle appeared.

"Come here, I want you to meet someone," said Rabbi Loew. 'Chaim, this is Joseph'. He turned to the golem. 'You must stand up when you're introduced. Joseph, this is Chaim.'

Joseph stood. He was four feet higher than Chaim was. Joseph's face was blank. He saw, he registered, that was all. Chaim, on the other hand, wanted to stare and he wanted to run.

"It's a monster," Chaim said at last. "Where did you find him? Is he safe?"

He was like a boy, thought Loew, who had stumbled into the presence of a giant.

"It's a long story," said Rabbi Loew. "I found him in the street. He's a mute. And although he's big he's harmless. He does exactly what I tell him. Watch me." He coughed. "Joseph, turn and face the stove." Joseph turned. "Sit on the box." Joseph sat. "See, anything I say," Rabbi Loew continued, "and he does it. He'll jump in water or walk through flames if I command him to do so."

"I see," said the old beadle.

"But don't be telling him what to do," said Rabbi Loew. "He answers to me alone. There'll be trouble if anyone else but me gives him instructions." Rabbi Loew lowered his voice to a whisper. "A cobblestone has got more brains than he has. You see, Chaim, he's completely stupid."

"Oh, I see," said Chaim. He felt better now. There was little likelihood that this simpleton would usurp him. "I'll go back to my work then," he said, cheerfully. "I'm chopping firewood. See you later, Joseph."

Over the days that followed the enormous silent stranger, who either attended to the fire or sat motionless on the wood box with his head down and his hands resting on his lap, made an enormous impression on the Jews who passed through the courtroom. A freckled boy of sixteen named him Joseph the Mute. And before very long that was how he was known in the ghetto and in the Christian Old Town beyond. He was Joseph the Mute.

14

The flood

The world turned on her axis. The days grew just a little longer, the nights a little shorter. The moon changed from a curved dagger to a swollen ball of chalk with little black smudges on her cheeks. In the pleasure grounds around King Rudolph's elegant palace, little sticky buds appeared on the trees. In the yard behind the rabbi's house, in the places sheltered by the old lopsided walls, tender green shoots pushed out of the cold wet earth.

With Passover now not far off, Pearl followed custom and began to clean her house. She proposed to start at the attic, and work her way down to the brick-lined cellar, where she stored cheese, apples and salted fish over the winter. She began work on Sunday but had to keep breaking off. She had grandchildren to care for and meals to cook and many other duties.

By the fourth day Pearl was grumpy. She ought to have been in her cellar by now but owing to the numerous interruptions she hadn't even finished the first storey yet. She ate breakfast hurriedly and climbed the stairs to the big festive room, which was traditionally used at Passover by the whole household. Here they would have their Seder, the ritual supper of remembrance.

She pushed open the door and went in. The room was dark and there was a smell of old plaster and mould. It had been shut up for months.

Pearl crossed the room kicking dust up as she went. The little particles soon made her nose itch and her eyes smart. She opened the shutters and lifted the windows that looked over the yard below. A cold breeze blew in. She turned to examine the room.

A thin skim of furry dust covered the floor – other than where her footprints were – as well as the walls and ceiling. The whole room would have to be washed. She needed to fetch water up from the well. If only she could have it here without having to tire herself out even more by carrying it.

The next thought came effortlessly. As her husband was out, why didn't she get Joseph to do the job? She wasn't supposed to use the golem but Rabbi Loew need never know she had. She could have the job done and Joseph back on his box in the courtroom before he got back. And as he was a mute, well, Joseph would hardly tell on her. So there'd be no need to mention the matter to the rabbi later, either. Pearl knew what she proposed wasn't quite right, but she didn't think it was quite wrong either.

She got two empty barrels from the scullery and carried them to the festive room. Then she hurried towards the courtroom.

Hearing her footfalls, Joseph, on his box, looked up. When she came in, he saw a woman wearing an apron with little hoops of gold dangling from her ears.

"Follow me, Joseph," she shouted.

Of course he had been told he was only to follow Rabbi Loew's instructions. But Joseph was not a man who could retain complex information. He was in effect a machine and this new order, barked out in an authoritative tone, obliterated what was there before and switched him on. He jumped to his feet. He was ready to do whatever he was told.

The woman hurried off. He hurried after her. She led him to a first storey room.

"Well, yard," said Pearl pointing out the window. Then, she continued, pointing at the barrels, "Take barrels, fill with water, and bring water here. I'll be back." With that she rushed out.

Joseph got the barrels, one under each arm, and he jumped out of the window. He ran to the well. He filled the barrels quickly. Then, with a full barrel tucked under each arm, he jumped up through the window and into the festive room without spilling a single drop. As Pearl had set no limit, Joseph would now go on bringing water until told to stop.

He emptied out the water onto the floor and, performed the same action hundreds more times. He moved so fast that each circuit only took a couple of seconds. And he moved so carefully that he didn't spill a drop. The large room soon began to fill up with water.

At the same time, some of the water Joseph brought up squeezed out through the space under the door, sloshed down the stairs and began to form a puddle in the corridor outside the kitchen door.

While this was happening, Rabbi Loew returned unexpectedly early to his courtroom. When he discovered Joseph wasn't on his box, he was perplexed. He decided to ask Pearl if she knew where Joseph was.

As he moved towards the kitchen, not looking where he was going and utterly absorbed by his thoughts, Rabbi Loew stepped into the puddle. The water soaked straight through his shoes and wet his toes. He stopped. He looked down. Water. Was this coming from outside?

He stepped back and, at the same time, he heard a noise – the unmistakable gurgling noise of flowing water. He turned. No, the source of the puddle wasn't outside. Water was sheeting down the stairs from the floor above. Then he heard the unmistakable sound of feet in clogs clumping around.

"Pearl," called Rabbi Loew, opening the kitchen door.

Pearl was at the table cutting the wicks of candles.

"You'd better come out here to the hall," said Rabbi Loew, urgently.

Pearl lifted her skirts. She dashed through the kitchen doorway and splashed straight into the puddle that was rapidly becoming a small pond. Then she heard the noise upstairs. Her cheeks reddened.

"Is that my friend Joseph, possibly?" asked Rabbi Loew. His tone was mild.

Pearl saw the stairs and the water pouring down. Her mouth opened. Her hand automatically flew to her lips. There came a strangled, "Oh dear," and a gasp.

They hurried up the stairs and rushed along the gallery to the door of the festive room. Lapping water sounded on the other side of the wood.

Rabbi Loew opened the door – it opened outwards – and a great wall of water gushed out around their legs. Joseph, at that very instant, could be seen leaping daintily in through the window, a barrel under each arm.

"Joseph," called Rabbi Loew as the golem tipped the barrels. "Stop."

The expression on Joseph's face was the closest to surprise he could get.

"Water – fetching – over," said Rabbi Loew.

From the far end of the room, Joseph stared at Rabbi Loew and the woman standing in the doorway with water flowing around their feet, as he waited to be told what to do next. Through the open windows behind Joseph stretched a white Prague winter sky.

"Drop – barrels," continued Rabbi Loew.

Joseph obeyed. The barrels splashed in the thin depth of water remaining and rolled away.

"Pearl, would you mind, in future, sticking to the arrangement we agreed? From now on it's just me who tells Joseph what to do."

"Certainly," Pearl said quietly. She coughed. "Can you ask him do something then?"

"Yes."

"Ask him to get an old blanket from the press outside our room. He can mop the water up with it and then wring it out of the window. He'll get this room dry quick enough. Then he can go and mop up downstairs. And you know what the best part of it is?"

The rabbi shook his head. The bulk of the water

had drained away down the stairs though there was still a skim on the floor of the landing and in the festive room. He wriggled his wet toes inside his soaking shoes. When he had heard Pearl out, he thought, he'd go and sit in front of the kitchen fire and get dry.

"He won't grumble like a normal servant at having to undo what he's just done."

The rabbi told Joseph what he was to do and the golem went off.

"You know something else strikes me too," began Pearl.

Rabbi Loew tilted his head. She had a gift for finding something to say when anybody else would be dumb. He would enjoy this.

"I know as much about making watches as Joseph knows about gathering water."

"Shall we go down to the fire?" he suggested. They turned and together began to squelch slowly down the stairs, warning each other as they went to be careful and not to slip on the wet wood.

The story of what happened, complete with Pearl's punch line, spread through the ghetto. Within weeks, "You know as much about watch-making as Joseph the Mute knows about carrying water," had become a standard rebuke issued to incompetents in the ghetto and in greater Prague beyond. And it remained in currency for hundreds of years, long after its origins were forgotten.

15

The guard

Rabbi Loew woke with a start. He lay still in his bed. His heart was beating. He heard Pearl at his side taking shallow sips of air. The room was quite dark. It was the middle of the night and he was wide awake. He realised he would not get back to sleep now.

Passover lay a few days ahead. This was when the haters of Jews were most likely to contrive to make the Blood Libel come true. It had happened at the moment of his birth. It could happen again.

He remembered having read somewhere that a dead body, no matter how heavily it was weighted, would always float up to the top in water. Wasn't this the same? His anxieties about the future, which had been lying at the bottom of his mind, had risen suddenly to the surface. They were what had woken him.

The rabbi considered lighting a candle. He would have liked the comfort of the pale yellow light coming from the trembling wick. But what if he woke Pearl as he lit it? She would want to know why he was awake and what he was feeling. In the end, however ingenious his excuses and denials, she would extract the truth from him. She always did. The remainder of the night would then be terrible, he thought, with both of them terrified, and there was no profit in that.

No, he would just have to lie still in the dark. He would say his prayers. He would remember his life. He would speak to God. He would promise to try harder. He would ask that his inadequacies be understood. He would explain that he tried and he intended the best but it did not always come to pass that he did as he intended. He was a man, just a man – and to be such a creature was to fail.

And in this way, while his thoughts shot from his head and flew away to the ear of the all-seeing, all-hearing, omniscient creator, the hours would pass. Then, at last, the first light of dawn would glimmer outside. The new day would have come – just as it had every day of his life so far – and then he would set in motion the rescue plan he had made.

At nine o'clock that morning, Rabbi Loew strode into his courtroom with a bundle of clothes under his arm. He immediately smelt burning.

Joseph was at the stove at the far end of the room, riddling the embers.

The rabbi hurried across the room. Joseph had his arm inside the stove. He was turning the embers by hand.

"Take your arm out and stand up," said Rabbi Loew sharply, throwing the bundle of clothes on to the wood box.

Joseph pulled his enormous arm – it was the thickness of a small tree – back through the hatch at the front and stood up.

"Don't do that again," said Rabbi Loew. "Now show me the hand you just had in the fire."

Joseph proffered the hand, knuckles uppermost. Rabbi Loew turned it palm upwards. On the finger ends there were no blisters or other signs of burning at all. Joseph was partly made from fire, so it was hardly surprising he did not burn.

The rabbi was about to drop Joseph's hand when he noticed for the first time that there were no lines on his palm. The rabbi was not surprised. Joseph's fate was whatever he, the rabbi, determined. Joseph had no lines because he had no volition. If his future was anywhere, it was on the rabbi's palm.

"You may be immune to fire," said the rabbi, "but your clothes aren't."

Joseph nodded. It occurred to Rabbi Loew, watching the huge head rocking backwards and forwards, that he had only told Joseph to keep the stove going. He had never shown Joseph how to do it. He now realised he should assume nothing and explain everything.

The rabbi picked up the poker and waved it at Joseph.

"From now on, use this in the stove to turn the coals and not your hands. Right, off you go, prove to me you know how to do it."

Joseph seized the poker and used the end to turn the coals. As he watched, the rabbi rejoiced that he had surprised Joseph. If Joseph's clothes had caught fire, the golem would have survived but the courtroom would not.

Joseph threw wood and coal on to the hot red fire bed inside the stove. Then he closed the stove door.

"Good, thank you," said Rabbi Loew. "Now I want you to put these on."

Rabbi Loew held out a coat. It was a vast shabby shapeless woollen garment. It had once been black but age and soiling had made it grey.

"I think that should fit," said Rabbi Loew.

Joseph turned and rammed his thick arms back and down through the sleeves. Whatever else he was, when it came to obligingness, Joseph could not be faulted.

"Turn."

Joseph faced forward and Rabbi Loew pulled the coat closed over his huge chest. There were a half dozen buttonholes down the coat's front but no buttons to put through them.

Rabbi Loew turned and took from the chair a piece of thick greasy rope. The guard dog it once secured had chewed it. There were teeth marks up and down its hairy length.

"Lift your arms, Joseph," said Rabbi Loew in a polite voice. Because he still tended to bark at his helper he was really making an effort to speak to him more sweetly.

Joseph lifted his arms. Rabbi Loew threaded one end of the rope through a buttonhole and then walked, holding the other end, right round Joseph. When he got back to where he started, the rabbi reached the other end from the buttonhole and pulled the rope tight, closing the coat in the process. Rabbi Loew had a talent for knots. He made a lovely double-bow, but then thought that if Joseph were going to pass himself off as a Christian porter, this would look inauthentic. He pulled his handiwork apart and made an ugly nondescript knot instead.

"Now," said Rabbi Loew, quietly, "the final touch."

He held a red hat. It was made of felt. It had a battered crown and a huge brim that drooped badly.

"Put that on your head."

Joseph put the hat on.

"Walk round the room would you, please?" said Rabbi Loew.

Joseph walked in a circle, his feet clumping on the floor as he went. The drooping brim of the hat covered most of his face.

"Very good, excellent," said Rabbi Loew. He was pleased that Joseph's face was almost invisible. It was a strong ugly face and as such it was too memorable. For what he had in mind, the less Joseph was noticed and remembered, the better.

Rabbi Loew left Joseph walking in a circle. He went to the door to the storerooms, opened it and called, "Chaim."

The beadle came into the courtroom a few moments later carrying a small axe. As usual, at this time of day, he was splitting wood.

"If you saw him in the street," asked Rabbi Loew, pointing at the trudging golem, "what would you take him to be?"

"A porter."

"Sure?"

"Absolutely."

The porters were a group of forty or fifty Christians, who gathered just beyond where the ghetto ended.

They were ill-educated but physically powerful men, and for a small fee they would carry anything for anyone, anywhere. If you lived in the ghetto, by custom, you had to employ one of these men if you wanted anything carried.

"So he'd definitely pass for one?"

"Oh yes," said Chaim, "that's a porter."

At that moment Pearl entered.

"What's with the porter?" she asked.

"Don't you recognise him?" asked Rabbi Loew, smiling. "Joseph, show your face to Pearl," he called out.

"Why is Joseph dressed like that?" Pearl asked.

"Because he is going to be a porter," Rabbi Loew said. "Or he's going to pretend to be one at any rate. And he's going to guard us."

Chaim went back to cutting wood. Pearl told her husband to come to the kitchen and left the courtroom. Rabbi Loew clapped his hands.

"Joseph, come here."

Joseph broke off from his circuit and went straight to the rabbi.

"This is what you're going to do for me, Joseph," he said. "You're going to patrol the outskirts of the ghetto tonight and every night. Watch out for someone carrying a sack, or driving a cart with a sack on the boards at the back. If they look as if they're worried they're going to be spotted, stop them, look in their sack. If you find a body inside – man, woman, boy or girl – you tie the man up and you take him and his sack to the police at the city hall."

16

Joseph traps Vasek

It was two nights later. Joseph stood on a street that ran between the ghetto and the Old Town. The night was dark and the space between the houses was packed with fog.

A workman appeared, pushing a wheelbarrow. It was filled with glistening wet coal. A spade stuck up from the pile at a jaunty angle. Joseph stepped forward. He stopped the cart and pushed the spade deep into the middle of the heap.

"What are you doing?" the man asked, astonished by this giant.

Joseph rotated the spade through the coal as effortlessly as a paddle in water. He was looking to see if anything was hidden in the middle. There was nothing. Joseph dropped the spade and disappeared into the fog.

The man pushed his handcart forward and mumbled, "I don't understood. Why do people think they can just do whatever they want?"

Joseph did not hear. He cut down a lane and emerged into another narrower foggy street that connected the Jewish and Christian quarters. He could only see a few feet ahead and he carried no lantern. The lights in the windows of the houses he passed only showed when he was close. Two or three steps on and they vanished into the murk.

He slid forward over slimy cobbles. He moved so gently, despite his enormous feet, that he might as well have been creeping on felt. He heard a burst of song. Then he smelt a burnt smell.

As he moved on, the smell grew stronger. He was approaching a baker's shop that had caught fire a few weeks before. The heat had melted the glass in the three small front windows. This dripped down and formed puddles in front of the building. In the evening, after the fire had burnt out, some local children carried the hardened puddles away in triumph. They believed they were the tears of an angel.

The scorched smell was overwhelming now. He had reached the building. Joseph slipped into the blackened doorway. Here he was enveloped by the smell of soot and charred wood. Though he could not know this, these were some of the smells present at his creation.

At this point Joseph heard metal-bound wheels rolling at a furious pace. A handcart was hurtling towards him. He withdrew further into the doorway. Suddenly, out of the murk, a handcart appeared. As it drew closer, Joseph saw there was a bundle on the boards, exactly as he had been told to look out for. A figure with a blanket thrown over its head was leaning on the handrail at the back, propelling the cart along.

The golem stepped out of the doorway. He dropped an enormous hand onto the shoulder of the cart owner. There was a gasp. The voice was deep. It was a man.

His name was Vasek. He was a pork butcher. As soon as he felt the heavy weight of Joseph's hand on his shoulder his heart began to race. He had assumed, because the night was so horrible, that everyone would be indoors.

Vasek knew that whatever he did he must not scream. If he acted frightened, he might be asked to explain why was he in the street at this time? And worse, what was that in the bag on the barrow?

Vasek needed to see who had stopped him. If he looked friendly, he might be able to persuade the fellow to let him go. When circumstances required, Vasek could talk quite well.

Legs trembling, stomach curdling, Vasek turned. He saw a giant in a hat with a drooping brim that covered his face. Vasek guessed it was only a porter. He was certainly dressed like a porter. Vasek relaxed. Then, he was angry.

"What do you think you were doing," asked Vasek, "jumping out like that?"

The giant said nothing.

"I don't know if you've noticed," Vasek continued, "but porters normally wait to be asked."

Vasek braced himself for an angry reply. Porters tended to be rough men. If the row really got going, he wondered would people come out of the surrounding houses to gawk?

In a nearby house someone laughed, but the giant neither spoke nor moved. This combination of silence and stillness unnerved Vasek. Perhaps his tone had been too harsh? Perhaps, what he needed now was to make his peace. The giant was obviously slow. He was clearly stupid. He probably spoke badly. He might even be drunk. Vasek needed to show this big fellow that he was not one to harbour grudges.

"Oh well, what does it matter?" Vasek started, but he got no further. A huge hand closed over his mouth and enormous fingers squeezed the places where his jawbone hinged.

Suddenly, Vasek was in pain. He tried to cry out. He wriggled at the same time. The fingers on his face squeezed harder. He was, he realised, to be silent. The trembling and curdling in his stomach returned. He was under attack. His opponent was much bigger and he looked as if he had no qualms about using extreme violence.

Instinctively, Vasek formed a plan. Kick out as hard as possible, once, twice. Then wrench free from the terrible hand round his face, turn and run. It was too bad that he would have to leave the barrow. But if he could get away in this fog, the authorities could never connect him and his cargo. He had stolen the cart only that morning.

Vasek lashed out with his booted foot. The giant's leg, when Vasek connected, seemed like a bar of iron. He kicked a second time. Same again. He tried the other foot against the other leg. This was a truly ferocious kick. It would have snapped any ordinary man's shin. It made no impression on the giant, however. He did not even cry out. Instead, the giant tightened his grip. His teeth, thought Vasek, were going to crumble under his cheeks if the pressure on his face continued.

Vasek felt first his heels, and then the balls of his feet separating from the cobbles. He had been lifted into the air and his body hung by his throat. He found it hard to breathe. This, he thought, was what it was to drown.

He put his hands up and tried to prise the fingers away. They were like bands of brass. He kicked out wildly. It was futile but he couldn't stop himself.

Suddenly, the fog was sliding past and so was the dark building he could just make out through the gloom. The giant was manhandling him along. They were walking round to the front of the handcart.

Then, as suddenly as they had started they stopped moving. And now Vasek was vaguely aware that the giant, with his free hand, had got the sack. The giant up-ended it. The pig tumbled out. The giant wrenched open the slit in the pig's belly revealing the bare stark unalterable evidence of his crime. It occurred to Vasek, dimly, that he was done for now. He assumed the giant was going to throttle him and throw his body into the Moldau. It was as he was having this thought that Vasek passed out . . .

A long time after this, Joseph returned to the rabbi's house, where he explained, in the few words he had, what he had done. Loew went to bed relieved. The ghetto was saved, that night at least.

17

⸑ather Tadeus on the warpath

"Come on," a voice said, "wake up. I want to talk to you."

Vasek heard the voice. He wondered who was being addressed? He decided it couldn't be him. Unless, of course, he was lying on his back on the bottom of the Moldau River, and the voice came from a stranger on a bridge above.

He felt a hand shake his shoulder. No, he was on dry land and alive. Vasek opened his eyes. He saw shiny, wet cobbles stretching away into fog. He saw wrinkled boots with breeches stuck into them and the tip of a sword scabbard. At least this wasn't the giant.

He lifted his head. It was a policeman. He wore a three-quarter length coat with a sash from which sword and scabbard dangled. The policeman's moustache was spotted with drops of mist.

"What's your name?" The policeman wore a floppy hat with a wide brim.

Vasek told him and shivered. His clothes were

damp. He tried to move. His arms, he realised, were tied behind at the wrists.

"Stand up."

Vasek tried to stand but because his arms were tied and his legs were stiff, he couldn't manage. The policeman took him by one elbow and lifted him to his feet.

"Is this your handcart?" The policeman indicated that the object in question was behind.

Vasek turned and his stomach somersaulted. There was his handcart and there on top of it was the pig, and there, worst of all, was the small hand of a dead child extending through the slit in the belly of the pink carcass.

Vasek considered and rallied. He had been in trouble with the police before. The funny thing about the police was that if one told them the truth straight away they never believed it. The police believed the truth could only be dragged out. The police had a special place for doing this. It was a dungeon under the police station proper. Vasek knew that if he blabbed now he would be taken down there and tortured. The trick would be to make them hurt him a little, now. Then they would believe him when he told them the truth.

"It's not my handcart," said Vasek.

The policeman drew his sword and slapped Vasek several times on the head with the flat of the blade. He made two or three deep cuts in Vasek's scalp as he did this. When the blood began to drip down his face, Vasek decided he had resisted enough.

"It is my handcart," he squealed. "I'll tell you everything."

"Go on."

"I'm a butcher. Sausages are my specialty. I owe the money-lender Mordecai Mayzel five thousand crowns. I can't pay him back. This child," here Vasek indicated the hand sticking out of the pig, "was a neighbour's child. He just died of ague. Last night I went to the graveyard. I dug up the coffin. I took the corpse. I carried it to my shop where I had this hog already slaughtered and waiting. I cut the corpse's throat to make it look as if he was murdered and then I put him inside the animal. Then I put them both in a sack and loaded them onto a handcart that I'd stolen. I was on my way to Mayzel's house. I was going to throw it all into the basement of his house and then report him. I was going to say Mayzel killed the child for his blood to make unleavened bread for Passover. I never touched the child, I swear. The child was dead when I dug him up."

The policeman lightly hit Vasek twice more. This

time he used the sharp edge of his sword and he cut the prisoner badly.

"One blow's for being a fool and the other's for getting caught," he said. "Right, we're going inside. You can tell me the whole story again and I'll write it down. And you'd better face the fact that you're going to prison."

As the policeman led the butcher up the stone steps towards the entrance of the city hall, a man came out of the door, coming the other way. It was Cardinal Sylvester's secretary, Karel.

The secretary instinctively glanced at the prisoner to see if he knew him. He didn't recognise the butcher's face, but he did know despair when he saw it. Now Karel thought of himself as a good man. He would help him.

"It can't be that bad," he said to the prisoner cheerfully.

"Oh it can," said Vasek gloomily.

It was such a surprising reply Karel stopped and addressed the policeman.

"Is it really that awful?" he asked.

The policeman recognised Cardinal Sylvester's secretary.

"Well, he is in quite a bit of trouble," said the policeman.

"How so?" asked Karel.

"I'll tell your honour," interrupted Vasek. "I had this body. It was a child. I dug him up. Last night I was going to dump the corpse in the house of Mordecai Mayzel – you know, the money-lender?"

Karel nodded.

"Just before I got to the ghetto this huge giant came out of nowhere. He stopped me. He found the body. I passed out. When I woke I was right here in the square and this policeman was with me."

"Is that what really happened?" Karel asked.

"So he says," said the policeman.

"Oh dear," said Karel, "I'm not surprised you don't sound happy. That sounds like a horrible night. Oh well, I must be going, goodbye."

Karel arrived, many minutes later, breathless and very excited at Father Tadeus's parochial house.

He knocked on the door. Gerda the housekeeper let him in and brought him to Father Tadeus's study.

"I have some information for you," said Karel. "Last night, some miserable butcher went into the ghetto with a corpse. He was going to dump it in the basement of that money-lender, Mayzel. Anyhow, this is where it gets interesting. He was caught, entering the ghetto, by a giant."

"Are you sure about this?" asked Father Tadeus.

"Oh yes," said Karel.

Karel left. Father Tadeus sat on by his fire. He had heard rumours of a Jewish giant. Now he knew both that he existed and that he was a defender. He was to keep the ghetto and its occupants safe.

And from where did this figure spring? It had to be Rabbi Loew, didn't it? Well, this giant would have to go and his master along with him. And he, Father Tadeus, would have to be the one to do it. No one else could.

But how would he achieve this? He had no idea. He would have to wait. Something completely unexpected would turn up. Life or fate had a way of throwing opportunities his way. He would just have to be patient, and more importantly, he would have to be alert, so that when the opportunity came he would know to seize it with both hands.

He stared right into the red-hot core of a burning length of wood. It was fragile. A smart blow from the poker and the log would shatter into glowing fragments. Yet there was so much power in that burning heart. Nothing could withstand the power of fire, could it? Perhaps that would be the means by which he would destroy this giant and Rabbi Loew along with him?

Two years passed before Father Tadeus saw that the

chance had at last arrived. Rabbi Loew would be
challenged as never before.

18

Lenka's mistake

Lenka was an eighteen year old servant girl. She lived in the ghetto with Widow Frankel and her grown-up children. Lenka was a Christian. On Sabbath days, after she had lit Widow Frankel's fire, she made extra money by lighting fires in other Jewish homes, including Rabbi Loew's. Lenka did this because Jews on the Sabbath could undertake no work. She was so well known in the ghetto that boys, when she passed, would chant, "Hey, Lenka the firelighter."

It was morning, a few days to Passover. Widow Frankel found Lenka in the yard chopping wood.

"Take the sheets off all the beds and wash them," said Widow Frankel.

Lenka collected the linen and took it to the laundry room. She filled the copper with water and banked the fire below. Before they were washed the sheets had to be boiled.

Widow Frankel rushed into the laundry room at that moment.

"Lenka," she said brusquely, "get to the kitchen. There's a heap of vegetables to peel."

Lenka ran to the kitchen. She began peeling and quite forgot the copper.

Suddenly, Widow Frankel smelt burning. "You've forgotten the washing," she shouted.

Lenka and her mistress ran to the laundry room. The copper had boiled completely dry and the sheets lying in the bottom against the hot metal were now brown.

"Stupid girl," shouted Widow Frankel. "My best sheets are ruined."

"I'm sorry," Lenka said, her eyes filled with tears.

"Sorry is no good to me," said Widow Frankel.

Lenka agreed to pay for new sheets from her wages. However, when she went to bed that night she began to regret this. It would, she calculated, take her a year to pay off the debt. A year of work stretched ahead and she would have nothing to show at the end of it. And the scorched sheets weren't even her fault.

Lenka knew Widow Frankel well. She wouldn't let her leave, until after she'd paid for the new sheets.

Well, thought Lenka, there was only one way out of this. Her parents lived in the country, miles to the north. She could leave now and walk there overnight. And once she was gone, the Widow would probably never chase after her. She couldn't be absolutely certain about this, but Lenka had half an idea the old woman didn't even know where she came from.

Lenka got up, dressed, put her belongings in a sack and crept out of the house. It was the middle of the night. The ghetto's streets were almost deserted. The only activity was at the house of David Moritsy, a doctor. As Lenka approached, the door from the yard at the back creaked open.

Lenka did not want to be seen. She stepped into a doorway but kept her eyes on the door into Moritsy's yard.

A girl emerged. She wore a cape and the hood was pulled well over her face. Perhaps, Lenka thought, she was also running away. Jewish girls did sometimes fall in love with Christians and flee their homes in the night.

The girl closed Moritsy's yard door silently and moved away up the street quickly. She was heading in precisely the direction in which Lenka wanted to go. Lenka followed her, but took care to stay well behind.

The girl reached the point where the ghetto ended and the Old Town began. There was a booth at the side where the night watchmen sat. Lenka expected her to stop, bribe the night watchman and go on. To Lenka's surprise, the girl bolted past the booth and hurried away up the street on the other side.

Lenka followed. As a Christian she was allowed to pass between the two areas at night. As she passed the booth she looked through the open door. The night watchman was asleep at the table inside. The mysterious girl had been extremely fortunate.

Lenka hurried forward. The girl was still in front of her. What a coincidence, thought Lenka, if she left the city by the very gate I want to leave by? If this happened, Lenka decided she would wait an hour to let the girl get well ahead of her.

They continued moving through the silent Old Town. They reached the Green Church. Lenka had sometimes come to Mass here on Sundays. The priest was the famous Father Tadeus.

On one side of the Green Church stretched a courtyard and this, in turn, was bounded by a high wall with a small door in the middle.

Suddenly, as the mysterious girl reached the doorway, she darted sideways and beat the wood three hefty whacks. The door opened instantly. The girl ran in, the door slammed.

Who, from the ghetto, was visiting the priest at this time of night? The gossip in the ghetto over the next few days would be wonderful. It was a shame she would miss it. However, she reminded herself, that life was behind her now. She was on her way home. And what was more, she had miles to go. She would have to hurry as she wanted to be in the kitchen when her parents came down in the morning.

Now the mysterious girl was Moritsy's daughter. When she knocked on the door in the wall, Father Tadeus was waiting on the other side. She had been seeing him secretly for months. This night, she was going to move into one of the priest's guest-rooms. These were in the yard beside the caretaker's house. Moritsy's daughter, Mathilde, wanted to convert. When she was ready, Father Tadeus would baptise her.

And why did Mathilde do this? It was partly her age. It was partly her character. It was partly Father Tadeus's powers of persuasion. It was partly bad luck.

Mathilde was young and clever, far cleverer than her mother or father. They had known this. As a result they had always spoilt her. They had constantly told her she was destined for great things.

On the day of her sixteenth birthday – six months ago – it had suddenly struck Mathilde that her parents were wrong. She wasn't destined for anything. She was a girl from the ghetto. She would marry a merchant or, if she were lucky, a rabbi. She would live in the ghetto. She would die in the ghetto. That would be her life.

The idea of such a future appalled Mathilde. She had put on her cloak and hurried off. Once she was outside in the street, she did not look where she was going. Her feet simply moved one after the other and carried her out of the ghetto. Suddenly, she looked up. She was greatly surprised to find herself outside the doors of the Green Church.

Now, with all those feelings still surging through her, she stared at the polished brass handles in the middle of the doors. She had never been in a church before, had she? Jews were not allowed. And was that not typical, she thought, of the poverty of her experience? And was that to be her life until she died?

At that exact moment one of the doors of the Green Church opened and Father Tadeus put his head out. He was as surprised to see Mathilde as she was to see him.

"Who are you?" he asked.

"Mathilde," she said naïvely.

"Mathilde who?"

"Mathilde Moritsy."

"You're from the ghetto?"

"Yes, sir, I am."

"What are you doing here?"

"I don't know," she said.

"Have you ever seen inside a church before?" he asked quietly.

"No."

"Would you like to?"

"Yes."

"Was that really why you came?"

"Maybe. I don't know. I think so."

He threw the door wide.

"Come on, come inside, I'll show you what we have in here."

Mathilde climbed the steps and timidly went through the door.

"Welcome to my church," said Father Tadeus. "Know you are always welcome here, at any time. Everybody, whatever their faith, is welcome in here at any time."

They walked about. He showed her the font and the nave and the altar. He sensed Mathilde's deep unhappiness. It occurred to him that here was an opportunity. She was ripe for conversion. He talked about his faith. He was charming, gentle and engaging. Mathilde listened, fascinated . . .

So started the process that culminated with her flitting across Prague in the middle of the night and disappearing into the Green Church. What Mathilde could not know was that this would threaten her parents, Rabbi Loew and her whole community.

19

Mathilde's lie

The next morning, when she found Lenka gone, Widow Frankel rushed round to the police station to complain.

"How dare the girl disappear without telling me!" she exclaimed to the first policeman she met. "She owes me for bed sheets she destroyed."

"Go away," said the policeman nastily to Widow Frankel. "We've got better things to do than chase runaways."

Widow Frankel was so appalled she went into the street and started complaining to everyone who would listen. Within hours the story had spread throughout Prague. It was his housekeeper, Gerda, who told Father Tadeus the story.

Pondering what he had just been told, it occurred to Father Tadeus that the means to attack the mysterious giant beadle and his master, Rabbi Loew, had just fallen into his hands. It was the missing Lenke.

He rang his bell. Gerda reappeared.

"Get Mathilde," he said.

Gerda fetched her.

"Mathilde," Tadeus began. "Cardinal Sylvester is going to ask you why you want to convert."

Mathilde nodded.

"I want you to say Rabbi Loew's beadles – the small one Chaim and Joseph the big one, who doesn't speak – came to your house one night. They handed your father a flask of blood. He paid them. They left. This was to make unleavened bread at the coming Passover. That was why you ran away and came here. This business of killing for blood to make bread drove you from the faith of your fathers."

Mathilde listened carefully to what was said. She had realised that she was not only unwelcome in the Jewish world she had left behind but in the Christian world to which she hoped to move, as well. Many Christians, because she had been Jewish, did not believe in the sincerity of her intention to convert. Several had made it clear that even after she was baptised, they would not accept her as one of their own. Once Jewish, always Jewish, they said. There was no way round a bedrock truth like that.

These boorish people and their nasty opinions had caused Mathilde much unhappiness, no matter that Father Tadeus had dismissed them as curmudgeons without compassion or intelligence. But with her own world lost now to her forever, the priest's words weren't enough. She longed for the certainty of complete and unequivocal acceptance as a Christian.

Now, listening to Father Tadeus, it occurred to her that if she agreed to say what he asked, that could only help to change the hearts of the doubters. What better way to prove she was a true Christian than to embrace each and every one of their beliefs, even if this meant she agreed to tell a lie? That it might hurt the community she had left seemed quite irrelevant, for she was never going back to the ghetto, was she?

Mathilde nodded, signalling assent. Father Tadeus nodded back, indicating both his gratitude and his certainty that she was doing right.

"I want you to add that you do not want your father reported," he continued. "You must say he has surely been punished enough by the loss of his daughter. Do you understand?"

"Yes," said Mathilde.

Father Tadeus made no mention of the missing Lenka although she was much a part of the scheme as Mathilde. The blood Mathilde would say she saw her father buy from Joseph and Chaim had to come from someone and the conclusion the authorities would come to was that that someone was the missing serving girl, Lenke. However, the priest knew he had no need to make this connection. He knew he could rely on the police to factor Lenke into the story. When one had an untruth one wanted to spread, it was important not to tell the whole of it. It was better to hold a bit back and let people add that in themselves.

At Mathilde's baptism, Cardinal Sylvester did ask, "Why are you converting, Mathilde?" and she explained as she had been instructed. And at the finish she said, "But don't report my father. He has been punished enough by losing his daughter."

Standing in the congregation, Cardinal Sylvester's secretary, Karel, heard what Mathilde said. That evening, in the tavern, he told the wonderful story to some of his friends of what the Jewish convert said at her baptism.

And Hirsch, the tavern owner, overheard Karel telling his story. At the end of the evening he walked to Rabbi Loew's house and told him. This was what Father Tadeus had expected would happen. He knew how a good story, once it was out in the world, would spread.

Rabbi Loew, having heard Hirsch, now worked out what would happen. And the lines his thinking followed, once again, were precisely as Father Tadeus had calculated. Mathilde, reasoned Loew, had asked Cardinal Sylvester not to report her father, and he hadn't. However, the rabbi doubted the drinkers in Hirsch's tavern had such scruples. They would tell the police, who in turn would come to arrest his beadles. If he hoped to save them, Rabbi Loew didn't have a second to lose.

At the end of the rabbi's street there lived a mute called Lehmann Mayer. He was a bulky middle-aged man. He didn't have Joseph's stature but in the dark and in the right clothes he might just pass as the golem.

The rabbi ran to Lehmann's house. Lehmann's wife, Frieda, opened the door.

"Frieda, get your husband up," said Rabbi Loew. "I need to borrow him for a few days. And don't worry – you'll get him back safe and sound."

Lehmann was produced, sleepy and confused. His wife kissed him goodbye. Rabbi Loew dragged Lehmann up the street and into the courtroom.

The only light in the room came from the stove. The door at the front was open. The darkness was good, thought Rabbi Loew.

As usual Joseph was on the wood box. His eyes were open. He was just lying there utterly still, looking up at the ceiling. He might have looked like a very large man but he was really a machine that was idling and waiting to be turned on.

"Up," shouted Rabbi Loew.

The golem sat up then stood. The flames from the fire were reflected on his skin. He looked at his master.

"Right, Joseph, switch hats, coats and clogs with Lehmann here."

Joseph and Lehmann did as asked.

"Joseph, fetch a bottle of wine and open it. Bring it here and a glass."

Joseph went off and returned.

"Give the wine and the glass to Lehmann. Joseph, you are now to go to the attic room right at the top of the house. When you close the door behind – lock it. Get into the bed. Pull the covers over your head. Pretend to be asleep. That means you actually have to close your eyes. Do not unlock the door or leave the room until I come for you."

Joseph left the courtroom and went upstairs. Rabbi Loew indicated to Lehmann that he was to drink. Lehmann, who liked to drink, drank the bottle off in ten minutes flat, then lay down on the wood box and went to sleep.

Rabbi Loew went through to his synagogue. He stopped in the middle of the darkened room and looked up. Then with his inner voice he began to speak.

"I have brought an innocent man into my house," he said. "I am about to pass him off as someone else.

In a little while, I think or I'm almost certain, the police will come and arrest him. He doesn't know what is about to happen.

"This is a terrible thing I am about to do. I do it in the full knowledge it is wrong. I do it because I do not see what else or how else I can get around the difficulties that face us.

"I must preserve Joseph at all costs. If he is arrested, then I will lose the best means at my disposal. If anyone can help us at this time, it is Joseph.

"So it is to preserve him that I am offering Lehmann and I faithfully promise that I will not abandon him. Whatever happens, he will come to no harm even if I have to go to the authorities in the end, and confess my duplicity. Please believe that I offer this promise in all sincerity."

20

Joseph's search

In the early hours of the morning, as Loew had anticipated, a detachment of policemen came and pounded on his back door. The rabbi had prudently changed into his nightclothes and was in the kitchen waiting for them. He opened his back door with a great show of fatigue and surprise.

"Where's Joseph the Mute?" shouted the sergeant.

"My beadle," said Rabbi Loew. He sounded humble and frightened. "Why do you want my good beadle?"

"You are not entitled to ask questions – only to answer them. Do you understand?"

"Yes," said Rabbi Loew.

"Where's Joseph?"

"In the courtroom."

The sergeant turned to the constables. "Courtroom. Arrest him."

The constables charged off.

Rabbi Loew began to sniffle and rub his eyes with his cuffs. The sergeant hoped he wasn't going to cry.

He did not want his constables to return and find their sergeant with a blubbing old rabbi. It would reflect badly on his virility.

"Why do you want my beadle?" repeated Rabbi Loew, in a trembling voice.

"I'll tell you if you promise not to let yourself down."

"I promise," whispered Rabbi Loew.

"Dry your eyes. Stand up straight."

Rabbi Loew smeared his cuffs across his face and threw his shoulders back.

"Murder," said the sergeant.

"Murder," wailed Rabbi Loew. His eyes moistened, his shoulders drooped.

"You said you wouldn't let yourself down," snapped the sergeant.

"Yes," said Rabbi Loew.

"Well then," said the sergeant, fiercely. "Pull yourself together. And yes, I said murder – but he didn't do it alone."

"What!" exclaimed Rabbi Loew.

"We've arrested your other beadle as well."

"Not Chaim!"

"Yes, we took him from his house."

The Rabbi blew his nose and wiped his eyes. "Who are they supposed to have harmed?"

"Lenka, the firelighter. She's disappeared you know."

Rabbi Loew nodded. "Not Lenka," he said painfully.

"No one's seen her and we've got a witness who saw a well-known figure in the ghetto buying blood from your beadles. It all adds up, I'm afraid."

A bewildered Lehmann appeared, with the constables shoving him from behind. Lehmann's hands were tied behind his back. He was groaning and staggering.

Lehmann was thrust out the door into the Prague night, the constables following.

"You'll be hearing from us," said the sergeant. He walked out and slammed the door after himself.

Rabbi Loew felt queasy. Lehmann had gone to sleep drunk but happy. Now, angry policemen had hurried him from the rabbi's house. They would throw him in a police cell with his co-accused, Chaim. They would be interrogated. Lehmann and Chaim would protest their innocence. Whatever had happened to Lenka, the rabbi knew his beadles had nothing to do with it. But knowing you were innocent when the police thought otherwise counted for nothing. Once they realised they were going to be punished for something they didn't do, he knew Lehmann and Chaim would be gripped by despair. It was hateful to imagine what they would endure, but because of the situation engineered by Father Tadeus, their pain was

169

the least worst alternative. They must suffer in order for the rabbi to have time to act.

Rabbi Loew lit a candle and went to the attic room where Joseph was.

"Open, Joseph," he shouted through the wood.

Inside, Joseph jumped to his feet and unlocked the door. The rabbi went in.

"You'd recognise Lenka," he asked, "the girl who lights fires?"

Joseph nodded. He had seen her in the rabbi's house once or twice.

"Follow me."

The rabbi then went and woke up the Widow Frankel. He asked her to tell him the whole story of Lenka's disappearance.

"So where do you think she went after she left you?" asked the rabbi when the widow finished.

"After her midnight flit, you mean?" said the widow, peevishly. "Well, she didn't get a job with another family in the ghetto. And if she'd gone to the Old Town I'd have heard by now. No, she went home, didn't she? Her parents live out in the country somewhere. She wrote to them when she was with me. She could read and write a bit in German – actually quite well."

"Do you have an address?"

"What for?"

"Her parents."

"Why would I?"

"I just thought you might."

"No, why should I? I wasn't writing to them."

"Do you know the name of her village?"

"Of course I don't. I didn't go out into the countryside looking for her. She came here looking for work. And I took her in, fool that I am. I'll know better next time than to employ a country girl like her. She destroyed all my sheets. That's why she fled. Didn't want to pay."

"Yes, yes," said Rabbi Loew, "but north, south, east or west of Prague – do you not even know that?"

"No, and I don't want to know either. I never want to see that awful girl again."

"Was it far, Lenka's home?"

"No, I think I remember her saying she did it in a day from there to here."

Well, that was something. Rabbi Loew thanked the Widow Frankel. He led Joseph home and into his study.

"Wait," he said.

He sat at his desk and wrote a letter in German:

Dear Lenka,
I have spoken to Widow Frankel. I know about the

copper boiling dry. Had I been in your position I would also have run away. I know you have gone home but I need you to come back. I need you to save the lives of two innocent men.

Joseph, the bearer of this letter has money. Put your hand out and say, "Joseph, give me the money". He will do what you tell him. He will always do what you order.

Use the money to hire a horse and cart. Come back to Prague. You will find me at the synagogue or at home. I will pay you handsomely for your trouble. Moreover, if you want a position, in my household, for the rest of your natural life, it's yours for the asking.

Yours, Rabbi Loew.

PS. If you were to burn our sheets like at Widow Frankel's, my wife, Pearl, would never make you pay out of your wages. We know accidents happen.

Rabbi Loew folded the paper in half and sealed it. He handed this along with a bag of gold to Joseph.

"You will perform this task as fast as possible. Visit every house within a day's walk of Prague. And I mean every house. You will find Lenka in one of them. Give her this letter. When she's read it, she will hire a horse and cart. Bring her to me in Prague. If she doesn't hire the horse and cart, but sends you away, you come and find me and bring me back to her."

Joseph ran out of the house, through the ghetto, through the Old Town and out into the countryside. When he arrived at the first house he came to he knocked at the door. It was the home of a woodcutter, his wife and their eight children.

The wife answered. Joseph pushed her aside and hurried straight in. The wife screamed. The woodcutter ran from the kitchen and collided with Joseph. The golem's body was like granite and the woodcutter was knocked to the floor. Joseph walked through the rooms. He stared into the faces of every female over sixteen. The children wailed. The woodcutter fetched his axe. He never got the chance to use it. Joseph stomped out the back door and raced off across the back meadow to the next house he saw. This scene was repeated hundreds and then thousands of times over the days that followed. During this time Joseph never stopped to eat or sleep. As a golem he was free of such needs. As a golem, he could keep going forever.

21

The trial

In Prague, meantime, a trial date was set for Lehmann and Chaim. As day followed day, and still Joseph did not return, Rabbi Loew grew more and more anxious. Never in his life until now had he done wrong like this. Substituting Lehmann for Joseph weighed on him. Like a bad toothache, this thought harried him day and night. His appetite waned. He slept badly. He prayed for forgiveness frequently but this brought no release. Wrong was wrong, even when it was done with the best of intentions, and there was no escaping that.

One cold damp day he was in the Old Town, on his way to an appointment when he passed the public gallows. A workman was oiling the hinges on the trap. When a man was hanged, this flapped down, the condemned man fell through the hole, and the rope snapped his neck.

The gallows were being got ready for Lehmann and Chaim. Unless Rabbi Loew could produce Lenka, alive, the court was sure to convict the pair of her murder.

He wouldn't let that happen. He would own up. He would die in their place if he had to. But once the trial started, Prague's Christians were going to become enraged and then there was going to be trouble. A mob would storm the ghetto. Christians would vent their rage at Lenka's murder on every Jew on whom they could lay their hands. In principle the police were supposed to defend the innocent. In practice they would cover their faces and join the mob. They always had before.

Rabbi Loew decided not to go to his appointment. He went home and found Pearl in the kitchen slicing a pickled beetroot for soup.

"I feel terrible," said Rabbi Loew. "This trial, when it comes, is going to cause so much trouble."

"No sign of Joseph then?"

"Well, I'd have told you if there was, wouldn't I?"

It was unusual for her husband to speak sharply. Pearl said nothing but glanced at him instead.

"I suppose it's intolerable living with me at the moment?" he said.

"You can be a bit churlish now and then, not that I mind, you understand. You're worried."

"I'm terrified," he said quietly.

"Yes, terrified. But it will work out – I have no doubt of that."

"You're sure?"

"Of course, I am. Don't you think so?"

"I hope so."

"The truth will always out in the end, you know."

"I want it to come now, not later."

She pushed the blade through the heart of the beetroot.

"Where's your faith in God? Don't you remember our betrothal?"

He said nothing.

"So, no sign of Joseph yet?"

"None."

"And what will you do if he's not back and the trial starts?"

"If he doesn't return?"

"Yes."

"Let the process run its course."

"I can see that," said Pearl tactfully. "Give Joseph the maximum time you can."

The rabbi shrugged but said no more. He certainly wasn't going to tell her he would get the men's conviction overturned by assuming responsibility for Lenka's murder. But that was in the future. First things first. Now, he had to get his family to safety.

"I want you to go away. I want you to take the children, the grandchildren, the kitchen boy, everybody. And I want you to go now."

"Can I finish chopping?" Pearl's fingers were stained red.

"I want you to pack and go at once."

Pearl put the knife down. Her husband was right. She and the household set off immediately for a town several hours from Prague. The rabbi there was a friend of Loew's from his yeshiva in Przemysl. He was happy to take them in. He said they could stay as long as they wished.

That night, Rabbi Loew slept alone in an empty house. He kept a candle burning continuously in his bedroom. No mob came. No windows were broken.

When he woke in the morning, he was grateful and relieved nothing had happened, yet he was still filled with dread. He prayed especially fervently that morning, and asked for the courage to face whatever ordeals arose.

Time passed and the day of the trial arrived. Rabbi Loew decided Joseph was not coming back. He wrote out his confession and hid it in the inside pocket of his coat. If needed he would give it to the magistrate just before he pronounced the death sentence.

Rabbi Loew locked the synagogue and walked to the courthouse. Inside, he found the public benches packed with spectators. They had come for vengeance.

Rabbi Loew took his place at the front, as he was entitled by King Rudolph's order. His presence was mandatory at trials that involved the Blood Libel. Frieda, Lehmann's wife, came and sat beside him. She had been ordered to attend to interpret Lehmann's gestures.

The rabbi glanced at the witness bench. David Moritsy sat forlornly at one end and his daughter, Mathilde, at the other. Father Tadeus sat between them. Father and daughter had not spoken since Mathilde ran away from home.

The two defendants were put in the dock. Their legs and arms were chained. There were jeers and catcalls from the public benches. A court official demanded silence. The presiding magistrate took his seat behind the high desk at the front. Rabbi Loew felt his heart beating.

The magistrate cleared his throat and turned to the dock.

"Lehmann," he called, "do you confess to the crime of distributing Christian blood for Passover among the Jews of Prague?"

Frieda repeated the question. She spoke slowly and at the same time she gestured.

Lehmann, hearing the question, smirked as if what had just been asked did not deserve the dignity of a serious reply. He shook his head for good measure.

"He denies the charge," said his wife.

"Show him the phials," said the magistrate.

A court official held up some glass tubes filled with a mixture of raspberry juice and water.

"Have you ever seen anything like those before?"

Lehmann smirked again and gestured to his wife.

"He says, is it plum brandy and can he have it now?" she said. "He hasn't had a drink for a month and he's desperate."

Lehmann, who was watching Frieda, now mimed a man knocking back a drink and then pretended to stagger like a drunk.

There was wild laughter.

"Stop that now," shouted the magistrate.

An unpleasant silence followed.

"Show him the knife."

The court official produced a knife. He drew it across his throat. Lehmann's expression was a mixture of surprise and disgust.

"Lehmann, did you cut the throat of Lenka, the Widow Frankel's servant?" asked the magistrate.

Frieda repeated the question with a trembling voice.

Lehmann went white and shook his head emphatically.

"No," said Frieda, "my husband says he did not

cut the Widow Frankel's servant's throat."

The same questions were put to Chaim. In reply to each one he answered emphatically, "No."

Mathilde took the witness stand and told her story. It was the same story as she had told Cardinal Sylvester at her baptism but with one small addition. She said that when her father took the phial of blood, Chaim the beadle had said, "You know Lenka, the woman who lights fires in the ghetto, this is her blood."

Mathilde left the stand. The magistrate turned to Chaim.

"Did you say that, Chaim?" he asked.

"No, I never," said Chaim, "and neither was I ever in Dr Moritsy's house."

"Are you saying Mathilde made the story up?"

"Yes."

"Lehmann, did Chaim say, 'You know Lenka, the woman who lights fires in the ghetto, this is her blood'?"

Lehmann stared back at the magistrate and shook his head. His expression was appalled.

"Is that no?" the magistrate asked Frieda.

"That's no," said Frieda. Her voice quivered. Her face was pale.

"But why would Mathilde tell such a story?" persisted the magistrate looking at the two accused men. "It's not to her advantage in any way. She's not going to get anything out of lying, other than the arrest of her father. And do you seriously expect me to believe a daughter would lie to get her father arrested?"

"I was never in her father's house. I never sold him blood," said Chaim. Lehmann shook his head, and gestured with his hands as if saying, "Me neither".

"You still haven't answered my question. Why would a daughter lie to get her father arrested?" said the magistrate.

The courtroom was still. Rabbi Loew wanted to stand, pull out his confession and shout, "I'm the one to blame. Leave them alone. They're innocent."

"You don't know, do you?" said the magistrate, staring angrily at the accused.

Chaim and Lehmann glanced at their rabbi and Loew looked straight back at them. His expression mingled strength and sympathy. It encouraged them to keep going. It reassured them he would never let them down.

However, what they could not know, he would only intervene once the court process was over. Every second that passed was another second for Joseph to find Lenka. It was cruel of course. But if the community was preserved perhaps Chaim and

Lehmann would, in time, come to see their trial was justified.

"Why would a girl lie to get her father arrested?" the magistrate repeated. "There isn't a good reason why. If anything, a girl does nothing, in a situation such as Mathilde finds herself in. She stays silent.

"And that, to all intents and purposes, is what Mathilde has done. Mathilde never came to the authorities with this story. It was drawn out of her at her baptism. She also told our Cardinal she specifically did not want her father arrested or charged. A very interesting detail, I should say.

"The reason Mathilde never told the truth before was that she knew it would cost her. She knew it would hurt her father.

"Now, in this court of law, she tells us because she knows we know and she knows she has to tell us. And of course, she knows the difference between right and wrong.

"You two on the other hand," he continued, glaring again at Chaim and Lehmann, "have a very good reason for denying the truth. You want to save your lives. You do not want to hang. I don't think you necessarily killed Lenka. In fact, I don't think you or your accomplice is either smart or vicious enough. But you know who did it and you know they're probably sitting in this room. If you confess the truth, now, to me, that Lenka was murdered and by who, and that you sold her blood to David Moritsy, I will commute your sentence to life imprisonment. But if you persist in denying the truth I will have no alternative but to order both of you to be hanged by the neck until dead. Then I will order the arrest of your partner in crime."

In the witness box, Chaim looked at the floor, while Lehmann moved his hands backwards and forwards in front of himself. It was a desperate gesture of denial.

"What is he saying?" the magistrate asked.

"He's saying," said Frieda, "he's saying . . ."

Rabbi Loew felt Frieda shaking beside him. Then he heard her let out a great cry of incoherent grief.

All over the courtroom the spectators wriggled in their seats. Some were distressed. Others were excited.

"Settle down," shouted the magistrate.

A hush fell over the courtroom. Frieda sobbed on.

"We will wait until Mrs Lehmann has composed herself," said the magistrate, "and then she can tell us what her husband said."

While the court waited, rumbling wheels, incoherent shouting, a whip cracking and hooves clattering on cobblestones could be heard outside. Next, running feet and echoing voices could be heard inside the courthouse. Finally, the double doors of the courtroom burst open. There, on the threshold, stood Joseph. He carried a woman in his arms. He set her down carefully. She turned to face the front of the court.

"I," she said, "am Lenka. This strange fellow has brought me here. I have a letter. This is a matter of life and death apparently. Will somebody explain to me what this is all about?"

Lenka took the witness stand. She told her whole story.

"We came into Prague this morning," she continued, "and went straight to the synagogue. It was locked. A passerby told me to go to the courthouse. The rabbi was at a trial. A matter of life and death, he said. That's what the letter said, too.

"We rushed across the city to the courthouse. Joseph picked me up and ran here with me in his arms."

Lenka left the stand slightly breathless and very excited. For the first time ever in her life, she had had something important to say and everyone had had to listen to her. The magistrate cleared his throat.

"I find the accused not guilty of the charges," he declared.

The spectators rose from their seats as one. There

were gasps of amazement and cries of dismay. There were catcalls. There were handclaps.

"I order their immediate release," continued the magistrate. "Strike their irons at once."

Frieda ran over to the witness box and threw her arms around Lehmann. Hammer blows filled the room as the rivets on the irons were knocked out.

"Clear the court," shouted the magistrate. He vanished through a door behind.

Soldiers rushed out of the anteroom and into the courtroom. Father Tadeus and Mathilde began heading for the doors.

"Mathilde," Moritsy called after his daughter.

The crowd closed around his daughter and the priest. A second later the soldiers began pushing everyone towards the double doors with the shafts of their spears.

Mathilde did not turn round to her father. Moritsy sat on the bench alone. He had hoped his daughter would ask to come home and he would have taken her too, whatever anyone in the ghetto said. He knew now that would never happen. Great tears ran down his cheeks and dripped onto his hands. Rabbi Loew said nothing. He just took off his scarf and gave it to Moritsy to wipe his tears.

The soldiers pushed the spectators out of the room.

They left the Jews where they were. Rabbi Loew soon heard the crowd shouting and jeering beneath the high windows of the courtroom. The Jews still made no move to leave. No one wanted to meet any of the disappointed spectators below.

After a couple of hours the street outside finally fell quiet. Rabbi Loew, Frieda, Lehmann, Chaim, Dr Moritsy, Lenka and Joseph left together. When they passed the gallows, no one spoke. They all just looked down and hurried on.

A few minutes later it started to rain. The rain fell from the sky in thick heavy spears. Soon there were sheets of water gushing off the eaves of houses, streaming over the cobblestones and pouring along the gutters.

In the countryside beyond Prague the rain was falling furiously as well. In the hills to the north it spattered against the windows of a convent. Inside, the Mother Superior sat at her desk. Opposite sat a young woman whom Father Tadeus had just delivered.

"If you join our order," explained the Mother Superior, "it is a condition that for the first seven years you do not talk."

Mathilde nodded and muttered, "That is what I want."

As darkness fell the rain stopped. A hush fell over

Prague. Rabbi Loew went to his bedroom. He could hear Lenka in the room above his. He had offered her a job. She had agreed to stay. She was now washing the floor.

He put on his nightgown and got into bed. He felt neither joy nor relief at the verdict. He felt only anguish and distress. The day had so nearly ended in tragedy. He had been so close to confessing to a crime he hadn't committed.

In the darkness, he prayed again for forgiveness for risking the lives of Lehmann and Chaim. He prayed as well for an end to the sufferings of the Moritsys.

He fell asleep suddenly. At some point he dreamt that Joseph was throttling him with his huge hands.

Rabbi Loew cried, "No," and sat up in bed.

"It's only me."

The rabbi was most surprised to see Pearl was standing by his bed. She was shaking him. It was morning.

"Why are you here?" he asked.

"Why am I here?" said Pearl. "Because yesterday evening we heard the verdict. I thought, now it's safe to go home, why delay? We came stright away."

Rabbi Loew lay back on his pillow.

"You see, I didn't want to leave you here on your own for one moment more than was necessary.

You'll only brood on things and get morbid."

"I don't brood and I'm never morbid."

"That's what you think," Pearl replied.

Somewhere downstairs he could hear his children and grandchildren charging about and shouting.

"By the way, why is Lenka in the kitchen?"

"I've given her a job."

Pearl nodded.

"You don't mind?" said the rabbi.

She shook her head. She'd have preferred to choose Lenka herself of course, but she wasn't going to argue about it now.

"What were you dreaming just now?" Pearl asked. "You cried out you know, when I touched you. You sounded terrified."

"Oh, I don't know," he said, finally. "I can't remember now."

"That's funny, you usually remember your dreams."

And on the wood box in the courtroom below, Joseph lay by the whispering stove. His eyes were open. He was staring up at the ceiling. He was waiting for his next orders.

22

The feast

Claude closed his exercise book and said, 'That's the end of the first half.'

There was hearty applause.

Claude bowed.

'Bravo,' shouted Agatha.

'Yes,' agreed Mina.

All the adults spoke at once. They praised Claude both for what he wrote and how he read. Saul, on his box, let the words wash around him. He concentrated instead on what he saw with his mind's eye. What he saw was Joseph. The golem was stretched out on the wood box in the darkened room. His eyes were open. The stove at his side whispered as embers settled. Saul did not want to leave this extraordinary invented world and go back to his everyday one.

'Enjoy that, Saul?' he heard his uncle asking.

Why couldn't they leave him where he was? Why must they talk at him?

He closed his eyes.

'Saul?' This time it was his father who spoke. 'Are you all right?'

Keeping his eyes closed, Saul nodded slowly.

'Why have you closed your eyes?'

'He wants to stay in the world he's in,' said Agatha. 'I remember, when I was read to as a child, I was the very same. A story would produce a fantastic world in my head that I wouldn't want to leave. I'd stay in it for hours, for days if I could. I think it drove my parents mad.'

A hand touched his shoulder.

'Saul?' It was Agatha again, this time with her mouth close to his ear. She spoke in a low tone.

'Come to the cave and help me carry some things. I won't talk to you, I promise.'

'Promise?'

'I won't.'

Saul opened his eyes.

'So you enjoyed that then?' This was Uncle Hugo again.

'Don't listen, Saul. Come on,' said Agatha. She took his hand and pulled him to his feet. 'Follow me.'

She pulled him away from his family and together they struck off through the trees in the direction of the cave. When they had gone a short distance she dropped his arm, stepped ahead and motioned him to follow.

They moved on. With his mind's eye Saul could still see the huge golem lying motionless in the courtroom but the intense feeling of being in the ghetto was receding. He regretted the loss, but at least his sense of the imaginary world was fading gently. If he'd had to answer Hugo's questions it would have been quite different. It would have been like waking up before he was ready. When that happened he always felt awful for the rest of the day.

His eyes were fixed on Agatha just ahead of him. Her hair was piled high with a crown of wild flowers sitting on top. He'd never seen Agatha like this before.

'You've got flowers in your hair,' he said.

'I do, yes.'

'Why?'

'Why? I'm wearing flowers because this is an occasion, Saul. When you lived at home and your parents went out at night, didn't they wear different clothes from the ones they normally wore?'

He could remember vaguely. His mother would wear a long skirt and carry a stole. His father would wear a jacket with shiny lapels, a brilliant white shirt and a black bow tie. On these evenings what impressed him the most was their smell. His mother's scent and make-up and nail varnish, his father's cologne and the Bay Rum with which he dressed his hair.

'Yes, they wore their good clothes,' he said.

'We haven't got access to our wardrobe here,' said Agatha. She laughed. The peal was light and airy and quick. 'Wardrobe, now there's a word I haven't used in years. But we decided that even if we didn't have nice things, we were still going to make the effort for Claude's story. We were going to the theatre, we said, so we would dress appropriately. We girls have all made ourselves crowns of flowers. And bracelets.'

She shook an arm. A small chain of yellow flowers dangled from her thin wrist. 'Didn't you notice?'

'No,' he said. 'Not until just now.'

'Did you notice anything else about us?'

'No.'

'We've cleaned our clothes, and washed our hands and faces and the men have all trimmed their hair.'

'Oh,' he said, 'but I didn't.'

'Well, you're just right. Why should you be like them?' She dropped back and touched him on the shoulder. 'You're a boy, aren't you? You should just be allowed to be one.'

He didn't follow what she meant but he understood from the tone that she meant well and that she liked him in her own odd way.

On the very edge of his thoughts a quite unexpected one now began to emerge. He had been wrong to take against her. Agatha was quite nice really.

He glanced sideways at her face. She was still walking beside him. She had a small nose. Her skin was slightly golden.

Agatha, sensing the boy's glance, half-turned her head and quickly winked at him with her left eye. Then she sped forward and resumed her place in front.

They came to the cave. Inside the air was chilly and still and there was the familiar whiff of wet stone. They walked to the ledge towards the back where the food was always stored.

'Now,' said Agatha, 'this is what we have to carry back.' She pointed at two old orange boxes and two bulky squares made of old flour sacks sewn together. In the bigger box there were wine bottles. The glass was green and the wine inside, seen through the green glass, looked almost black. The corks had been pulled and then pushed halfway back into the necks.

'There's wine,' said Saul.

'That's right,' said Agatha. She glanced humourously upwards in the direction of the gendarmerie.

'Courtesy of Henri,' she said. 'He sent cheese too,' she continued. She nodded into the smaller box as she handed it to Saul. He looked down. He saw a couple of parcels wrapped in greaseproof paper.

'It's hard cheese but after what we've been eating it'll be like manna.'

Agatha rested one of the folded squares of flour sacks on top of Saul's box. Then she took the other bigger box, the wine bottles clinking as she lifted it, and set the other flour sacks on top.

'We'd better get a move on,' she said, 'they'll be screaming for their food.'

They left the cave and retraced their steps. This time they walked side by side.

'This may be the last meal we have,' Agatha said suddenly.

'Why?' he asked, 'Are we going to run out after this?'

Agatha grinned. 'No. I didn't mean that. We could survive here for a couple more months, easy. There's plenty of berries and wild sorrel around. Not that I ever want to eat either again. No, I mean it might be the last because we're leaving here very soon. Well, you know that, don't you?'

He nodded.

'As soon as the Allied soldiers appear, Henri will come down and get us. Or send a message down in the basket. They're so close. For all I know they have arrived already. After Claude finishes at the end of this afternoon, we might even come back to the cave and find Henri or his message waiting. Wouldn't that be wonderful? Then tonight we might all sleep in a bed, and tomorrow we might all have a hot bath,' she added in a voice that sounded simultaneously subdued and excited.

'And then tomorrow I can have hot bread and jam and hot milk,' Saul said.

This was what he ate for breakfast when they lived in Nice. And this was what he always imagined to himself when he thought about life after they went back home. This was what he would eat again. It would be delicious and it would banish the pain of being empty, a pain he had lived with since they came to the cave. And what would come in its place, once he had put the food into his belly, was a feeling he could remember well. This was the glorious feeling of being replete and full and free from hunger pangs.

They walked on. The thought then occurred to him. If this ended that afternoon, then they would each go their separate ways.

'Will you go back to England?' he asked.

'I might but then again I might not. I might stay. I haven't decided. I have to see whether I'm going to be welcome or not,' she added mysteriously.

'Do you want to go back to England?'

'I do and I don't.'

It occurred to him that she was really talking about Henri but that she wasn't going to say so. It also occurred to him that he shouldn't ask any more questions. She didn't want to talk about it, did she? Then he had an inspiration.

'I could come and visit you in England if you went back.'

'Would you?' She sounded a little surprised but not unhappy about the idea.

'Yes. I'd like to as well. Is it very cold and foggy? Claude says it is.'

'Unfortunately yes, the weather's awful. France is much better. But it would be nice if you came.'

'Where would you be if I came?' he asked.

'In Eltham probably, that's where my parents are, that's where I'd go I think. It's in London. Well, on the outskirts.'

They walked on.

'I hope you come,' said Agatha.

'What happens if you don't go to Eltham?'

'Then I'll be here somewhere,' said Agatha quietly.

'Then you could come and see us,' said Saul triumphantly. 'We'll be in Nice. We're not far from Nice here, are we?'

'Not really,' she agreed.

'You could bring your baby.' He baulked for a

second at what he had said – he had never alluded to the baby before – then decided the best course was to go on. 'There's a park with swings near our house,' he continued. 'We can go down to the sea and eat ice creams. And there's a merry-go-round in the square near the town hall.'

'That sounds a lot better than Eltham,' said Agatha. She knocked him with her shoulder to emphasise what she said. 'I shall come, nothing will keep me away, with my baby.'

It sounded to Saul as if she really meant what she said. It occurred to him that what he had said was simple yet it had produced such a strong effect. It had made her friendly. It had made her really like him. And he liked her.

He decided not to say more in case he undid what he had achieved. They went on. After a while they heard laughter through the forest. It was Hugo. He had a surprisingly deep pleasant laugh.

'Someone's enjoying themselves,' said Agatha cheerfully.

He saw the others now though the trees. They were all laughing and talking. When he came close to them his sister Nelly got up and came towards him. She wore a chaplet of flowers on her head, a necklace of flowers round her neck and bracelets of flowers on her wrists and ankles. Her dress looked clean. She smiled at him. She looked pretty. He had never had such a thought about her before.

'Hello,' she said. She pulled his nose gently and smiled again. 'Don't stare. I know, I'm wearing a lot of flowers,' she whispered. 'Don't tell anyone. Let me take the box,' she continued.

She took the box from him. Everyone else now got up. The men stretched the flour sacks on the ground. The women unpacked the food. Saul stood at a slight distance and looked at everybody. Now that Agatha had drawn his attention to it, he saw that everyone did indeed look cleaner and tidier. All the women wore wild flowers. Everyone was smiling as well. These weren't big smiles. They were contented, quiet smiles. These were the smiles people showed when they were cheerful. Everyone, he realised, was happy. It was the first time, since they'd gone underground he could ever remember them all being like this.

'Right, everyone sit round,' said Mina. Everyone sat in a circle. The food was laid out on wooden platters that the Jews had made themselves and on old chipped plates supplied by Henri. There were cold roasted mushrooms sprinkled with wild sorrel and thyme, chunks of stale bread, and heaps of sour blueberries. There were also two huge pale white hunks of cheese and the four wine bottles, one with the cork out.

'Right, first a toast.' This was Uncle Hugo. 'Hand the cups around, hurry up. Give the boy one as well.'

Their chipped cups were handed round. Saul felt a mug with no handle being pressed into his hand. It was Agatha who gave it to him.

'Everyone hold out your glasses,' said Uncle Hugo.

'They're cups,' said Mina.

'I know,' said Hugo, 'but let's pretend.'

Everyone stuck their arm out. He filled each cup expertly with a measure of wine and emptied the last of the bottle into his own cup.

'One down,' he called, putting the empty bottle carefully on the ground. 'And three to go.'

He indicated the three remaining bottles.

'I propose a toast to Claude, our master story-teller.'

There were murmurs of assent.

'To Claude,' said various voices.

'Now drink up and drink down,' said Uncle Hugo, 'and Saul, that's all you're getting today. We don't want you falling asleep in the second act.'

They all drank, Saul lagging slightly behind the adults. The wine had a strong, sharp, slightly vinegary taste in his mouth. It made his eyes water. But after he had swallowed it back, he felt a slight warm glow, first at the back of his throat, then in his stomach below. A mild sensation of excitement and a small surge of happiness followed this.

He put his empty mug down and took a flat piece of bread. He covered it with mushrooms. He took a bite. The moisture of the mushrooms soaked into the stale bread, making it softer to eat. The taste of flour and the faintly meaty taste of mushrooms mingled in his mouth.

His mother and father were smiling at him. He smiled back. There was something about them that seemed intensely familiar. Then he remembered. They were smiling just like they were in the big wedding photograph that stood on the piano in the house in Nice.

'Isn't Claude good?' his father asked.

'Yes,' he said.

'Saul, you're talking with your mouth full,' his father said breezily, 'but I'll overlook the offence this time.'

He couldn't remember when he had last seen his father this cheerful. Nonetheless, he took care to close his mouth before he chewed any more.

'I bet you're glad you don't live in the ghetto in the sixteenth century. It must have been dreadful,' his father continued. 'Imagine being made to live in one place like that. And I bet it was horrible too – cramped and insanitary and claustrophobic.'

'As opposed to what – our conditions now?' Hugo interrupted.

'Hugo, I hope you're not going to be rude,' his wife Ida added. 'I won't have a word said against this forest or our lovely cave.'

Saul guessed, from the laughter, no one was going to say anything nasty.

'Do you remember,' said his mother, 'when we saw the cave the first time? Wasn't it awful?'

A piece of cheese was put into his hand.

'It wasn't that bad,' said Hugo.

Saul took a bite. It was hard and crumbly and when he chewed the insides of his cheeks tingled from the taste of it.

'You just couldn't see the potential of the place,' continued Uncle Hugo. 'But I knew that with a few bits and pieces from Henri and what we could make ourselves, it would be fine and it has been.'

The adults continued to reminisce. Saul decided what he was hearing was boring. Blanking out their laughter – it was his mother who was laughing loudest – he turned his thoughts back to the story.

In his mind's eye he saw the fog-filled street, the

burnt-out bakery and the golem pressed into the doorway. He heard the wheels of Vasek's handcart rumbling on the cobblestones. He felt a little thrill of delight. He had all that he had heard to draw on. And by the end of the afternoon he would have more. The thought of what was coming made him happy. He took another mouthful of the cheese. The strong taste he registered inside his cheeks was more pleasant this time.

'My son is happy,' said Al. 'Look, everybody, he's smiling.'

Everybody in the circle was looking at him. A light red blush crossed his face. He looked down.

After he had finished eating, Saul found himself yawning. He felt tired. He lay back on the forest floor. His plan was to lie still for a few minutes. Then, suddenly, Claude was clapping his hands and calling, 'All right everybody, back to your seats.' Saul woke, realised he had slept and sat up. He always felt marvellous after a little snooze.

'You must have been tired,' his father said. His voice was gentle and pleasing.

'I'm not surprised,' his mother said, 'he's been concentrating that hard.'

She stood over him.

'Come on,' she continued. 'Give me your hand. I'll help you up.'

He put his hand in hers and she pulled him up. Then she embraced him, holding him very tightly around the shoulders.

'You're squeezing me,' he said.

She released him slightly and he was able to step back half a step. Her eyes he saw were green and she was peering at him closely. He threw his own arms around her then broke away quickly. There was no point in overdoing the hugging. It would only give her ideas.

Everyone walked back to the circle of seats. Saul sat on his box. The others resumed their places. Claude walked back to the front and put his glasses on his nose. Hugo clapped.

'You don't clap now,' said Saul's mother lightly. 'You clap at the end, or, if you must, at the end of the first half. But you don't clap at the end of the interval.'

'At a proper play or a classical concert maybe,' said Hugo, 'but at the shows in my theatres the audience clapped as loudly when the girls came on as when they went off.'

'Well, this isn't one of your theatres or one of your shows,' said Mina. 'This is the equivalent of a classical play, isn't it, Claude?'

Claude shrugged. 'Whatever you say,' he said.

'Now is everyone ready? Shall I begin?'
'Oh please,' said Saul, 'please can we go on?'

23

Rahel

Father Tadeus sat by his fireplace and stared at the old piece of pine burning on the hearth.

It was clever, he thought, of Rabbi Loew to have substituted Lehmann for Joseph the Mute. But for that – and the rabbi could never repeat the trick – Lehmann and Chaim would have been found guilty. That, in turn, would have led to Rabbi Loew's arrest on Mathilde's evidence. If Joseph hadn't produced the girl, Lenke, the rabbi and the other two would have been hanged like common criminals.

Triumph had been so close and yet it had eluded him at the last moment. Perhaps his mistake was trying to strike at Joseph and his master simultaneously. Maybe, he thought, he should try to convert someone significant from the ghetto and get at Loew that way. The right conversion might turn the ghetto Jews against their famous rabbi. But who might it be?

He stopped thinking and stared into the flames.

They were mostly red or yellow or blue, but every now and again they went an iridescent green. Waiting for such a flame to show, Father Tadeus got the whole plan in an instant. Every Thursday evening Gerda presented Father Tadeus with the week's bills. He would start then . . .

The evening arrived. Gerda duly handed him the bills. Father Tadeus examined the first, signed it and told Gerda to pay the tradesman in question on Friday morning when he called. He worked his way through the others, issuing the same instruction in every case, then returned the pile to his housekeeper.

"Don't rush off," he said. "Wait while I write a letter. I want you to drop it round to Berger, my wine merchant, tomorrow." There had been no bill for wine in the pile because Father Tadeus always paid Berger in cash.

"Certainly," Gerda said, and she waited while the priest wrote:

> *Dear Berger,*
> *I would like to open an account with you. In future, you send your bill – if there is one – on Thursday. I will authorise payment and on Friday your proxy can come and collect the cash from my housekeeper. As this is how I pay all my other tradesmen I hope*

you won't mind doing the same. Please indicate to the bearer of this letter if my proposal is agreeable.
Father Tadeus.

"When you deliver this you must wait for an answer from Berger," said Tadeus, handing the letter over.

The following morning Gerda appeared.

"Berger said yes," she said.

It was the answer Father Tadeus had expected.

Over the following months Father Tadeus bought his wine each week on account. Every Thursday, Father Tadeus authorised payment. Every Friday, one of Berger's servants collected the money. Both parties pronounced themselves happy with the arrangement . . .

It was now a Thursday in high summer. There were big clouds in the sky above Prague. From his study window Father Tadeus surveyed the enclosed courtyard. His parochial house formed one side. The Green Church, to his left, formed the second. The buildings opposite that included the caretaker's house and the guest-rooms formed the third. The long, high, thick wall to his right made up the fourth side. In the middle of this was the low door through which Mathilde had entered. At the far end of the courtyard, Johan, the caretaker, was carefully digging out any weeds that had grown up between the cobbles with a small trowel. This was a job he did every week in the growing season. Father Tadeus insisted the Green Church and its environs were never less than immaculate.

There was a knock at the study door.

"Yes."

Gerda came in with the bills.

Father Tadeus signed each in turn "Pay". Suddenly, he stopped.

"I'm not paying that."

Gerda looked faintly alarmed.

"Which one would that be?" she asked.

"This one from Berger, the wine merchant." Father Tadeus tapped the bill. "It's for ten bottles I never had. When his servant comes tomorrow you tell him I'm not paying this. Oh no, I tell you what, wait. I'm going to write you a letter to give the servant.

"These Jewish tradesmen really are too much. They think they can give you any old bill and you'll pay it. Well, Mr. Berger, you are in for a rude shock."

Dear Berger,

Today I received a bill for ten bottles of wine I have not had. I am not happy. I thought you were a

reputable tradesman. Can I suggest you send Rahel
with the ledger? It won't be long before careful study
of your accounts will prove your latest bill is a fiction.
    Father Tadeus
    PS: Sunday afternoon is convenient if Rahel wants to
call then.

He looked up and caught Gerda's eye.

"It is Rahel, the daughter, who does the accounts, isn't it?" he asked, although he knew perfectly well that she did. He was anxious that not even his housekeeper should guess Rahel was whom he hoped to catch.

"Yes it is," agreed Gerda.

"When you give this to Berger's servant tomorrow, tell him I'm very cross. Tell him I am seriously considering taking my business elsewhere. And tell him, finally, that under no circumstances is he to tell Berger what you've said. This, of course, is the only way to guarantee that he will tell his master."

Gerda smiled. "I understand," she said.

The following Sunday afternoon, Gerda announced, "Rahel's here."

"Show her in," said Father Tadeus. "And come in yourself. You might learn how to deal with tradesmen."

Rahel stepped across the threshold. She was a

small, very pretty eighteen year old with a dimpled chin. Her eyes were greeny-brown. Over her head was thrown a shawl and she did not take it off. All the women from the ghetto kept their hair covered in this way at all times. She carried a large black book, the Berger ledger. The housekeeper followed behind.

"I have to say, I am surprised," Father Tadeus began.

He rose from his seat and moved towards Rahel.

"Sending me a bill for wine I haven't bought, it's really not good enough, is it?" he continued gently.

Rahel said nothing. Father Tadeus quickly added, "You don't mind if I call you Rahel, do you?"

The light that came through the window lit up her shawl. He noticed it was so black it was blue.

"Now here's my bill." Father Tadeus cleared his throat. "9 June, Rhine red, ten bottles. Well I never received them." He looked at Gerda. "Isn't that right?"

"I don't know," the housekeeper said, confused. "If you say you didn't, you didn't, I suppose."

Father Tadeus turned back to Rahel.

"Do you remember me taking this wine?" he asked.

"I'm in the office," said Rahel quietly, "not the shop. I don't remember you taking it."

"How would you know I had?"

"If wine goes out, the details are written on a docket which comes to me, and I write the details in the ledger."

"Oh," said Father Tadeus. "All right then. Go on, you check in that ledger of yours. You'll find I never had them. And once you've confirmed that fact, you can say sorry to me very nicely. Go on. Sit in that chair if you want."

Rahel sat on the edge of a chair and opened the ledger. Then she began to run her finger down the entries, moving her lips and reading each silently. Her finger stopped halfway down the page. She coughed. "9 June, Rhine red, ten bottles, Father Tadeus."

"What! You're joking. Are you telling me it says I had the wine?"

"It's what's written down here," said Rahel quietly.

"Let me see. There must be a mistake."

He leant over Rahel's shoulder and peered at the ledger.

"Show me."

She pointed a slender white finger at a line.

Father Tadeus read it aloud. "9 June, Rhine red, ten bottles, Father Tadeus."

Father Tadeus straightened up.

"Oh dear," he murmured. "What have I done? Oh, I'm a fool. I've accused you of the most terrible impropriety. Please forgive me. Rahel, I am completely at fault. I apologise unreservedly.

"Of course I had the wine. It's in your ledger, in ink. It's irrefutable. And you know what, Rahel? I'm so ashamed, I can barely bring myself to confess this. I remember buying the stuff now. But when I got it home and uncorked a bottle, I found it had gone off. This is my excuse. I meant to send it all back. I'm just far too busy at the moment. My housekeeper here will tell you that. I forgot. Then like the fool that I am, I acted as if I'd never had the wine in the first place. All this trouble the followed for which I am completely to blame."

He turned to Gerda. "There's a basket immediately inside the cellar door filled with bottles. That's the wine I'm talking about. Bring two bottles up and Rahel can taste it." He turned to Rahel. "It's absolute poison, like vinegar. You'll see for yourself."

The housekeeper left. Rahel sat with her heart pumping. Gerda returned. The first bottle was opened. A glass was poured and handed to her. She was so overwrought she completely forgot the prohibition on alcohol. She swallowed a sip.

"It tastes fine to me," she said.

"That can't be. Oh no," said Father Tadeus. He turned to Gerda. "Open the other bottle." Gerda looked puzzled.

"Yayn nesech," said the priest. He explained to his housekeeper this was the ordinance by which Jews were forbidden to take wine from the same bottle from which a non-Jew drank.

"How do you know that?" Rahel asked. She was impressed, and relieved that he would take his wine from a different bottle to hers. In a strange way this made the fact she'd drunk wine somehow seem less bad.

"Oh, you'd be surprised," said Father Tadeus quietly. "I know about a lot of things, and that includes Judaic law."

The second cork was pulled. Two more glasses were filled. Father Tadeus tasted one and the housekeeper tasted the other.

"A moment ago I claimed I knew things," said the priest. "Well, pride comes before a fall. The truth is that actually I'm the most stupid man in Prague. There's nothing wrong with that wine. It's perfect. What was I doing saying it tasted like vinegar?"

He turned to Gerda.

"It's good, isn't it?"

"Yes, Father," she said nervously. She wasn't used to drinking wine with her employer.

Father Tadeus took another gulp. "In fact it's delicious? Don't you agree?"

This question was addressed to Rahel. She wasn't

used to drinking either but out of a mixture of politeness and relief, she swallowed another mouthful. It was a large one. After the wine slipped down, she felt a warm pleasant glow at the back of her throat and deep in the middle of her body. A moment or two later, she had an unexpected rush of happiness and a conviction that all was well in the world.

"Listen," said Father Tadeus smoothly, "if you breathe a word about this, I'm finished. Can you imagine the fun my parishioners would have with this? Think what it'll do if I, their priest, the one who gets up in the pulpit every Sunday and delivers an interminable sermon, become known as the one who can't remember what he's bought and can't tell wine from vinegar?

"If they discover that they'll never trust me again. They'll start calling me Father Vinegar behind my back. I'll be ruined, finished. I'll have to leave Prague. I'll have to go to some horrible village in Silesia where everyone is hairy and ugly and unwashed. I'll want to leave and go somewhere nicer but no other parish in Bohemia will take Father Vinegar. Oh no, woe is me, if you won't promise to keep silent, Rahel, I'm finished as a priest."

The housekeeper smiled. Father Tadeus had a lovely sense of humour when he chose to show it.

Rahel smiled as well. Ever since her father told her to take the ledger to the parochial house, she had been dreading this visit. In the event, for which she was not prepared, Father Tadeus had turned out to be funny and winning. She was enjoying herself.

"I promise, you don't need to worry," said Rahel quietly. She took another gulp of wine and then another. Her throat and down inside her body felt warmer still.

"You mean my secret's safe with you?" said Father Tadeus.

"Of course it is. Well, just as long as you keep coming to Berger's for your wine."

"That is blackmail," Father Tadeus thundered humourously. "But I suppose I've only got myself to blame, fool that I am. Oh well, I assure you, yes, I'll only buy from Berger's. I'll do anything not to be known as Father Vinegar."

By the time she left, Father Tadeus had made a considerable impression on Rahel Berger. She had dealt with Christians all her life but this was the first time a priest had talked to her. She found his conversation interesting as well as witty. She also found his manner kind. She found his eyes, which were brown, surprisingly warm. She had not expected any of this. It was all very perplexing.

The following morning Father Tadeus wrote a pleasant chatty note to Rahel. He signed it Father Vinegar and added, after a PS: "I've signed it Father Vinegar so no one will know who I am."

Gerda called at Berger's wine shop in the afternoon and slipped the letter to Rahel when her father wasn't looking. Rahel hid it inside her ledger.

This was the start of a secret correspondence between Father Tadeus and Rahel. At first, Tadeus's letters were airy and entertaining (they were always signed Father Vinegar), while Rahel's were joshing and curt.

But as month succeeded month her letters gradually became longer and more serious. She began to express feelings she had always had but never articulated before. She wrote to the priest about her faith and the life of the soul. Had she been a boy she would have had a chance to explore these in study. But this was denied to her. She was a girl and these were not matters with which girls concerned themselves. Their sphere was the home or the place where they worked.

Until this correspondence started she had had no one to talk to deeply. Now she did. The effect was extraordinary. Her mind expanded and with it her appetite for meaningful contact. After a while, she even found it necessary to meet Father Tadeus now and again in private in the parochial house to talk.

Rahel had considerable faith but she was also burdened with huge intelligence. If she had been less intelligent, it might have been a different story. But there you are. Sometimes our assets are not always the help they might be.

Father Tadeus knew that the moment he recommended conversion their friendship would end. He knew that the only person on earth capable of converting Rahel was Rahel herself. And he knew he had to act in every way opposite to how a priest seeking conversion would behave.

So he always told Rahel to pray to God for solace and comfort and advice. He told her to talk to her rabbi about her doubts and anxieties. He told her to read her scriptures. He told her to strive harder and then harder again. Of course all this made her think not so much about her own Judaism as about his Christianity.

The idea gradually took root in her mind that there must be something essentially good and generous about the system of belief that had created Father Tadeus. Otherwise, why else would a priest go to so much trouble to urge her to be a better Jew?

Next, she began to wonder why couldn't she immerse herself in this generous faith that had produced such an exceptional priest?

One evening she came to the parochial house and, sitting in Tadeus's study and drinking tea in front of the fire, she said, "Why can't I become a Christian?"

"Well if you want to, fine," said Father Tadeus, carefully hiding his delight. "But I hardly see why you need to. Your faith is a sturdy ark. It will carry you through this world and into the next. Why change to another vessel? In fact, the more I think about it the more, it seems to me, I must make you stick to what you know. No, no you may not convert."

After several hours of heated conversation Father Tadeus finally threw his hands in the air like a man who had been defeated in argument.

"All right, if you insist, you can convert," he said, "and I shan't stand in your way. And yes, you can live here, in one of the guest-rooms while you prepare for baptism.

"And of course I will help you. I will do whatever you want. But as your friend, I feel duty bound to say that I still think you should go home to your mother and father. I still think you should tell them what you plan to do. But if you want to walk away from your old life, and start your new life, right now, right this moment, I will not stop you. If you know in your heart that this is what you want to do, it must be the will of God."

"I'm sure it is," Rahel said earnestly.

That night Rahel did not go home. Father Tadeus asked Gerda to bring her to a guest-room across the courtyard. It had stone walls, bare rafters and pigeon-coloured slates. The bed was slightly damp. The sheets and the bolster smelt of lavender.

The next morning, Mikhel Berger and his wife, Eva, found their daughter's bed empty, and their only child missing. They searched their house. They made frantic inquiries in the ghetto. Nobody could tell them anything. Nobody had seen her. Rahel had disappeared as surely as if she was a stone dropped down a well.

24

The marriage proposal

Rahel now began to prepare for baptism. She read the New Testament. She learnt her catechism. She was studious, she worked hard but it seemed to Father Tadeus, after a few days, that she was growing despondent. At first he thought her faith was wavering. But then he realised Rahel was lonely.

A few miles outside Prague lived the widower, Milan, Duke of Teplice-Sanov, with his only son, Kaja, who was eighteen. Father Tadeus was an old friend of the family. He knew Milan wanted a wife for his son. It occurred to Father Tadeus that Rahel might be the one. She was pretty. She was clever. And she was alone.

Father Tadeus invited Milan and Kaja to lunch with him and her the next Sunday. Rahel sat beside Kaja. The two young people made a powerful impression on each other. Father Tadeus arranged for Kaja to visit frequently. Over the following weeks, Rahel and Kaja became first attached and then passionate about one another. If this hadn't happened there is no doubt that Rahel would have begun to miss her parents or, at the very least, to feel guilty. She might even have sent a message or a letter. After all, she had run away and she hadn't spoken to them since. But Rahel neither missed her parents, nor regretted the way they had separated. She thought of no one else but Kaja. For the first time in her life she was in love, and the elation was so intense everything else was blotted out.

After several weeks of courtship, Kaja and his father appeared one afternoon at the parochial house. The priest immediately noticed their mood was deliberate and purposeful.

"On his last visit," said Milan, "my son, Kaja, measured Rahel's finger with a piece of thread. Since then, he's had a ring made for her and he's had his name and a message inscribed inside. My son wants to marry Rahel."

"It's no good asking me," said Father Tadeus. "I don't own her. Kaja," and here he broke off to look at the young man, "you'll have to ask her yourself."

Father Tadeus walked across his study to the window. He pointed through the glass and across the courtyard.

"Come here, Kaja. Do you see the blue door at the other end of the courtyard?"

"Yes," Kaja said.

"Rahel's in the room on the other side of that door. If you want to know if she'll marry you, you'll have to go over and ask her."

"May I?"

"Well I certainly won't stand in your way," said the priest.

Kaja left the room.

"Why don't you join me here at the window, Milan, and we can watch proceedings. It's not often one sees a proposal of marriage enacted in front of one."

"No, that's true," said Milan, joining the priest at the window.

The two men watched Kaja walk across the courtyard. They watched him stop in front of the blue door.

"Oh dear, one does feel for him," said Father Tadeus. "He must be so nervous."

"I'm sure he is," said the duke, "but we all have to go through it. If there's something we want, we have to learn how to ask for it."

"Never were truer words spoken," agreed the priest.

The blue door opened and Rahel stood in the doorway. Suddenly she stepped back and Kaja stepped forward into the guest-room. The door closed.

"Well," said Father Tadeus, "we'll know the worst or best soon enough."

Several more minutes passed. Rahel came out. Kaja followed. They were both smiling. Rahel stopped, waited for Kaja to draw level and then slipped her arm through his.

"We've got an answer I'd say," said Father Tadeus, "wouldn't you?"

"Oh yes," said Milan cheerfully, "we got the answer I prayed for, anyway."

"I'll announce the banns at Mass on Sunday. Then, unfortunately I have to go away to Krakow for the archbishop's convocation. But when I get back, and I won't be gone that long, I propose to baptise Rahel and marry her to Kaja on the same day. Do you think our two young love birds will like that?"

Father Tadeus's proposal was put to the couple when they came in. They agreed, happily. Father Tadeus then asked Milan and Kaja to go home and not to return until the wedding day.

"Apart from my visit to Krakow, or when I'm doing something I can't get out of, like saying Mass," he explained humourously, "I want to spend every minute with Rahel, getting her ready."

"For my glorious new life," Rahel added.

25

Joseph the angel

The next Sunday, Father Tadeus told the congregation he was leaving for Krakow later that day. He also announced the marriage banns of Rahel Berger and Kaja, son of Milan, the Duke of Teplice-Sanov.

Rahel was a stranger to the congregation, though they guessed from her surname that she was a Jewess. But they all knew Kaja. After all, he was the only son and heir of a duke.

News of the betrothal quickly spread through the Old Town and then into the ghetto. Mikhel and Eva Berger soon heard that their daughter was to be married to Kaja in the Green Church by Father Tadeus. And once they knew this, they were able to deduce the rest.

The priest had their daughter somewhere on his property. She was in the throes of conversion and at the end of this process she would marry this Christian fellow, Kaja.

The Bergers went to tell Rabbi Loew. When they

finished the Rabbi asked, "You're sure he said he was going to Krakow?"

Mikhel Berger thought the question strange. But he also knew he had to answer his rabbi.

"We're only saying what we heard third or fourth hand. But yes, that's what he said, apparently."

"Do you have any relatives who don't live in Prague?"

"I have a brother Max in Amsterdam."

"What does he do?"

"He's a wine merchant. We all are."

"Go home," said Rabbi Loew. "Early, tomorrow morning, have a carriage with two strong horses and two strong men waiting at your house. Your daughter will be returned. You are to put her in the carriage. You are to send her to your brother. And she is to stay there with him. She is not to come back. You cannot keep her in the ghetto here. Do you understand?"

The Bergers began to weep. First they lost their daughter. Then she was discovered although, alas, this news came tangled up with the revelation that she was not only converting but marrying a stranger. Then their rabbi gave them instructions of which the clear implication was they would have Rahel back. And then finally, he told them, they couldn't keep her and must send her away.

Still crying, the Bergers left Rabbi Loew sitting at

his desk. He flattened a piece of paper and wrote the following:

> *Dear Rahel,*
> *I am your angel. I have come down from heaven.*
> *Jump in my sack. Do not ask why. Just do as I ask.*

Rabbi Loew blotted and folded the paper. Then, having collected a sack, he went and found Joseph sitting on the wood box.

"Up," said Rabbi Loew.

Joseph jumped to his feet.

"Follow me."

Rabbi Loew and Joseph made their way to the Green Church. They arrived just in time to see Father Tadeus being driven off in his carriage in the direction of Krakow. Rabbi Loew brought Joseph to the long wall bounding the courtyard beside the Green Church.

"You will come here tonight, Joseph," said Rabbi Loew. "You will cover your face. You will pull your hat down and your collar up. I will give you a scarf as well. You will jump over that wall. You will search every room off the courtyard behind the wall. You will find Rahel Berger. She is a young girl. She is Mikhel Berger's daughter. She has just become betrothed so I imagine she has a new ring on her hand.

When you find Rahel you will give her this to read."

Rabbi Loew handed Joseph the letter.

"Now put it under your hat and keep it safe."

Joseph did as he was told.

"Once she's read this letter she will climb into this sack. Here, take it."

Joseph took the sack.

"You hold it open for her so she can get in."

Joseph nodded.

"You will carry Rahel in the sack to the house of Berger, the wine merchant. You know their house?"

Joseph nodded. He knew where everyone lived in the ghetto now.

"You will deliver the sack with Rahel to Mikhel and Eva. You will come home to me with the empty sack. Do you understand?"

Joseph nodded.

"Right, come back home with me now and I'll get that scarf. I don't want you to be seen. You only return when it's dark."

A little after midnight, with his face covered, Joseph jumped the wall and landed silently in the courtyard of the Green Church. He entered the caretaker's house first and went into one bedroom after another. He found no young girl with a ring on her finger.

Then Joseph went into the guest-room next door. Joseph knew at once when he saw the ring on the hand that he had found Rahel. He lit a candle and nudged the sleeping girl on the shoulder. She sat up abruptly, saw a giant with no face leaning over her, and opened her mouth to scream. Joseph clamped his huge hand over her mouth before she could make a sound and handed her the letter. Rahel shook with terror and dropped it. Joseph picked it up and put it back in her hand and pointed at it. Rahel understood she was to read. She unfolded the paper and held it up to the candle.

When she had finished reading she said, "You are my angel and you have been sent to fetch me."

Joseph said nothing but opened the sack as Rabbi Loew had instructed him to do.

Rahel looked at the huge figure whose head nudged against the ceiling. She had always imagined angels were thin and fine and dressed in white whereas this one was thickset and heavy, dressed like a beadle from the synagogue and had his face swathed in a scarf. Perhaps he was in disguise because he was on earth?

Joseph shook the sack, indicating she was to get in.

Did angels normally carry people about in sacks? This was peculiar. And why had he come for her? Of course, she realised it was because of her forthcoming baptism and marriage. Both these must mean a great deal to God.

But if she left now she must break her promises to Father Tadeus and Kaja. She would not be baptised. She would not marry her fiancé. Her heart pounded at the thought. Father Tadeus and Kaja would both be appalled when they discovered her gone.

But could she choose not to go? No. God was calling her. She could not bear to hurt Father Tadeus and Kaja, and yet she was elated that God was calling her. Her priest and her fiancé would surely understand why she had left? God was the supreme authority.

Rahel jumped out of bed in her nightdress and climbed into the sack. She felt the drawstring being tightened above her. The inside of the sack went black. It smelt of carrots and earth. She felt her angel set the sack on his shoulder. She sensed him striding across her room, jumping the courtyard wall, and moving off through the streets.

She was happy, jiggling about inside the dark, earthy sack. Her recent life had been so full of incident and surprise. But it had also added to her confusion and perplexity. Now that was all over. God had sent an angel for her. Henceforth, everything would be clear and straight and just. Even Kaja would understand eventually, she felt sure, although, for all her certainty, there was still a little part of her that ached at the knowledge of what he would feel when he discovered she was gone. This too, she decided in the end, was part of the plan God had for her. Having contracted to marry him, it was inevitable and right she would feel pangs of guilt. One couldn't just obliterate the past and expect to feel nothing. It would be quite wrong if only Kaja suffered. She must as well.

Rahel now sensed her angel had stopped. She heard knocking, a door scraping open and muffled voices. These sounded like those of her father and mother. But this was too extraordinary. It couldn't be them. This wasn't right.

She felt the sack being set gently on the ground. She felt the drawstring being fiddled with. She looked up. She saw a small white pinhole opening out into a wide mouth. It was like looking up from the bottom of a well. And then two faces appeared. They looked in and down on her. It was her mother and father. They were smiling at her and they were crying.

And as Rahel saw her parents, after so many weeks away from them, she felt a great wrenching sensation deep in her being. Her eyes filled with tears. She had missed them horribly. It was just that at the Green Church she had been able not to think about them because she had thought of no one else but Kaja. But feelings denied do not go away. They live on in secret in the mind until something happens. Usually it is something unexpected or shocking, and then what is hidden can erupt into the light. Like now. Seeing Eva and Mikhel she felt huge sadness bordering on grief, and simultaneously she felt fantastic joy. The angel had been sent to bring her home, she realised. That was his purpose.

She threw her arms around her parents. She was vaguely aware of the door opening and closing, as her angel left, but she did not care. All that mattered was that she could touch her mother and father.

Later Mikhel told her she would have to go to Amsterdam to his brother Max's. She accepted this, as she accepted everything else that night, as one more sign of the will of God. Also, it made sense. By coming home, even at God's wish, she could be sure of two things. She would have earned Father Tadeus's undying enmity. And she would have broken Kaja's heart. It was right to leave now before Father Tadeus returned from Krakow and Kaja discovered she had left the Green Church. To be sure she would cause pain with her actions, but as she believed God's will came before man's and this was His will, she did not doubt for a second that her course was right.

The time came to go. She climbed into the carriage. She closed the door. She saw her parents, with their wet, white faces. The coachman cracked his whip. The wheels turned. Rahel's journey to Amsterdam had begun.

26

Johan's deception

Every morning Johan the caretaker brought Rahel warm water so she could wash. This morning was no exception. He carried the steaming pitcher carefully to the guest-room door, set it down on the cobbles and knocked.

There was no reply. He knocked again. He knocked a third time. Was Rahel sick, perhaps? Calling, "It's Johan, I've your water. Are you there, Rahel?" he opened the door. He saw the bed with the covers thrown back. He saw Rahel's dress laid out on a chair. He saw embers smouldering in the grate. The girl was gone.

Johan's first thought was Father Tadeus. When he got home from Krakow and found Rahel had gone he would go berserk. And his fury would be directed entirely at his luckless caretaker.

Johan's heart began to race and his stomach to tremble. He would have to do something – what?

He set the pitcher outside his front door. He rushed to the Green Church. He went down into the crypt.

This dark dank room was lined with stone shelves divided into alcoves. In each lay a human skeleton, the bones higgledy-piggledy.

Johan selected an alcove and pulled all the bones out. He found a sack and threw them into it. Then he took a selection of bones from several other alcoves and threw them into the empty one. No one would ever know of the theft.

He carried the sack back to the guest-room. He emptied the bones on to the bed and laid them out in the shape of a skeleton. He left to fetch a flagon of lamp oil and a burning candle. He poured the oil on the bed and the sack. Then he threw the burning candle into the middle of the bed. The lamp oil caught fire with a whoosh.

Johan hurried from the guest-room, taking care to close the door behind him. He retrieved his pitcher and went into his own house. His wife and children were at breakfast. There was hot milk sweetened with honey, bread and cheese. He sat down.

"What kept you?" his wife Vera asked. She had wide cheekbones, watery blue eyes and hair the colour of straw.

"You know the empty barrels?"

She did. They had warned their children not to play with them.

"A stray cat got stuck in one," he explained, "and I had to get it out."

"Funny, I never heard it screeching," said Vera.

"It was so frightened it was beyond that," said her husband.

"And how's Rahel this morning?" Vera asked.

"Not so good," said Johan, absentmindedly. "She's not feeling well. I had to fetch wood and bank up her fire. She said she's staying in bed."

"She didn't want her hot water even?"

"No, I brought it back."

"She must be ill."

The room was filled with the sound of chewing.

"I know why she's sick," said Vera.

"Why?" asked Johan.

"Worrying about her wedding, I bet."

Silence descended. The family ate. Suddenly, Johan's oldest surviving child, a boy called Andres, sniffed the air.

"I smell burning," Andres said.

Vera lifted her head from her plate. She twitched her small pointed nose.

"Something is burning," she said. A look of appalled understanding had crossed her face. She exclaimed, "Johan – the guest-room!"

Johan and Vera, followed by their five children,

rushed outside to the courtyard. Vera had been right.

There was a small window by the door of the guest-room. Behind the thick glass great yellow flames shimmered. Plumes of smoke rose from the keyhole. Tufts of smoke curled around the edges of the door. The sound of the fire within the room was like a distant waterfall. Johan kicked the door back and a tongue of fire leapt out at him, followed by a wave of abysmal heat. Everyone fell back with smarting eyes. The fire was too fierce for Johan to go in and rescue Rahel.

"Get the fire tender," Vera ordered Andres. The boy headed off for the city hall. His father opened the gate at the corner of the courtyard.

A few minutes later, four black horses galloped through the gateway. The firemen and Andres were sitting on the tender behind.

The tender hurtled over the cobblestones to the guest-room and stopped. Two firemen began to work the pump while two others unrolled the hoses, and pointed them at the open doorway. A stream of water arched in through the doorway. The water collided with the roaring jumping flames. Soon there was hissing and billowing steam.

It was hours before the fire was out and the firemen said it was safe to enter what was once the guest-room. Johan and Vera picked their way into the charred sodden stinking space. In the corner, where the bed had stood, they found the bones.

"Poor Rahel," said Vera. "I hope she was asleep when it happened. I hope it was a quick death."

Johan blessed himself and muttered a prayer. When he had finished he said, "What do we do now?"

"Fetch the police," said Vera. "They'd better see this for themselves. And when they come, tell them everything, don't keep anything back. Tell them Rahel was a Jewess and Father Tadeus was instructing her for baptism."

"Why would I do that?" he asked, alarmed.

"Her parents may have reported her missing."

"Yes. So what?"

"Think what they might do when they discover she's burnt to death, here, in this church, and that you were the last person to see her."

Johan looked at his wife. "I don't understand."

"Well they might accuse us – or you, actually – of having killed her because she's a Jew and you're a Christian."

"But I didn't," her husband said plaintively.

"I know that. But if you say she was here and she was going to convert, then the world will know we had no reason to harm her. Her parents certainly won't be able to accuse us."

"Oh I see, yes, I understand now," said Johan.

Andres was sent back to the city hall. He returned with a policeman. Johan told him everything, then showed him the blackened bones. The policeman touched them with the tip of his sword.

"And these are the remains of this Jewess," he asked, "who was staying here until her baptism?"

"And marriage," said Johan, "yes."

"I'll have to make a full report."

"Oh yes, of course," said Johan, "you do that."

"I'll want to see Father Tadeus when he gets back. I'll want a statement from him as well. Be sure and warn him."

"Certainly," said Johan. The thought of telling the priest made his stomach curdle.

27

Father Tadeus vows vengeance

When Father Tadeus got back from Krakow, the first person he met in the parochial house was Gerda. He was surprised to see she was dressed entirely in black.

"Something dreadful has happened. You'd better talk to Johan."

Father Tadeus found Johan in the courtyard weeding between cobblestones. He too was dressed in mourning clothes.

"Oh Father, your honour," said Johan, standing as his employer approached, "there was a fire, and the Lord have mercy on her soul, wasn't Rahel burned to a cinder."

Pity and fury washed through the priest. But he did not show what he was feeling.

"Where did this happen?" asked the priest, coolly.

"In the guest-room. It's been left exactly as it was so you could see."

Johan and priest filed through the charred door and into the sooty room.

"Those are her remains," said Johan, pointing at the blackened bones.

The priest blessed himself, closed his eyes and prayed for several minutes. At last he opened his eyes.

"A candle or something must have caught fire and she burnt to death in her bed," said Johan. "The police have all the details. And they want to see you."

"Oh," said Father Tadeus. The shock he had felt when he first heard the terrible news was subsiding. Prayer had stilled him. His mind was starting to work again. He did not like what he was hearing. He did not believe it either. Johan was never this fluent normally.

"How did the police become involved?" he asked quietly

"The firemen," Johan said quickly. "They said we had to tell the police and we didn't want to disobey them. A policeman came and he asked us to tell him the truth. We knew you'd expect nothing less, so we explained about Rahel coming from the ghetto and preparing to convert and to marry. We said she was living in the guest-room until that happy day."

Now the priest was quite certain. Johan had prepared his story in advance. That could only mean it was a lie.

Staring down at the bones, Father Tadeus's mind started turning. It was so obvious, it struck him as amazing that Johan thought he could get away with his lie.

While he was in Krakow, he decided, Rahel's faith wavered. She decided she didn't want to convert or to marry. She wanted to go home instead. She must have contacted Rabbi Loew and asked him to help her.

The rabbi, of course, was cunning. He knew if she just went back home to the ghetto, there was always the possibility that he or Kaja would go after her and try to bring her back. Or make trouble.

Rahel needed to vanish off the face of the earth. Having decided she wanted to go she went to Johan. She offered him money to make it look as if she'd burnt to death. Johan said yes. Tadeus was certain of that. He was always a greedy fellow.

Father Tadeus revealed nothing of his conclusions. He nodded instead at his caretaker and blinked sadly.

"I know you did your best. And in this world, Johan, you can only do your best. Get back to work," said Father Tadeus. "I'd better go to the police station."

Inwardly, as he walked away, he was livid. He was disappointed. He was hurt. He was bewildered. He had extricated Rahel from her family. He had found a fine husband for her. He was going to baptise her and marry them. He had hoped, with this, to hurt the Jews, it was true. But he also believed it was right. He believed he would secure a better afterlife for Rahel's immortal soul. And he liked her, enormously.

All was ruined now, and all because of money. But it was ever thus, he thought grimly. Hadn't Judas Iscariot betrayed Jesus Christ for thirty pieces of silver? Johan was no different.

This reasoning didn't improve the priest's mood. It was dreadful to think human nature didn't change. His mood darkened and his thoughts turned to vengeance as he tramped on. One day, he decided, somehow, some way, he would pay Johan back. And if, while hurting Johan he also hit Rabbi Loew, well, that would be poetic justice.

28

Kaja in mourning

The next day a letter arrived at Milan's castle. A servant took it to the old Duke in the music room. He was practising scales on his flute.

"A letter, your grace," said the servant.

Milan recognised the handwriting as that of his old friend, Father Tadeus.

Milan broke the seal, opened the letter and read:

Dear Milan,

I have some terrible news for you, old friend. While I was away in Krakow, Rahel stayed at the Green Church in one of our guest-rooms. One morning, last week, a fire broke out in her room and she burnt to death. Alas, with Rahel not being baptised, her remains will have to go into unconsecrated ground. I will do this tomorrow. Do not feel either you or Kaja need come. There are some experiences a man can do without. This, surely, must rank as one.

Yours, in sympathy,
Father Tadeus

Milan told the servant to fetch Kaja. Five minutes elapsed. Milan did not move from the spot where he stood. Kaja came in. He saw his father's face and knew immediately that something was wrong.

"What is it?"

"Kaja, I want you to sit down," said Milan quietly. "I want you to steel yourself. The news I have will split you in two."

Kaja sat on the edge of a large chair covered with red velvet.

"I just received this letter from Father Tadeus. I am going to read it to you."

Kaja stared at the corner of the rug lying on the floor near his feet. Milan read the letter. After he finished there was a long silence.

"The goldsmith who made the engagement ring said it would protect her," Kaja said finally. He had his face down and Milan could not see if Kaja was crying.

Inside, Milan felt a strange, feverish sensation. This was grief. He remembered it from the time his wife died. But would his feelings be as powerful now as then? He doubted it. Milan had only lost his future daughter-in-law while Kaja had lost something much greater.

He had lost the one, above anyone else on earth, whom he believed would make him happy. In the coming months, Milan had no doubt, it would seem to his son as if his very life was over.

"I want to see the remains," Kaja said. "I want to go to the funeral."

They went to Prague, to the parochial house. Gerda opened the door to them.

"Come in, your honours," she said, gently. She was sorry for the pair, especially for Kaja. She was in no doubt he had been very much in love with Rahel. She had grown fond of the girl herself. Everyone had.

"The remains are where she died," said Gerda. "It was the best place for the coffin."

The two visitors knew what she really meant by this. If Rahel had been baptised, then her remains would have been in the Green Church. Kaja and Milan followed Gerda through the house, and across the courtyard. As they approached the guest-room they saw Johan. He was stacking the few roof slates to have survived the fire.

Hearing footsteps Johan stopped and turned. He drew himself to his full height. He removed his hat.

"Your honours," he said, as Milan and Kaja, drew close. "You'll find her in there."

Milan and Kaja took off their wide brimmed hats and handed these to Gerda. Milan coughed and indicated to Kaja that he should go through the doorway first. Kaja nodded and went forward.

Inside he found himself in a gloomy sooty space. This was the room where he had proposed to Rahel. This was the room where she had agreed to marry him. Now, how different. The damp ground was uneven and strewn with debris. The stone walls were smeared with black furry dust. Apart from a couple of charred rafters the roof above was gone. Blue sky and white cloud filled the square. There was an overwhelming smell of burn and wet stone.

The only thing that bore no signs of the recent fire was the coffin. It was in the corner, where the bed once stood. It rested on trestles. It was a plain coffin, made of pine.

Kaja heard his father come in and stop somewhere behind.

"Is the caretaker still outside?" Kaja asked his father.

"Yes he is," Milan said.

"Johan," Kaja shouted.

The caretaker appeared in front of the two visitors. He knew exactly why Kaja had called him in.

"Can you take the lid off?" Kaja asked.

"Oh yes," said Johan. "It's just tacked on."

He gripped the crowbar he had brought to do this. The coffin top rose like a kettle lid buoyed by steam. Johan repeated the process at the other three corners. Then he looked at Kaja and asked, "Are you ready? There's not a lot in here, you know."

"I didn't expect there would be," said Kaja.

Johan lifted away the lid with a single fluid movement. Kaja and his father looked down. The inside of the coffin was white and deep. Rahel's blackened bones were arranged on the base exactly as they would have been in her body. All the bones were held in place with pieces of wire tacked to the coffin floor. Kaja guessed – rightly – it was all Johan's work. It was beautifully done.

"Did you find a gold ring?" asked Kaja.

"No," Johan said. "It was a ferocious fire. No gold could have lasted in the heat inside here."

Rahel's bones had resisted the fire yet her ring had melted and trickled away. On balance, Kaja decided, it was the best way round. At least there was something left to prove she had once existed.

Milan and Kaja sat up with the coffin all that night. The next morning, along with Father Tadeus, Gerda, and Johan and his family, they followed the coffin through the Old Town and out into the country, to the public graveyard. The remains had to go outside the graveyard wall, where suicides, apostates and those who were not baptised were buried. Here they watched as the coffin was lowered into the hole. They listened as Father Tadeus recited Psalm 107, then waited as black Bohemian earth was shovelled down on top of it.

Bumping towards home in their carriage later, Kaja stared out the window and cried quietly. Milan knew better than to speak. Words, whether intended to comfort or distract would be insufferable. When grief was at its hottest and brightest, as Milan recognised Kaja's was, the best course was to watch the sufferer to ensure they did not harm themselves, and otherwise to leave them alone. He knew, like everything else in life, extreme grief did diminish in the end.

Three months later, Kaja came to his father and said, "I have decided I want to go away. I want to enrol at the university in Venice. I want to study medicine."

This delighted Milan. Since Rahel's death Kaja had been in darkness. He had known only misery and pain. But now, as Milan had always known would happen, Kaja's grief had started to moderate. His son's gaze was starting to shift away from himself and back towards the world.

"If that is what you want, of course you can go with my blessing."

"It is what I want," said Kaja but he was lying. He needed a pretext to leave home and this was it.

Kaja had come to a startling conclusion. He had decided to convert to Judaism so that when he met Rahel in the world to come, he would share her faith. Kaja was nowhere near the end of the white-hot grieving period.

Kaja travelled by diligence to Trieste and then by boat to Venice. It was raining when he arrived and the streets were slimy with wet.

His priority was to find lodgings. In a small lane by a dark canal he came on a house with a notice tacked up in the window: Rooms to Rent. He knocked on the door. The landlord answered. He was small and dark, not unhandsome, with beautifully-manicured nails.

"Have you a room to rent?" asked Kaja.

The landlord gazed at the speaker. He saw a tall young man with regular features and an unhappy expression. A man with a broken heart, he guessed. He also noted that this stranger wore very expensive clothes.

"Of course." The landlord decided to ask for a little more than he had planned.

He showed Kaja a large room on the first floor with a bed, a table and a wardrobe.

"How much?" said Kaja.

The landlord told him.

"I'll take it," said Kaja. "I'll pay you now for this year. In a year's time I will pay you for the next year. I will not always be in residence. In my line of business – I'm a cloth merchant – I have to travel a great deal."

The landlord nodded. He didn't believe what he was hearing for one moment, but that was no business of his. All that mattered was that he got paid.

"If anyone should call for me," said Kaja, "while I'm away, you must say I will be back but you do not know when. You will make a note of their name and the time and date of their visit. You will leave a list of my visitors along with any letters that arrive for me here on this table. And many letters will arrive here for me and you must keep them safe here in my room ready for me whenever I visit."

"Of course," said the landlord and he took receipt of the first year's rent.

That night Kaja wrote a brief note to his father:

Dear Father,
I am in Venice (address at the head of this). I

have enrolled. My studies are going to take up my every waking hour. I doubt I will be able to write as often as you would like. I will try, of course, but trying and succeeding, as we know, are two very different matters.

Your loving son,
Kaja

The next day Kaja left Venice. He travelled north. In a perfect world he would have gone now to Rabbi Loew in the Prague ghetto. But how could he? His father would hear of it in no time. So would Father Tadeus. The priest would incite his parishioners to storm the synagogue and save him from Rabbi Loew.

Kaja had settled on middle Europe's second most famous rabbi, Loew's sometime pupil, Jacob Gintzberg. He lived in Friedburg, a town in the principality of Hesse, where he had gone a few months after he had helped to make the golem.

Kaja arrived in Friedburg. He presented himself to Rabbi Gintzberg.

"I want to convert," he explained, bluntly.

The rabbi was appalled. He couldn't convert this youth from Christianity to Judaism. His religion had no tradition of conversion. It didn't proselytise. He also knew that the host community would be furious. He would be accused of having put a spell on Kaja in order to get him to convert. Why else would a young man want to ally himself with the people that he had been taught from the cradle had crucified Jesus Christ?

"I can't," said Rabbi Gintzberg politely. "It will lead to strife, it will lead to trouble."

"But you must."

"I can't."

"What would Rabbi Loew say?" Kaja asked.

"You know him?"

"I have heard of him. Who hasn't?"

Mention of Loew's name provoked a long conversation. This was followed by many more over the following weeks. As they spoke, Rabbi Gintzberg found Kaja to be charming, sincere and interesting, and very intelligent. The more contact they had, the more difficult it was to go on refusing to convert the youth. Finally, Rabbi Gintzberg agreed. However, he stipulated conditions. It must be done in strict secrecy. Kaja must stay in the synagogue all the time. And he must not talk to anyone except the rabbi and his immediate family.

Kaja agreed. The master and his new pupil began their work together. A year later Kaja converted at a small ceremony attended only by Gintzberg's family. In the course of the initiation he ceased to be Kaja and became Abraham Yeshurun instead. After the ceremony, Gintzberg asked his protégé what he wanted to do next.

"I want to study the Talmud with you."

"You know that study involves being able to know by heart every rabbinical commentary ever written . . .? Of course you do. Why do you want to do this?" he continued.

"I feel I've only begun to scratch the surface. I want, I need, to go further and deeper."

"I can't take another pupil," said Jacob Gintzberg, "not if he's as clever as you clearly are. You'll wear me out. But I will send you to the yeshiva in Amsterdam. They should be able to help. All I have to do is get you in."

Gintzberg sent Abraham to Amsterdam, with a letter of introduction in his pocket. Abraham found the rabbi in charge and presented the letter. This is what it said:

Dear Master,
The bearer of this letter was once called Kaja. Now he is Abraham. He was once a Christian but he has converted. I believe he will be a brilliant scholar.

Abraham was admitted. He began his studies. He was a diligent and conscientious student. He was so gifted and so clever, word of his academic prowess spread through Amsterdam. Marriage brokers began to visit Abraham. Sometimes they brought portraits of the girls they represented. Abraham declined all offers. He had decided that if he couldn't have Rahel as his wife then he would have no wife at all, though this was going against his duty. He would live a celibate life and he would devote himself to his faith instead.

After a few months intensive study Abraham took leave of absence. He returned to Venice, to the room he rented. He found his father's letters piled on the table. He sat and wrote a long and largely fictitious reply. He asked for money to be sent to a bank in Venice.

Writing this letter was wrong of course – he knew that. But how could he tell his father what he had done? It would lead he did not dare think where. It was far simpler to wait until they were all in the world to come. Then Milan would understand why his son had done this small wrong. He would see his son had no alternative but to switch to the faith of his true love.

The following day Abraham returned to

Amsterdam where he continued his studies. He filled his head with words from books but his heart was empty.

29

Andres's accident

Father Tadeus and his vestrymen were seated at a table in a meeting room at the Green Church.

"What about the repair of the guest-room?" one vestryman asked. He was a small officious little fellow with a big moustache that he liked to stroke while he was talking. Father Tadeus couldn't abide him.

"What about it?" said Father Tadeus. His tone was deliberately light although in truth his feelings were quite the reverse. He wanted to leave the place he connected with the loss of Rahel as it was and let it rot.

"Shouldn't we get the repairs under way?" insisted the vestryman.

"Why?"

"It's become a playroom for the caretaker's children. I even saw them playing in there with a dog on my way to this meeting."

"Oh yes, the dog – he's new. I think they call him Peter."

The vestryman was also called Peter. He felt, in

some way that he couldn't exactly put his finger on, that he had just been insulted.

"At the moment it's just a playroom," he repeated.

"What's wrong with that?" said Father Tadeus.

"What's wrong with it? I'll tell you. It's on church property. It's an eyesore. It should be fixed."

Father Tadeus smiled, but in his heart he was smarting.

"One day, yes," he replied, "but at the moment I want to spend what money we can afford on something much more important. I want to build some houses, for the poor and the old, the lame and the halt, the sick and needy of our parish. I agree the guest-room is a monstrosity but not nearly, to my eyes, as ugly as the sight of a child and his mother sleeping in the street."

The vestrymen murmured approvingly. Father Tadeus really wasn't like anybody else. He did put the interests of other people first. He was a good, kind, Christian man. Peter regretted the way he had just spoken and decided to let the subject drop.

So the guest-room was not repaired. The caretaker's children went on playing inside. Then, one afternoon, when they were chasing around inside, Andres fell. As he hurtled towards the ground, he put his hand out. He did not see the nail sticking out of the earth. It was a large old rusty nail that originally held a floorboard in place. The nail went right through Andres's hand and came out the other side. Andres burst into tears. He jumped up and ran next door to his mother in the kitchen.

"Oh my hand, my hand," Andres wailed.

His mother cried, "Oh my God!"

Vera got a bottle of spirits from the cupboard, pulled off the cork and doused Andres's palm. The alcohol ran into the bleeding wound and stung horribly. Andres cried out in pain. Vera, without warning Andres what she was about to do, took hold of the nail and plucked it out. Then she poured more liquor on the wound. Andres screamed again. By this stage his brothers and sisters had followed him into the kitchen and were watching in appalled silence.

"From now on," Vera shouted, "none of you are to go into that guest-room. It's cursed, it's dangerous, and if any of you disobey, you'll have your father to contend with."

She told Andres to go bed.

"Why? I'm not ill."

The next morning he had a temperature. His hands and feet were freezing. His breathing was rapid. He had a cramp in his stomach. He was drowsy. There were splotches all over the arm above his wounded hand. They were dark red, irregular. It looked as if old strawberry jam was smeared randomly under the surface of his skin. These daubs were blood pools. It was septicaemia caused by the rusty old nail.

A doctor was summoned. He put a poultice of mustard seed on Andres's weeping hand and another of lavender on his head. He burnt herbs in the sickroom to drive away the evil vapours that he believed had made Andres sick.

The following morning the splodges had spread across Andres's shoulder and down his back and front. A surgeon was summoned. He cut a vein in the sick child's good arm. Blood flowed out with slow constancy. He collected the liquid in a glass bowl and held it up to the light. He pronounced the operation a success. He had purged the malignancy, the surgeon said.

The following day the blood patches had spread up Andres's neck and across his face. They were getting bigger as well. Over the following days, more and more of the child's healthy pink flesh was taken over by these vile blots.

Several nights after his fall, Andres lay in bed, shaking, perspiring and murmuring. His mother drowsed in the chair beside him. Suddenly Andres sat up. Vera woke with a start.

"I see a rainbow," he muttered. He pointed into the furthest corner where the walls met the ceiling.

"Do you see a rainbow?" his mother asked. "Do you really?" Her heart raced. At last, she thought, a sign that he would recover.

He lay back on the bolster. His mother took his good hand. A slick of cold sweat covered his skin. His breathing grew quieter and fainter.

Her hope was misplaced. Of her eight children three had already died and now the fourth was about to follow.

"Johan," she called to her husband, sleeping with the children in the adjacent room, "he's going. Come in and bring the children and send for Father Tadeus."

The caretaker sent Andres's brother Vaclav for the priest and came into the room with his other children. They were sleepy. The youngest, the girl, Dasha, rubbed her eyes and bit her lip. They stood in a circle around the bed. What followed was like the moment when a candle burns to the end and all that is left is a puddle of wax, and the floating wick swells up and contracts before finally snuffing out. Their brother's breathing rose, then fell, then rose, and then, finally, stopped.

When Father Tadeus reached the caretaker's home

a few minutes later, he could tell by the crying that the child was already dead.

It was not until the early hours of the morning, that Father Tadeus got back to the parochial house. He did not go back to his bedroom. He went into his study and lit the lamp. He opened his calendar. He made calculations. Passover was soon. When God struck Andres down, he not only punished Johan. He also delivered to Father Tadeus the means to strike at Rabbi Loew.

He put the light out and went to sleep.

30

Rabbi Loew's dream

As Father Tadeus drifted towards sleep later, Rabbi Loew found himself standing outside the Green Church. He stood at the top of the front steps before the double doors.

He closed his hand around one of the polished brass handles. He pushed. The door did not budge. It was locked.

Rabbi Loew turned. He went down the steps to the square at the bottom. He walked to the end and turned right. On one side rose the Green Church while on the opposite side of the road there loomed one of the most interesting buildings in the Old Town, the old Five-Sided palace.

Everything in the building was a multiple of five. Besides its five sides it had five floors. At ground level, there were five archways, inset with five doors. Each of the floors had five windows. And along the parapet at the top were five carved stone figures.

The Five-Sided palace was an ancient royal

residence. It was rumoured that a hundred years earlier, when there was tension in the city between Protestants and Catholics, the reigning Habsburg monarch, who was Catholic, had had a tunnel built under the street to connect the palace with the Green Church. This allowed the royal family, when they were in residence, to get to the Green Church secretly and safely.

If the tunnel did exist – and for all Rabbi Loew knew this was only a story – it was no longer used. The Habsburg kings now either lived in their palace at the top of Vysehrad hill, or more usually across the river in a newer palace on top of the Hradcany hill.

The Five-Sided palace was now the home to hundreds of beggars and their families. They camped out in its once sumptuous rooms and threw their rubbish into the basement. Every year or two the city authorities would send in the police. The beggars would be thrown out. The glassless windows and doorways would be boarded up. But it would only be a matter of time before the beggars broke in again.

Standing in the street, his back to the Green Church, Rabbi Loew surveyed the Five-Sided palace. From inside it came music and laughter. The beggars were famous for their music. He heard snatches of song mingled with the beat of a drum and the trill of a flute.

Rabbi Loew's attention was drawn to a window on the first storey. A white sheet was stretched tight and nailed to the frame. Judging by the shadows he saw, the people in the room behind were dancing.

A cry came from inside the room. It was as surprising as it was terrifying. The stretched sheet grew suddenly white and bright. Then it was wrenched away violently. In the room behind there was a terrifying smear of red. In the foreground there was a dark silhouette.

"Fire," shouted the silhouette desperately, "fire."

Rabbi Loew raised his eyes. Along the entire length of the roof there were tongues of flame jumping into the night. There were beggars shouting at every window and running from every door.

Someone tugged his elbow. He shrugged them off. His elbow was tugged again.

"Please, leave me alone," he shouted. "Go away. Can't you see I'm busy?"

"No, I won't. Come on, it's time to get up."

Rabbi Loew opened his eyes. He was in his bed at home, his head on the bolster, looking up at Pearl.

"Do you know what you just did?" asked Pearl.

"No."

"When I was shaking your arm, you told me to go away."

"Oh."

"I should think an apology is in order."

"Sorry," said Rabbi Loew mechanically.

"You don't sound as if you mean it."

"Oh I do."

"Then say it properly."

"I'm sorry."

"Oh no, that's not enough. You have to say, 'I'm sorry for speaking to you the way I just did.' Go on," continued Pearl, "say that as well."

"Do I have to?"

"Yes."

"All right," said Rabbi Loew. "I'm sorry for speaking to you the way I just did."

"That's better." Pearl smiled. "What was it anyhow?"

"What was what?"

"What was it you were dreaming?"

"The Five-Sided palace was on fire."

"That was what you were dreaming about?" said Pearl, incredulously.

"Yes."

"Why did you tell me to go away?"

"Well, it was fascinating and, ah . . . it was appalling as well of course, and I didn't want to be disturbed."

"Were there people in this dream?"

"Oh yes, there were beggars rushing about."

"It doesn't sound at all nice."

"It was only a dream," said Rabbi Loew.

"Speaking of which," Pearl said deftly, "I hope our lad in the kitchen hasn't dreamt the night away. If I find him asleep and the fire out, he'll find himself in a nightmare when he wakes up."

Pearl turned and left. Loew threw back the covers and swung his feet out. He put them down on the rug by the bed. He looked at his feet. Poor, tired feet, he thought. The veins stood up under the skin. His toenails were yellow and the ends were ragged. These were unmistakably the feet of an old man. An old man with a mission not yet completed.

He took off his nightcap and wiped it over his eyes.

"Why would I dream of the Five-Sided palace catching fire?" he asked out loud.

Then he answered himself: "It's a complete mystery."

31

Father Tadeus and the grave-digger

Two days later Father Tadeus said Andres's burial mass in the Green Church. After the service, while the church bell tolled mournfully, the congregation filed outside.

The funeral cart was waiting at the front of the church at the bottom of the steps. The small white coffin was put on the back. Father Tadeus, the family and the other mourners gathered behind.

The cart driver shook the reins. The black gelding hitched between the shafts took a step forward. The cart rolled forward, its wheels rumbling.

Father Tadeus took a small and careful step forward, using his right foot. He followed with his left. All the mourners fell into step with him.

The cortège moved up the little square, wheeled slowly round the corner and began to advance up the street that ran beside the church. On the other side of the street stood the Five-Sided palace. Hearing the church bell tolling gloomily, hundreds of beggars streamed out of the palace. They always came out when a funeral passed. They crossed themselves now and prayed. As the cortège moved on, thousands more strangers came out of their houses, in accordance with custom, to pay their last respects.

The procession passed through a gate in the walls and out into the country to the north of the city. A peasant in a field was fixing a fence. He looked up, saw the coffin and took off his hat. Then he crossed himself and prayed.

The funeral procession reached the gates of the graveyard, which sloped up a small hill. There was a stone perimeter wall, gravel paths and graves with headstones arranged in rows.

A boy stood waiting beside a brown hole, holding his spade. He was a big boned fourteen year old. His cheeks were red. His hair was red and curly. His eyes were grey and his hands were vast. His name was Jan. He was innocent, nervous in disposition, unintelligent and fundamentally decent.

Johan slid his son's coffin from the cart. He carried it through the gateway and up the gravel path to the waiting grave. Father Tadeus and the other mourners followed in silence.

The coffin was laid on the ground by the hole. The mourners gathered round in a circle. Father Tadeus began the order for the burial of the dead. When he finished the coffin was then dropped into the hole. Johan and his wife each took a handful of earth and showered it down on the box.

Father Tadeus signalled to Jan.

Jan dug his spade into the mound, got a heap on the end and threw this into the hole. The sound was so frightful Vera let out a cry. Jan threw down a second and then a third shovel's worth of earth.

"I think we'll stop now," said Father Tadeus, addressing Jan.

Jan usually filled the hole, or a good part of it, before anyone left.

"Certainly, Father," he said. He had only started work here the day after Rahel was buried, but he had already acquired the gravitas that he felt the post required.

"Haven't you got anything else to do?" continued Father Tadeus, addressing Jan. His tone was unexpectedly sharp.

Jan wondered what was wrong? He was waiting for everyone to go. Then he would finish off the job.

"I asked you a question," said Father Tadeus, even more sharply. "Didn't you hear?" the priest continued.

Jan's wide face went red. Earlier he had just thought the priest was bad mannered and churlish.

Now he realised he must have done something to offend Father Tadeus. He didn't know what it was. But priests were like that, weren't they? One moment they were your best friend, the next they were your worst enemy.

Jan opened his mouth. He closed it again. His hands felt hot. His thighs trembled. His throat hurt. He wanted to shout back. At the same time a voice at the back of his thoughts counselled calm. The priest had all the power. He had none.

"I've a grave over there," he said. He was aware his voice cracked as he spoke. He could feel tears welling up. He must not cry, he thought.

"I've to have it dug by this afternoon," Jan continued, pointing to a place below an oak tree where the turf had been cut away to leave a brown earth-coloured oblong.

"Why don't you go and do that then?" said Father Tadeus sharply.

There were quiet gasps from the mourners. They had never heard anything like this at a funeral. The young grave-digger had obviously done something terrible. Among his parishioners Father Tadeus had a reputation for softness and kindness and several of the mourners present were delighted to discover their priest had mettle.

The young grave-digger took his spade and walked away quickly.

A sigh of relief passed around the crowd of mourners. Johan with his wife and children formed a line. The mourners began to file past. They shook hands and expressed their regrets. Then they headed back along the road towards Prague.

When the last mourner left, Father Tadeus sidled over.

"I think the best thing now is that we all go home," he said. "If you want to make your way down, I'll go and have a word with Jan and settle up with him."

"Oh no," said Johan, his hand reaching into his pocket, "I've the money."

"No," said Father Tadeus firmly. He turned to Johan's wife. "Vera, have I ever ordered you to do anything?"

Vera, drunk with grief, could not understand why her priest would ask such a question but she was able to answer it.

"Of course not," she said.

"Well, there's a first time for everything. I am ordering you to go down to the gate, to the funeral cart and to wait for me there. I will pay Jan. I will then join you. Do you understand?"

Vera wiped her eyes. She trembled. At certain

times in life, the wisest course was to let others take care of things, and this was just such an occasion.

"Come on," she muttered to her husband. She took his arm and wheeled him round. Her feelings were numbed. But in the months to come, she would often remember this moment and when she did she would be filled with feelings of love for her priest. He was a real friend when he insisted on looking after Jan.

"Come on you children," she called, "follow us."

Vera led her husband and children along the gravel path towards the gate.

Father Tadeus stood watching their receding backs. He walked up to Jan.

"Hey, you," said Father Tadeus.

Jan was still both angry and terrified. He decided not to show his feelings but to ignore Father Tadeus.

"Do you want your money or not?"

Jan levered out a clod and threw it on the heap he had already made.

"You really are quite something aren't you?"

Father Tadeus threw a large heavy coin at Jan's head. It hit the youth on the side of his skull, just above the ear, then bounced away. Jan cried out and dropped his spade. His hand went involuntarily to where he had been hit.

"What was that for?" said Jan angrily, turning to face the priest.

"What was that for?" said Father Tadeus. "That's the money you're owed for your labours."

"No, what did you throw it for?" said Jan. Tears welled up in his eyes.

The crows in the oak trees above cawed brightly.

"Oh dear," said Father Tadeus in a childish voice, "we appear to have a cry-baby."

Jan's anger turned to fearfulness.

"What else could I do?" said Father Tadeus in his normal voice. "You wouldn't take it, so I had to throw it. Did I hurt you? I am sorry." His tone was insincere.

He made as if to turn away but then continued speaking: "Mind you, I'm surprised it hurt. Like all stupid people you've a thick skull. Anyway, your money's there. It's on the ground at your feet."

Jan bent down and picked the coin up.

"Where's the rest?" he asked. "This is just half what I'm owed."

"What do you expect? You've only done half the work, haven't you?"

"But I've got to fill it in still," said Jan.

Father Tadeus shrugged his shoulders.

"You do the job, I might consider paying. It'll have to be done properly, mind you. When you're done come and find me at the parochial house. I'll decide then. I've got to go now. Goodbye."

Well, Jan thought, he'd show him. He wasn't filling in the grave unless he was paid first. And when the parents returned on Sunday to their son's unfinished grave, he'd tell them the whole story. It was their priest's fault. Not his.

He levered a shovel full of earth away from the ground and tossed it onto the small mound at the side.

Down at the gate Father Tadeus joined Johan and his family.

"Let us go," he said quietly.

Father Tadeus was pleased. He was certain Jan would not fill in Andres's grave. His plan was going along very nicely.

32

The secret passage

Father Tadeus dressed and went out into the courtyard. The night was mild and dark. There was no moon. He had no lantern so he had to move with care. He found the handcart where he had left it earlier, standing close to the wall. He groped inside the well of the cart to check the tools he had put there earlier were still in place, on a layer of felt. They were.

He pushed the cart over the cobblestones, out of the door in the wall and into the street. It made almost no noise as he had tied strips of felt around the wheels.

Father Tadeus reached the gate and gave the nightguard a large coin. He took care to keep his face turned away.

The Judas door was opened for him. He rushed through and hurried past the gibbets with their dangling corpses and walked on through the silent empty countryside to Andres's grave.

It was, as he had expected, unfilled. He lifted the coffin with the help of a fork and laid it on the grass, still flat from the feet of the mourners. With a hammer and chisel he levered the lid off. A smell of old meat and wet dog hit him in the face.

Father Tadeus stood up and breathed deeply. This was not work he enjoyed. However, if he didn't do it, who would? For with this body and the help of God, he was going to destroy Rabbi Loew and his giant helper forever.

He wrapped the body in a sack and put it in the handcart. He piled a couple of large felt-wrapped stones into the coffin to give an illusion of weight. He nailed the lid back on. Then he dropped the coffin back into the hole taking care that it was upside down when it landed at the bottom.

Father Tadeus retraced his steps back through the dark countryside. No one saw him except a brown owl that he passed sitting hooting in a tree.

He re-entered the city by the Judas door. He crept along the Old Town streets, taking care to stay in the shadows.

When he was almost home he became aware of a watchman. Father Tadeus stepped into an alley. He waited until he could no longer hear the watchman's footfalls. He met no one else. He entered the courtyard of the Green Church. He left the handcart where he found it. He picked up Andres's body and carried it inside to his kitchen and put it on the table.

He paused. He listened. He could hear all sorts of noises of course but they were those that his house always made at night. A ceiling creaked. A doorframe sighed. The coals in the grate in the kitchen settled with a sigh. But there were no human noises. Gerda was fast asleep upstairs. There was nobody in all of Prague who knew what he had done, or who would know what he was about to do.

He put a candle in the fire and lit the wick. He put the candle in a glass-fronted lantern and closed the door. He picked up Andres's body, and holding out the lantern he went down to his wine cellar.

There was a table in the middle of the room with a sharp butcher's knife and a basket of phials. Each had a label tied to the neck with string that read "Rabbi Judah Loew".

He laid the body on the table with the head hanging over the edge. He peeled back the sacking. Christian teaching was quite explicit. It was wrong to interfere with the remains of the dead. But this case was different. Andres was taken not only to punish Johan. He was also taken to provide Father Tadeus with a corpse he could use to attack his enemy. Johan had helped Rahel to escape and now God had given his reply. It was as clear as the hand in front of his face.

He cut the jugular vein in the dead child's neck. Blood slowly leaked out. He caught it in a phial. When he had filled the phial, he filled two more. He put these in a basket. Then he tied a rag around the throat to stop the wound leaking. He re-wrapped the body in the sacking.

He moved to the farthest and darkest end of the cellar where no one ever ventured, and where a small filthy door was inset into the wall. He turned the old handle and began to pull. The door bottom grated on the flagstone floor.

Many years before, his predecessor, now dead, had shown him this. It was the door once used by the royal family. Father Tadeus had never shown it to anyone. He had always had a feeling that he would have to use it himself one day.

Father Tadeus sniffed. Cold, old air that had barely been disturbed for half a century wafted out.

What a stroke of genius, he thought, on the part of the builders to have brought the passage into the parochial house rather than the crypt. The crypt was below the church and in the church there were always people, whereas in his cellar there was never anyone except Gerda and Johan, and they never stayed long anyhow. They didn't like it.

He put the body over his shoulder and picked up

the basket with the phials. He took the lantern in the other hand. He walked through the passage. The previous afternoon, when he had checked it, he had heard carts in the street overhead. Tonight he heard nothing. Prague was still asleep.

He reached the end and another low door. He pushed and it juddered back. He stepped forward into the basement of the Five-Sided palace. He lifted his lantern and looked around. The room was filled with half a century's worth of junk and rubbish.

He dumped Andres's corpse behind some debris. He put the phials on the floor nearby. Above, he could hear a guitar playing . . .

Back in the parochial house, he took the knife from the table, carried it upstairs, washed it and put it away. Then he climbed up to his bedroom, undressed quietly and got into bed.

Father Tadeus felt quietly satisfied. His next task was to get the police to find the body and the phials. That would be Jan's task, though the idiot didn't know that yet.

In a few hours, Rabbi Loew would be finished.

33

The dream fire

It was still dark when Rabbi Loew found himself standing outside the Green Church again. He tried the door, found it locked, turned and walked round the corner to the Five-Sided palace.

From inside the building came snatches of song – though he couldn't make out the words – mingled with the beat of a drum, and the trill of a flute.

Rabbi Loew was drawn to a window on the first storey. Judging by the shadows he guessed the people inside were dancing.

There was a cry. It was as surprising as it was terrifying. The stretched sheet grew suddenly white and bright. Then it was wrenched away violently. In the room behind there was a terrifying smear of red. In the foreground there was a dark silhouette.

"Fire," shouted the silhouette desperately, "fire."

Rabbi Loew raised his eyes. Along the entire length of the roof there were tongues of flame jumping into the night. There were beggars shouting at every window and running from every door.

Rabbi Loew sat up in bed so violently Pearl woke up too.

"What is it? What are you dreaming now?"

"It's nothing," said Rabbi Loew. He lay back down on his bolster but he did not go back to sleep.

34

Father Tadeus returns to the graveyard

Father Tadeus combed his hair and washed his face. He put on a clean cassock. He walked out to the graveyard. As he approached the gate he could see Jan at work.

"Greetings," Father Tadeus called.

The young grave-digger started when he saw it was the priest. He turned back to the hole he was digging.

"Suit yourself," said Father Tadeus under his breath, "but I'm about to wipe the smile off your face, young man, just you watch."

Father Tadeus walked over to Andres's grave and shouted at Jan, "Come, quickly, hurry up now."

Jan turned. He saw Father Tadeus gesticulating madly. He heard the priest shouting, "Come on, come on."

The grave-digger buried the end of his spade in the ground and reluctantly walked across to Father Tadeus.

"You won't believe what's happened," said Father Tadeus, "it's terrible."

"What's happened?" said Jan coolly. He didn't trust this priest.

"Someone's interfered with the grave. The coffin's upside down. I hope no one's taken the remains."

Jan felt his knees sagging. He could lose his job for this.

"You can't be right," said Jan. Then he added, pathetically, "If I was paid properly I'd have filled the grave in."

"Oh come on," said Father Tadeus gently, "what's done is done. There's no point in us arguing. Now help me get the coffin out."

Jan lay on the ground and got his fingers under the end of the coffin. As he lifted it out, there was a hollow booming noise as the boulders rolled about inside.

They set the coffin down on the path. Jan prised the lid off. Inside, he saw the two stones, wrapped in felt and tied with string.

"Oh no," exclaimed the grave-digger, "I'm done for."

"Don't be ridiculous," said Father Tadeus nicely. "It's not your fault. I should have paid you properly. And I'm sorry I didn't now. Look, you're a good boy, you're a hard-working fellow . . ."

"And I've my mother and father to support," Jan interrupted.

"Of course you do. Look, there's an explanation for this, you know. All we have to do is go to the authorities. I know they'll believe us."

"What is it you're to tell them?"

"I'm not – you are," said Father Tadeus quickly.

"I'm not going to tell anyone I left the grave open all night." He struck himself on the head. "Oh, I'm a fool, I'm an idiot."

"The grave would have been robbed you know, whatever you'd done."

"Would it?" said Jan.

"It's Passover," explained Father Tadeus, wearily, as if it was tedious to tell what was surely so obvious. "If they don't kill a child they do the next best thing which is take one that's freshly dead."

"Who?"

"The Jews. Passover is coming. They often make the unleavened bread with blood from a Christian child."

"The Jews were here?" asked Jan on whom the truth was beginning to dawn.

"Well, one was," said Father Tadeus. "Several peasants told me on the walk out here. They saw him walking along the road, back towards the Old Town. He was a huge man in a big hat and he was carrying a sack with something inside, something heavy and about the size of a dead child."

"Oh," he said.

"Now I'm going to tell you what to do next. You do what I say, nothing will happen to you. No one need ever know the grave was open all night."

Jan nodded slowly.

"You will go straight to the Cardinal's palace now. On arrival, you will ask for the Cardinal's secretary. He's called Karel – he's a friend of mine. Do not mention me."

"I won't."

"You will say a grave was robbed last night. Don't say whose grave it was. Tell Karel that a huge Jew was seen in the area carrying a sack with something very heavy in it. You will remind him Passover's coming and you will ask him if that was why the grave was robbed. Say nothing else. Karel will tell the police. They will search the ghetto. They will find the body."

"And I don't say the grave wasn't filled in, do I?"

"I thought we'd been over that," said Father Tadeus. "Of course you don't. That's our little secret. You say you filled it in and this morning it was emptied out again. And just to prove how sorry I am about yesterday, let me make amends."

Father Tadeus took two gold coins from his pocket and handed them to Jan.

"Oh thank you, Father, thank you very much."

"All you have to do now is go to the palace and tell the story as we agreed."

"Corpse stolen by Jew and Passover coming," said Jan quickly.

"That's it," said Father Tadeus. "Go on, go as quickly as you can. There's not a second to lose."

"Yes," said Jan and he hurried away down the path towards the gate.

Alone, Father Tadeus thought his scheme was progressing well. He went home and got on with his morning. In the early afternoon he stopped to eat. He always ate in the dining room at the oak table that always smelt nicely of wax. There was a hyacinth in a pot on the sideboard behind. Its thick, lush smell filled the room.

The window was open and a warm breeze blew in. In the distance he heard cart wheels turning, the clip-clop of horses' hooves, the cries of children as they played.

There was a gherkin on his plate. He pushed a knife down through the tough rubbery skin and then the softer fruit inside. As the blade separated the round from the whole, watery vinegar leaked out and spread across his plate.

He cut a piece of dry white cheese and put this into his mouth with the gherkin. He enjoyed the combination of the sharp cold gherkin and the slightly musty crumbling cheese.

His visitor, he thought, should appear any moment now. The very next moment he heard a noise. Surely here was a sign, if he needed one, that his was a just enterprise and it was moving smoothly towards a just conclusion.

Gerda appeared. There were spots of gravy on the front of her apron. She was making venison pie, one of Father Tadeus's favourite dishes, for supper. The meat came from a grateful parishioner.

"Karel, the Cardinal's secretary," said Gerda. "I said you were eating but he says he still must see you."

"Oh show him in," said Father Tadeus. "And ask him if he'd like something to eat. He may be hungry."

Gerda disappeared.

"Come in, Karel," exclaimed Father Tadeus, a moment later. He waved his white flat hand. Karel stepped forward.

"I'm sorry," said Karel. "You are eating. I shouldn't have come but I had to."

Gerda came into the room behind Karel and he immediately stopped talking.

"Has Gerda asked you if you would like to join me?"

"She has and no I won't, thank you."

Gerda nodded and slid back, closing the door behind.

"You look like a man who wants to tell me something. Let me see if I can guess. Oh and by the way, sit down."

"You won't be able to guess."

"Let's play a game," said the priest. "You've come to tell me – unofficially of course – I'm about to be elevated. It has been decided to move me to the cathedral. I am to be made the Dean. No, I'm to go higher still. I am to be made bishop."

"Don't be ridiculous, of course you're not."

"Is it higher still I am to go? What . . . I hardly dare utter the words . . . am I to be made . . . a cardinal?"

"No," said Karel. "If it was anything like that you wouldn't be hearing it from me."

"Then why the smile, and the urgency. How could you, Karel," Father Tadeus continued, mock-solemnly, "build up my hopes only to cast me down?"

"The Jews are at it again," said Karel quietly.

"Oh no, it's about them you've come to see me."

"We had a visitor, only hours ago – a grave-digger – not very intelligent, but very agitated. A big peasant boy – name of Jan."

"Jan," said Father Tadeus, rolling the word around his mouth, "Jan, Jan . . ."

"You probably don't know him. He's in the graveyard, to the north of Prague."

"I know the place you mean," said Father Tadeus quickly. "I probably even know the grave-digger. Well, I'd know him by sight. I'm sure I do. Yes, so he came to see you. Go on, what did he tell you?"

"A grave was robbed last night – Jan only discovered it this morning. A child's corpse was taken, and a Jew was spotted with a large sack containing something about the size of a child."

Father Tadeus shrugged. "Yes, I see, terrible, but why are you telling me?"

"Do you know what time of the year it is?"

"Lent."

"And what else?"

Father Tadeus scratched his chin. "Lent then . . . Easter."

"This year, Passover is tomorrow."

"Oh, I understand you now," said Father Tadeus solemnly. Karel would never have guessed the relief Tadeus was feeling. Jan had actually delivered his story without fluffing his lines.

"When I leave here, I'm going to the police," said Karel.

"Oh good," said Father Tadeus. "You're going to get a search under way immediately."

"No, not immediately. I'm going to suggest the search takes place tomorrow. That way there's a really good chance of finding unleavened bread made of blood."

Father Tadeus wrinkled his forehead. He had been hoping for an instant search. However, he could hardly urge Karel to change his plan. He must appear absolutely ignorant.

"Oh tomorrow, right," said Father Tadeus.

"And not a word about this to anyone," said Karel.

"Of course not," said Father Tadeus. "I'll make it my business, though, to be out and about tomorrow. Obviously, if Christian remains are recovered, a priest may be required."

"I'll instruct the police to call here for you on the way to the ghetto. Ten o'clock, say?"

Alone again, after his visitor left, Father Tadeus picked up his knife. He cut off a large piece of gherkin, popped it in his mouth, and enjoyed its vinegary taste. The Jews were doomed now.

35

Danger warning

Later that day, Rabbi Loew stood with his feet apart. He distinctly felt the cold passing through his felt slippers and into the soles of his feet. He didn't normally notice such things. Perhaps, he thought, in a faraway sort of way, this was a premonition. This cold was how he would feel when he died.

Why was he thinking about his own death at this time and in this place? He was in his synagogue. He wasn't supposed to think about himself at Passover. He was here to serve his community. He was here to pray. To die now would be unthinkable.

Rabbi Loew peered ahead. He was aware of hundreds of pale faces turned towards him. The men were in front of him on the ground floor. The women were on the balcony upstairs. He was aware they were all breathing quietly, in and out, in and out. They were all breathing in unison, too. When people gathered that happened, he had noticed.

No one stirred. There was no fidgeting. Yet he was

aware of intense expectation. They were all waiting. They were waiting for him.

Earlier in the day, in homes around the ghetto, there had been the ceremonial search for unleavened dough. That was done. Now, with everyone gathered in the synagogue, it was for him to pronounce the Annulment of Leaven. This must be done before proceeding to the Feast of Deliverance. He must read the prayer in the book on the lectern in front of him.

He looked out again. His feet were still cold. Perhaps there was another meaning to this nagging cold, that had nothing to do with his mortality. His death was hardly something of which he had only recently become aware. No, this was a warning, surely. There was something malign in his world. There was some danger looming. He must be aware.

The eyes of everyone were still on him. No more thinking. He must pronounce the Annulment of Leaven.

He looked down at the book. A candle burnt on the lectern. By its yellow, faintly flickering light, he saw the thick Hebrew letters of the prayer sloping across the creamy page from right to left. He opened his mouth and breathed in. His vocal chords trembled and shivered, preparatory to saying the first syllable of the first word, the "A" of All. But, as the "A" was being born in his throat, the wick of the candle attached to the lectern trembled and went out. The creamy page darkened. He was unable to see the words clearly. The distinct smell of an extinguished wick hovered in the air. The congregation shifted in their seats.

"Chaim," Rabbi Loew called. His beadle was standing at the side, immediately behind. "Take the prayer book over to the sconce." He pointed at the bracket candlestick attached to the wall at the side. A long white candle burnt here. It lit up the wall immediately around with its lovely yellow light which made a shape in the air like an egg.

"You read the words of the prayer," said Rabbi Loew, "a sentence at a time, and I'll say them after you."

Chaim stepped up to the lectern. His legs were short but he moved quickly. He took the book. He put one hand on the spine below to support it. He put the other on top to stop the pages moving.

He walked slowly over to the sconce. He lifted the book into the penumbra of light cast by the wick. He saw the square Hebrew letters. He opened his mouth. The people were waiting.

"All the leaven that I five –" he said and stopped.

A deep red flush ran across his face. That was not what was written. Why had he said five? He could hear people sliding on their seats. He could hear their feet shuffling on the floor. He could guess their thoughts. What is the idiot doing? Why didn't he say the words of the prayer as they are written?

Chaim swallowed. A little bead of perspiration trickled out from under his left armpit and bumped down over his ribs, cooling as it went. His upper lip was suddenly and miraculously spotted with little spots of his sweat. He was wearing a fustian jacket over a linen shirt. He could feel the heat rising under his shirt, trapped by the jacket. He couldn't stop and put the book down and take his jacket off. He swallowed and glanced sideways. Rabbi Loew was looking across at him with a mixture of curiosity and surprise, shot through with a thread of anxiety.

The rabbi nodded at him. "Go on, say the prayer."

The sweat from the hand resting heavily on the book had seeped into the paper. Chaim took his hand away. He swallowed again.

"All the leaven that I five –"

He stopped. Well, next time, this third time, he was saying it right and nothing would stop him.

"All the leaven that I five –" he shouted.

There were little cries from the congregation.

Chaim's hair was suddenly wet right through, as surely as if it had been under water. At the same time his mouth was parched. Was this, he wondered, the first sign of madness? And would this end with him becoming one of those poor creatures who wandered round the ghetto, shouting incoherently, holding imaginary conversations and waving their arms?

"Ah," he heard Rabbi Loew saying. Chaim turned.

He saw that Rabbi Loew was still standing at his lectern, with one hand holding the edge. But the rabbi's face was turned towards the ceiling.

"Now I understand," said the rabbi. "I understand exactly."

The congregation was utterly silent.

"Where are we?" he asked. "Oh yes. There are people who want to hurt us. But I know what to do now."

Rabbi Loew shook his head again and looked directly at the people. They stared back with open mouths and troubled faces.

"Oh, you needn't worry, it's nothing that need concern you."

He slipped across to Chaim.

"Give me the book," he said.

Chaim handed it to him.

"Bring me a chair, can you?" he said gently. "I'm not as young as you, I need to get closer to the sconce light . . ."

He climbed up.

"All the leaven that I have . . ." he began. He went

slowly on, right through the prayer without stopping. At the finish he handed the open book to Chaim. Then his beadle helped him climb down from the chair. He walked forward, right up to the first row of watching men.

"You will all go straight home now," he said quietly. "Do not worry about what you have seen or heard here. Do not ask questions about it. Trust me. Just do as I say. Go home. Lock your doors. Stay there."

The worshippers stood, turned and began to file out. Nobody spoke other than some children who asked childish questions of their parents. Many of the adults, however, as they moved, kept throwing inquiring looks back in the rabbi's direction.

Rabbi Loew had decided not to tell them what he had just understood, that the imminent danger to his community lay in the Five-Sided palace. The truth now would create panic. Only when the danger had passed could the truth be told.

The last of the congregation left.

"Chaim," said Rabbi Loew, "we've urgent work to do."

He ordered three of the twisted candles to be put in glass lanterns. When this was done he said to Chaim, "You lead, we're going to the courtroom."

They left the temple and entered the courtroom.

"Joseph," Rabbi Loew shouted into the darkness.

The golem sprang to his feet and ran heavily across the room in his clogs to his master.

"Give him a lantern," Rabbi Loew said. "Now follow me. We're going to the Green Church."

They stepped into the street outside, and moved silently through the ghetto. When they came to the booth on the edge of the ghetto, the rabbi gave the night watchman a gleaming gold coin.

"You never saw us," he said.

The watchman nodded. The three men flitted through the gateway and went on through the Old Town. They reached the steps in front of the Green Church. The doors at the top were closed. The brass handles glimmered palely in the candlelight. In his dream, as Rabbi Loew remembered it, this place had a more real and powerful presence than it had now, but then that was often the way.

"We're going to the next street," said Rabbi Loew.

They moved to the end and turned. On the right was the church. On the left was the Five-Sided palace. There were lights shining in some of the windows. Laughter and singing came from within. Seeing the two buildings like this, separated by the road, Rabbi Loew remembered the rumour about the tunnel. If it existed, then that was where he had to go.

They crossed the road to the first door in the first archway. Rabbi Loew tried the door. It was locked.

"Open it, Joseph," Rabbi Loew whispered.

Joseph ripped the lock out and swung the door back.

They all stepped forward into the hall. Without warning a wind began to hiss around them. There was a smell of rotting fruit. A bat flew past, squeaking, and flitted out the door. In a room a fire burned and a figure moaned as he slept. From the floor above came a peal of laughter and a run of notes played lightly on a violin.

They moved to stairs at the back. The stairs that went up were filthy and broken but passable. The stairs leading down to the cellar, on the other hand, were completely choked with rubbish.

"Joseph, clear us a path down to the cellar but don't make any noise," said Rabbi Loew. "I don't want anyone to know we're here."

Joseph left his lantern and disappeared. The rabbi and Chaim heard strange furtive noises coming from the darkness. The sound of the wind changed from a hiss to a sigh. Joseph returned.

"Is it clear?" Rabbi Loew asked.

Joseph nodded.

"Lead me down."

Joseph took Rabbi Loew's hand. Chaim followed behind.

The trio reached the bottom. They were now in the cellar that extended the length and breadth of the Five-Sided palace. The wind was blowing harder now, howling rather than sighing. The candles in the lanterns wavered but did not go out. From the darkness, where the candlelight did not penetrate, came the sound of falling masonry. Dust swirled in the air and stung their faces. All three narrowed their eyes to stop the grit getting in.

"Joseph," said Rabbi Loew. "There is something here that should not be here. Go, search the entire cellar and bring it back to me."

Joseph disappeared into the darkness with his lantern. Rabbi Loew watched the little trembling flame of the candle as he went. Joseph moved further and further away. The light got smaller and smaller, but it never disappeared altogether.

After a while light from Joseph's candle began to swell. Joseph was returning. Rabbi Loew stared at the moving flame and held his head sideways. He was hoping to hear the golem's footsteps but the wind drowned them out. Instead, without warning, Joseph just burst out of the darkness. He had a bundle wrapped in sacking in one arm, and a basket in the other.

Rabbi Loew held his lantern over the basket. There

were three phials filled with a dark liquid. He presumed this was blood. Each phial had a label tied to the neck. The same name was written on each label: Rabbi Judah Loew.

"Open the bundle," said Rabbi Loew, although he already had a good idea what he would find inside.

Joseph parted the sacking and Rabbi Loew found himself looking at the pale dead face of an unknown child.

"Joseph," he said. "Make hole, here, now."

Joseph put the corpse down. He lifted a flagstone off the floor. He quickly made a hole in the damp earth. Rabbi Loew threw in the first phial, heard the glass break, and then threw the other two on top of it. He threw the basket in after.

"Fill hole, Joseph, and replace flagstone. Do it so no one could guess there's a hole here."

Joseph left it so no one would ever know what was underneath.

"Pick the body up, Joseph," said Rabbi Loew. "Lead us to where you found it."

Joseph picked the body up. The trio threaded through the darkness to the place.

"Somewhere round here is a secret door. Find it," ordered Rabbi Loew.

Joseph located the door.

"Open it," said Rabbi Loew.

Joseph opened the door revealing the passageway to the Green Church.

"Go down the passage," said Rabbi Loew, "taking the corpse with you. At the end you will find another door. Open it. Go through. You will find yourself in another room. Hide the body there. Then come back making certain you close all doors behind."

Joseph lifted the corpse on to his shoulder and, taking the lantern in his other hand, he entered the passage and walked away from Rabbi Loew and Chaim. Once again, Rabbi Loew watched the light getting smaller. There were a few muted and mysterious noises from the other end.

Then the light reappeared. Rabbi Loew heard the distinct sound of the door at the other end scraping as it was closed. The lantern swung in the darkness. There were footsteps. Joseph appeared in front of him. He nodded his head to show he had accomplished his task.

The two men and the golem closed the door between the passage and the cellar. They left by the way they had come in, and slipped back through the empty streets of the Old Town to the ghetto. No one saw them.

36

Father Tadeus's surprise

Gerda opened the door to a policeman. He held his wide brimmed hat in his hand.

"Father Tadeus?" asked the policeman.

"He's coming," said Gerda.

Father Tadeus appeared in the hallway a few moments later.

"We're about to start the search of the ghetto, Father," the policeman said.

"Oh yes, of course," said Father Tadeus, as if he had only just remembered. "I think I've got something very interesting to tell you," he added.

He stepped out into the street and pointed across at the Five-Sided palace.

"A little bird told me that what we're looking for is somewhere in there."

"Really," said the policeman, "my orders are to search the ghetto."

"If you were a Jew, wouldn't you want to put it somewhere no one was likely to look?"

"You might be right. Did your little bird give any information as to exactly where we should look? I know I've got plenty of men from the army," he continued, pointing at the soldiers in the street with pikes on their shoulders, "but the Five-Sided palace is not exactly small."

"I was told the cellar," said Father Tadeus. "But I warn you it won't be easy getting down. There's a lot of rubbish in the stairwells."

"Don't worry, we'll get down. We'll search the palace straightaway."

"Good," said Father Tadeus mildly. "And do come back and let me know it you find anything. And let's hope you do, then you won't have to bother with the ghetto."

The policeman walked towards the soldiers. Orders were shouted. The soldiers wheeled about. Father Tadeus went back into his house.

An hour later the policeman returned. Father Tadeus answered the door himself.

"Hello, again." His tone was muted, hiding his excitement. "How was it? Any luck?"

"No," said the policeman irritably, "nothing. We got down there. The place was a terrible mess, like you said. We formed a line and swept across, prodding the rubbish with our pikes. We found absolutely nothing."

"Nothing?" said Father Tadeus incredulously.

"Nothing."

"But I was told the body was in there."

"There's nothing there now."

"Are you sure?"

"I have two hundred soldiers," said the policeman. "Believe you me, if it was down there, we'd have found it."

Father Tadeus didn't understand.

"We'll now proceed to the ghetto as per our orders," said the policeman. "Maybe we'll have better luck there. Would you care to accompany us?"

"Oh goodness no," said Father Tadeus. He bowed his shoulders humbly and wrung his hands. "I think you can do without me. I think I've caused you quite enough trouble for one day."

"As you wish. Good morning," said the policeman.

Hand on sword handle, he walked towards the detachment and shouted, "Forward, march."

Father Tadeus retreated into his hall and, exercising great control, closed the door carefully behind him. What he really wanted was to slam it with all his might.

When the detachment of soldiers appeared on the edge of the ghetto, a terrified merchant sent a boy to Rabbi Loew with the news. Loew sent the boy back with the message, "Do not worry. They will find nothing." Loew's words were repeated round the ghetto.

The soldiers set to work. They searched every house with extreme violence. They smashed furniture, wrecked rooms, and ripped up floorboards. Householders who protested, they beat with the staves of their spears. Several Jews had their teeth knocked out or their arms and legs broken. No one died. The soldiers found nothing. As darkness fell, the policeman ordered the soldiers to march back to their barracks.

Passover came and went. Easter followed. The days were dry. On Easter Sunday afternoon Father Tadeus went to the kitchen. He found Gerda and Johan standing by the open kitchen door. Peter, Johan's mongrel dog, was lying stretched out on the ground with his red tongue hanging.

"Gerda," Father Tadeus asked, "go down to the cellar and get me a bottle of hock."

"Certainly," Gerda said.

"Put it in a bucket of cold water and bring it to me in my study," continued Father Tadeus.

Gerda lit a lantern and went away to the cellar, leaving Johan and his dog in the kitchen. A few minutes later Gerda rushed back.

"There's something down there," said Gerda

anxiously. "I don't know what it is but it's stinking the place out."

"Maybe it's a dead rat?" said Johan, grimly.

"Oh no, don't say that. I have to go back down there. I still haven't got him his hock yet."

"I'll come with you," Johan said. "Come on Peter," he continued, "there's a good boy."

The dog jumped to his feet. He followed Johan and Gerda into the cellar.

"Oh dear," said Johan. "There really is something smelling. Go on, Peter, see what you can find."

The dog disappeared. "I hate this place," Gerda said. The dog barked. Peter was in the farthest, darkest part of the cellar. When they got down to him they saw the dog was barking at a bundle on the ground.

"Oh no," said Gerda, and she blessed herself.

She held the lantern over the bundle. Johan crouched down and began to pull at the sacking. A face came into view.

Gerda let out a cry. "It's your Andres."

Johan fetched the police. Father Tadeus was interviewed. He claimed he was as mystified as everyone else was.

And there the matter might have ended except that a policeman was sent to talk to Jan. In no time at all the grave-digger told the truth about what had happened after Andres's funeral. The policeman called to see Cardinal Sylvester. The Cardinal was appalled. If those annoying Protestants, with whom he feuded continuously, ever discovered what his priest had got up to, his church would suffer. Something would have to be done about Father Tadeus.

Two weeks later, on a wet spring afternoon, Cardinal Sylvester summoned Father Tadeus to his palace.

"You are not allowed to speak," said Cardinal Sylvester. "You are just here to listen. Do you understand? Nod to show you do."

Father Tadeus, who had a good idea something awful was coming, did as he was told.

"I have decided, Father Tadeus," began Cardinal Sylvester, "that a priest with talents such as yours, should not be wasted here in Prague. There is a village in Silesia called Brieg. Charcoal-burners and miners inhabit it. The priest recently died, since when the congregation, I am reliably informed, has gone bad. The population is seemingly drunk every day and every night of every week. They need a strong shepherd to lead them out of darkness and back into the light. I have decided you are the one. Go home now, pack, say goodbye to your city congregation and go."

Father Tadeus could not decline. He went to Brieg.

It was a large ugly sprawling village of muddy paths, smoky taverns and vile people. At the start he was hated. He had to employ two burly gypsies as bodyguards. They were involved in several violent fights with the locals and on one memorable occasion, Father Tadeus had to fight off two footpads himself when they attempted to rob him.

Later, relations improved. Tadeus was able to turn his thoughts to other matters. He needed a housekeeper. He was repelled, however, by the thought of one of the village women living in his house. So he wrote to Mathilde's Mother Superior. He begged permission for Mathilde to be allowed to join him. The Mother Superior sent her. After a year in Brieg, Mathilde threw herself into a well and drowned. Tadeus had a large tomb built to house her remains in the bleak graveyard on the edge of town, and every day, for the rest of his life, he went there and said a prayer for Mathilde.

37

Lev and Rahel

One cold day, late in spring, Abraham, who used to be Kaja, sat at the desk in the house where he lived in a village outside Amsterdam.

On the other side of the window, a line of black and white cows lumbered along the road. Abraham was listening to the plaintive clang of their cowbells and watching the see-sawing of the beasts as they trod unsteadily along, when he heard a knock at his door.

"Yes," Abraham called.

The door swung open and Abraham recognised Lev, a marriage broker. Lev carried a flat package under his arm wrapped in black cloth. It was a girl's portrait. The girl was looking for a husband and Lev was acting on her behalf.

Lev had tried to interest him in girls many times before but Abraham had always declined his offers. Rahel, he believed, was the only woman who could have made him happy. But she was gone. What was the point of marrying someone else? He would be unhappy. So would his bride. Naturally, Abraham had never told any of this to Lev. He didn't trust him.

"Lev," said Abraham quickly, "before you say anything, the answer is no. As I tell you every time you come, I do not want a wife. I am a student of the Talmud. All I do, and wish to do is read, write and think. You will spare yourself a good deal of time and trouble if you just turn round and go."

Lev shook his head and smiled. He had not walked all the way from Amsterdam to Abraham's room to be rebuffed so easily. Besides, it was Lev's judgement – and he was an astute judge of character – that he really had, at long last, acquired a client who would interest Abraham. But Lev knew his approach would have to be subtle.

"I think you should look at this portrait," he said. He waved his package.

"I have seen portraits of your clients before," said Abraham. "I would not say they were bad. They were just not accurate. Their purpose was to find a husband, not to tell the truth about a face."

"That might be true but this," said Lev quietly, "is a portrait the like of which you have never seen before."

Abraham shook his head. "Every time a matchmaker opens his mouth, he always says the same thing: 'My client is the most beautiful girl in the world – look at her portrait and see for yourself.' Lev, if you want to persuade people to look, you've got to be more persuasive than that."

"And if you want to be a great scholar," said Lev, cheekily, "you're going to have to learn how to listen. If you'd paid attention you'd have heard me properly. I said I had a portrait the like of which you've never seen. It's the painting I'm talking about, not the subject."

It took Abraham a moment to recover from this sharp reply. "All right," he said, finally, "you can show me this famous portrait, and then you can go."

Lev marched in and closed the door behind him.

"With most portraits," said Lev, "it's the head and shoulders, taken from the front or the side. Am I right?"

Abraham nodded. Where, he wondered, was this leading?

"Well, I represent someone," said Lev, setting the painting, still covered, on a chair and angling it towards Abraham, "and I've seen her, and I know she's perfectly presentable. In fact, I'd say she's very presentable. However, she is so shy, so modest, she insisted on this portrait – a painting, in my experience, that is unique."

He whipped the cloth away. The painting in the

dull gold frame showed a woman painted from behind, side on. Her head was covered and her hair and neck were hidden. Of the face, the head being turned to the right, only a thin sliver of forehead, cheekbone, ear and chin were visible. There was nothing to see but, from the position of the head, the slope of the shoulders and the fall of the arm, Abraham was certain this was Rahel. But how was it possible? It just must be someone who looked like Rahel. She had no sister, he remembered that clearly, but perhaps this was a niece?

That was the moment when he noticed how the head was angled. The sitter was looking at her hands. There was a very good reason for this. Between the finger and thumb of her right hand the sitter held a gold ring at a curious angle to the plane of the painting. Her gaze, though hidden, was obviously absorbed by this object.

He bent forward to see the ring better and now that he did it seemed very familiar. Or did he simply wish to believe it was the ring he had once had made?

"Do you mind if I lift it over to the light?" he asked.

"So it interests you after all?" said Lev. It was just as he had calculated. The bright bookish Abraham was intrigued precisely because this portrait was unique.

"Please, be my guest," continued Lev. "You can

look at the painting for as long and as closely as you want."

Abraham picked the painting up and carried it over to the window. Bright hard spring sunlight shone through the thick greeny glass. Abraham tilted the portrait until it caught the light. He stared at the inside of the ring. There did seem to be something written there. He felt an incredible rush of excitement and at the same time, in another part of his intelligence, he thought, this was a ridiculous delusion. He had been in the guest-room. He had seen the soot-blackened walls. He had smelt the charred rafters. His ring had melted. The caretaker had said so, hadn't he? It was preposterous and absurd to imagine anything else.

But what words did the spidery letters he could just make out form?

Holding the portrait he lowered his face and lowered it again. The closer he got the less of the portrait he saw, and the larger the ring became. Gradually the letters swam into focus. When his face was so close to the canvas that he could smell the oil in the paint, the blur resolved into three words:

Kaja loves Rahel

This was the ring. This was the ring he had given her.

Why was it in this painting? He came up with the only logical explanation. It was painted before the fire, as a surprise for him. It pre-dated her death and somehow it had made its way from Prague to Amsterdam where it had fallen into the hands of Lev. He had taken it into his head to bring it round and show it to him.

"You'd be surprised how many people want to see what's written inside that ring."

"'Kaja loves Rahel'."

Lev nodded. "Strange name to have on her ring," he continued, quietly. "I asked her who it was but she refused to say."

Abraham set the portrait down on the chair. What was he thinking? It was painted in Prague. That was preposterous. The sitter was Lev's client and must be very much alive.

"She's here in Amsterdam?"

"Of course she is. I saw her last week."

"Would you take an offer of marriage back to her?" Abraham asked. He said this calmly and quietly. He didn't want Lev getting excited.

"Of course I will but I want to warn you, she may be awkward."

"I thought she wanted a husband?"

"I think it's more her uncle who wants her to be married."

A cowbell clanged in the distance.

"I don't know this for certain," said Lev, "but I don't know how much she wants to. That's why she's had herself painted holding the ring. It's her way of saying, 'This is the man I love, whoever he is, here's his name, it's on my ring, and I will love nobody else'."

"So why bring this to me?"

"You're clever and I suspected, if she took your fancy, you might see a way around this problem."

Abraham went to his desk and took a piece of paper. He dipped his pen in his inkwell and wrote these words in large bold letters:

Kaja still loves Rahel though now he is
called Abraham.

He blotted the paper, folded it over and handed it to Lev.

"You give her that," he said, "with my offer of marriage. This time she will agree, I promise. Tell her I will come to her uncle's at midday tomorrow. Report back to me that she agrees."

Lev called on Max Berger the wine merchant that evening. He handed Rahel the piece of paper. She read it. She shouted with joy.

"He wants to marry you," said Lev, "the man who wrote that."

The proposal was accepted. Lev returned to Abraham with the news.

That night Abraham wrote to Milan. He confessed everything. He was not in Venice and he was not training to be a doctor. He was in Amsterdam. He had converted. And he was marrying Rahel.

Milan wrote back:

> *My son,*
>
> *How could you? How could you have let me believe you were in Venice all these years training to be a doctor, when all along you were following a completely different course? I know what your answer is. I wouldn't have let you follow the path you'd chosen had I known you wanted to follow it. I would have stopped you. You are right, I probably would. I wouldn't have wanted you to leave what you were brought up to be and transform yourself into something else.*
>
> *I am also old and age, even if it does not bring wisdom, certainly brings a little humility. When you're young and lusty and twenty you think you can bend anyone and anything to your will. You think there is nothing on this earth that cannot be*

done or achieved. This is wrong. If another human being, having consulted their conscience, chooses to follow an alternative course to the one you would have had them follow, there is nothing to be done about it. You can't make people do what you want, especially when faith and love are involved. They will follow their star and that is the end of the matter. I know that. This is really what it is to be old. You have the ability to hold two contradictory ideas in your head at the same time. In my case, I believe I would have stopped you and I know, at the same time, I could not.

Now you are going to be married. I have been invited to attend. I am afraid, my dear boy, that because of who and what I am, I can't, I shan't, I won't. You see, just as I cannot make you do what you do not want, nor can you make me do what I don't want to do either. We must all be free to make our own choices.

Nonetheless, do not take from this that I am bitter or heart-sore or resentful. You have left our faith and the faith of our fathers in order to marry the woman you love. You believe this is the right course. Your judgment was always sound and I have no doubt you have made the right choice, for you.

I wish you, therefore, a long marriage, healthy

*children, a good and contented life. It will be yours
too. I am sure. Please remember me to Rahel, whom
I always liked, and please assure her that I do not
blame her any more than I blame you for this. There
must be a reason for what happened and in the
fullness of time that will become obvious.*

The wedding was solemnised with great joy. At least
Mikhel and Eva Berger were in attendance. Following
the ceremony, Abraham and Rahel remained in
Amsterdam. Milan died two years later without having
ever seen his son or his daughter-in-law. His son's
deception and conversion had hurt. But he knew his
son had done what he had because he was in love, not
because he was bad. Milan bequeathed his entire
estate to the young couple. If they can, a parent will
always try to forgive a child.

Abraham and Rahel returned to Bohemia and
before long they called on Rabbi Loew. They wished
to establish a school for Jews paid for with some of
the money generated by the estate Abraham
inherited. They found Loew in the courtroom.
Joseph, as usual, was sitting on the wood box in
the corner.

"I see," said Rahel, pointing at Joseph, whom she
recognised now as the giant who had come with the

sack, his face covered in a scarf, "you like to keep your angel snug and warm by the stove."

"I do," said Rabbi Loew, "I have to keep him warm."

During the conversation that followed Abraham pledged ten per cent of rents he received to the ghetto.

38

The end of Joseph

After the couple left, Rabbi Loew started thinking. He thought about all that had happened during the ten years that Joseph had lived in his house. There had been some extraordinary changes. Father Tadeus was gone. There had been no real trouble between the communities since he left. Even when Abraham, a convert, inherited his father's estates and title, there was no trouble.

Whilst there was trouble it was vital to have the golem. Without Joseph the rabbi did not doubt Father Tadeus would have succeeded. The Jews would have been driven out of Prague. But now those old dangers were over and in their place there were new ones. Joseph was a powerful figure. In the right hands, guided by the right man, he was a force for good. But in the wrong hands, guided by the wrong man, he would be a force for bad. What if the rabbi died suddenly and Joseph fell under the sway of someone who used him to do harm? As the incident in the festive room showed, when Joseph unwittingly flooded the house by following Pearl's instructions literally, this was not impossible. In Loew's absence, an authoritative figure who understood that the key to Joseph was clear orders, could easily have him doing their bidding, whatever that was, even if it was bad.

After several hours of thought, the rabbi came to his conclusion. He wrote to his former pupil Jacob Gintzberg in Friedburg. He told him to be in Prague on a certain day. He advised Isaac, his son-in-law, to be ready on the same day.

A fortnight later, the rabbi and his two helpers marched into the courtroom.

"Joseph," said the rabbi.

Joseph sprang off his box.

"Follow us."

The party went up to the room right at the very top of the building. This was where Joseph pretended to sleep on the night Lehmann was taken by the police. It was a storeroom really, almost hidden under the eaves of the synagogue building. No one ever came there.

"Lie on the bed, Joseph," said the rabbi. He pointed at the small dusty bed in the middle of the room.

Joseph lay down.

"Close your eyes."

"Right, everybody down to the head," said Rabbi Loew. The three men went to the top of the bed. They surveyed the golem's face with its heavy eyelids down.

Rabbi Loew left the younger men and began to circle the figure, moving anti-clockwise, reciting under his breath as he went. Joseph's finger ends twitched and jumped as his nails receded. All over his hefty hands the hair that grew there receded. The hair on his head receded. His eyebrows vanished. The hair disappeared from his nape and his ears. Then his pink skin began losing its crinkles and dimples as well as its colour.

Rabbi Loew finished his circuits and returned to his place. Joseph now looked as if he was made of compacted ash.

"Now, Jacob," said Rabbi Loew, "you will walk around the golem seven times in the same direction as I went, and as you do say these words under your breath."

He whispered the words into Jacob's ear. Jacob began his circuits. The room became as cold as a bitter winter night.

Jacob finished and returned to his place.

Joseph had turned to ice. Rabbi Loew and the others could see through his head, as if through glass, to the pillow below.

"Isaac," said the rabbi, "I want you to walk around the golem seven times, going from left to right and as you do, whisper these words."

He spoke the words into Isaac's ear. Isaac walked seven times around Joseph reciting under his breath.

As Isaac completed the seventh circuit the ice began to cloud. The temperature rose. Joseph turned to clay.

They covered the body with prayer shawls and phylacteries and left the room. Rabbi Loew locked the door behind them.

The next day Rabbi Loew walked to the Moldau and threw the key in the river. Then he walked home. He had a carpenter nail planks over the door of the attic room within which Joseph was lying. Then from his courtroom, he made two official pronouncements that were then promulgated throughout the ghetto. The first was that the attic room he had had sealed was never, under any circumstances, to be entered no matter what was heard coming from within. Second, he gave notice that Joseph the Mute had left in a rage and he doubted whether he would ever return.

The rabbi himself lived on for several years. He died in 1609 at the age of ninety-six. He was buried in the Old Jewish Cemetery, in the former Jewish quarter. He lies – or his remains lie – in a large chiseled vault covered by thousands of little stones, with thirty of his closest followers buried in a circle around him.

39

Claude's story

The high-pitched cry of a hawk came from above. Saul looked up without thinking. The canopy overhead was all dark green except for the little bright points where the sun streamed through. It was like the night sky scattered with stars.

Saul looked back at Claude. He was silent and still. Was this the end? wondered Saul. He glanced sideways. The grown-ups were sitting motionless. They didn't think it was over. They'd have been clapping otherwise, he thought.

That was the moment he noticed a shaft of sunlight that had squeezed through a hole in the canopy above and was now slanting past just in front of him. He stared into the column of light. He saw little dancing specks of dust. He followed the shaft to the ground. Here, it formed a sharp bright line. It looked like the edge of a buried coin sticking out of the forest floor.

'I presume,' said Claude, 'you are all wondering how I know this story. It is easily explained.

'Isaac – he was married to Loew's daughter – wrote the story down. This was after Rabbi Loew's death. He placed his manuscript in the rabbinical library in Prague.

'Unfortunately, at some point it got knocked off its shelf and fell into the space between the shelves and the wall behind.

'And there it stayed for centuries, until that is, I entered the story.

'I was in Prague. This was before this war. It was 1936. I was in the old rabbinical library. I needed the marriage documents of my grandparents who were married in Prague when it was part of Austria-Hungary.

'The library was somewhat less than it had been in its heyday. It was now a great document dump. I just had to start looking. It was slow work but not unpleasant. And whenever I got bored with my own quest, I explored. The library was crammed with the most extraordinary books and wonderful papers.

'One afternoon, marching about, I came across a book that interested me. I don't even remember what it was.

'I had a look at it and I was about to put it back when I noticed that there was something trapped between the back of the shelf and the wall behind. It looked like a cloth bundle.

'I must find out what this bundle is, I thought. This

wasn't easy – but I got it out. By now my hands felt itchy and dry from the centuries-old dust that leaked out of the sacking and on to my skin.

'The bundle was tied with ancient ribbon. The seams were closed with blobs of sealing wax. With my penknife I sliced the ribbon. It was so old it didn't cut, it dissolved. I ran my blade along the seam. The medallions of sealing wax crumbled like brittle mortar. I peeled the sacking away. Inside there was a pile of papers with writing all over them.

'At that moment the clock in the square began to strike four. I was born at four in the afternoon, 4 April, 1904. Four was my number and now here I was hearing the bell chime four times. This was a sign, I thought. It had to be. These papers must be intended for me.

'I began to read. My Hebrew was rusty. No, my Hebrew was terrible. But I understood enough. This was the missing account of the clay golem who lived in Prague. My grandparents had told me this story as a boy. I had thought it was just a fairy tale. But here, in my hand, I had the actual account of what really happened.

'I will take it with me, I thought. No one will notice. They don't know they have it so they won't miss it.

'I had a briefcase. I opened it. I put in the

manuscript. I closed it. All I had to do was to walk out.

'I decided I would practice walking briskly with the briefcase in my hand. I didn't want the man on the front door to catch me stealing. I picked up my briefcase. It felt as if there were two lead bricks in the bottom. I opened the briefcase, took the papers out, and weighted them. They felt light. I put them back in the briefcase. It felt heavy again. So it seemed I wasn't meant to steal them.

'At this point I had a better idea. I got this jotter. This very one I'm holding here.'

Claude waved the exercise book he had read from. Saul knew perfectly well that it came from Henri but he liked this story he was hearing far better than the truth.

'And I copied the whole story out,' continued Claude, 'not in Hebrew, but in French.

'The work went slowly. I wanted the story but with my embellishments. When you take a story on, you must make it yours. You must change it. In this way you make it your own. Otherwise, when you come to tell it, your version won't sing.

'It took me a week to complete my task. Then I put the bundle back where I found it.

'You are wondering why? I will tell you. I didn't want this version by Rabbi Isaac floating around and competing with mine when I gave it to the public. That was my intention, you see. First I was going to publish the golem. Then there would be a stage version – a musical of course – and perhaps even a film.

'But none of this happened. Events got in the way. The time was never right. Until now that is.

'So, finally, it is done. Ladies and gentleman, I thank you, for I have at long last, given you my golem.'

It was as he removed his glasses and went to bow that they all heard the barking of dogs in the distance. The entire audience stood and turned as one. They stared out across the pine forest, in the direction from which the barking came. It came from the road.

40

The surprise attack

Saul crouched down and grasped his spear without thinking. He would defend himself. He would go down fighting. They would not take him alive.

'Saul,' he heard his father say. His father's voice was sharp and cold. 'Run Saul, run and do not stop.'

He pointed away to the side, away from the direction from which the barking came.

'I told you – run!'

His father pushed him hard.

'Go on,' he said, 'run.'

Saul received another shove. It was a rule. He must always do what his father said. So he turned and began to run . . .

He ran and he did not stop even when he heard gunfire behind. Eventually he came to the road. He guessed he was a couple of miles on from the olive harvester's storeroom. He decided to go back there. Staying just inside the forest's edge, he doubled back until he found himself opposite the building.

The tarmac here had oil spots on it. The brush at the edge of the forest was broken. There were four spent Luger cartridges lying in the grass. A dog had made a large black mess by a tree. This, he guessed, was where they started with their dogs. And they must have returned here after they had finished. His mother, his father, and the others, he guessed, were still in the forest. Did he dare go and find them? No he decided. He did not.

He decided instead to cross the road. He would spend the night in the harvester's storeroom. In the morning he would decide what to do next. He might go back into the forest and get water. He might even go to the cave and find some food. He might even find them. But for now, he would stay here.

There was nothing coming in either direction. It was a still, utterly calm, late summer's afternoon. He walked across the tarmac taking care to avoid the oil puddles the German vehicles had left.

As he got close to the other side, he saw something lying on the grass. His heart trembled for he knew by the red cover what it was.

Saul picked it up and ran in through the storehouse door. It was hot inside the building and it smelt of dust and sacking and cigarette smoke. There was a butterfly beating its wing against a tile overhead.

He stared at what he had in his hands. It was Claude's book. He leafed through it slowly. Page after page was covered in Claude's tiny handwriting. It was all in pencil of course. He couldn't read it. His reading wasn't nearly good enough.

He stuck the exercise book down inside his shirt. He would look at it later. He sat down on the mattress and put his spear down on the floor. He was numb. He stared out the door at the road and the patch of sunlight that lay across it. Gradually the light leeched away. Evening was coming. Suddenly, he heard footsteps and quiet voices. The Germans had come back for him. His heart raced. He jumped up and bolted out the door and collided instantly with a soldier in green fatigues. As he fell sideways he closed his eyes. This was it. He was finished. And he hadn't even had a good stab at one with his spear. How could he? In his panic he'd left it behind inside.

He hit the ground. The shooting was going to start any second now, he thought. Instead, he heard someone speaking. It didn't sound like German. It turned out to be Polish. They were soldiers from the Eighth Army.

A Moroccan serving with the Free French forces was found somewhere and brought in to translate. Saul told the story of his day in French. The story was relayed to the Poles. The soldiers decided to search the forest.

As dusk was gathering, and armed with torches, they set off, Saul leading. He brought them to the place where Claude had read his story. Everyone was scattered around here, except for Agatha, and they were all dead.

41

The rescue

The soldiers brought Saul to a camp by jeep. One of the soldiers then brought him to an open-air canteen. An army cook gave Saul a tin plate of corned beef and dried crackers. He devoured the faintly greasy compacted meat in seconds, then turned and promptly vomited what he had just eaten on to the grass. After a diet of mushrooms, nuts, wild fruits and rabbit, he could not hold the rich meat in his belly.

'Oh dear,' said the cook. 'You're not very well, are you?'

Saul stared back at the army cook. He did not speak English. He did not understand him. At the back of Saul's throat was the acid taste that was always there after one was sick. He spotted a brown enamel cup on a trestle table and pointed at it.

'Oh, you want something to drink,' said the cook. 'I have tinned milk but I don't think we'll risk that. I think a cup of weak milky tea's all you can manage. And then I think we'll try you on some toast.'

That night Saul slept in a tent. The canvas was brown and the ground sheet smelt of dry grass. He woke in the morning to the sound of men chattering and singing. He poked his head out between the front flaps. He saw the row of tents that were opposite his tent when he went to sleep were gone. Only the oblongs of flattened grass testified to their existence. The camp, he vaguely understood, was being dismantled.

Later that morning Saul was taken by jeep again to a town hall. He was put in a room. It was filled with children. A doctor came and listened to everyone's chest through a stethoscope. When the doctor finished another man came and shouted in French, 'Everyone out, everyone into the square.'

The children obeyed. In the square they found a long blue bus waiting.

The driver shouted, 'Everyone get on board.'

Saul and the other children crowded on. The bus had been standing in the sun and the wooden seats were hot. It smelt of mint and disinfectant and dust.

The bus set off. The bus drove for several hours. The bus stopped.

'Everyone out,' shouted the driver.

Saul was the last to get off. At the bottom of the steps he found himself standing on a gravel square. There was a white flagpole. The French flag fluttered from the top. Ranged around the square were gloomy wooden bunkhouses. This was some sort of camp, he guessed. He remembered his spear. He would have liked to have it now. He did not know where he was or what was going to happen. He slipped his hand inside his jacket. He touched Claude's exercise book. He still had that at least.

'Quiet, everyone,' shouted a woman, though none of the children were talking. She wore a blue dress and a hat. She was a nurse.

'This is a camp for displaced and homeless minors,' she explained. 'You will stay here until your family members can be located, and you can be sent home. In the meantime, you will be cared for. We will feed and clothe you. We will give you somewhere to sleep. You will now follow me to the main assembly hall where you will be processed.'

The children followed the nurse to a hall with blacked-out windows and buckets of sand in the corners.

'I want boys at that end and girls at this end,' shouted the nurse.

The children separated into two groups.

'I want the boys to follow that man,' the nurse shouted.

The boys followed the man to a changing room.

'You are to undress,' the man shouted. 'Pile your

clothes there and form a line here. The barber will shave your heads. You will then shower.'

Saul undressed and joined the line of naked boys. He still had Claude's exercise book. He covered himself with it. His turn finally came. He sat in the barber's chair. The plastic seat was cold but sticky on his bare skin.

'What's that?' the barber asked, indicating the exercise book.

'It's my book of stories,' said Saul.

The barber brusquely set to work with a set of clippers. Each time the barber squeezed the handle, two sets of blades moved in opposite directions, cutting the hair caught between the teeth. Sometimes the strands of Saul's hair weren't cut completely and the barber would have to remove them by wrenching his implement. This hurt. Tears filled Saul's eyes but he said nothing.

'Right, that's you done,' said the barber.

Saul opened his eyes. His head was down. He saw the barber's right leg was shorter than his left one. He wore a raised boot and calipers. Saul went to stand.

'May I see that?'

Saul looked up. The barber was a middle-aged man with a toothbrush moustache and a pointed nose.

'Your book.'

He took the exercise book gently and began to leaf through the pages covered with Claude's small precise writing.

'There's a lot of writing in here,' said the barber. 'Did you do this?'

Saul shook his head.

'Your parents?'

'It was Claude's,' Saul said.

'Who's Claude?'

'He was in the cave with us,' said Saul quickly, then he blushed. He remembered what his father always said. 'Whatever anyone asks, you are always to say nothing.'

'So you were in a cave?' said the barber, curiously.

Saul said nothing.

'Where?'

Saul looked at the floor. He saw hair, his own and that of other boys, piled about like small drifts of snow.

'You can say you know,' the barber said. 'You're safe. The war's over. You don't have to keep secrets any more.'

'I want my book,' said Saul, looking up.

'Have your shower,' said the barber. 'I'll hold it. I'll keep it safe. I promise. Go on now. I've dozens more heads to shave today. I'm not going anywhere. Go and shower and then come back for it.'

Saul walked backwards to the shower, keeping the barber in view. When he was under the streaming water, he again kept the barber in view. As soon as he got out of the shower, he wrapped a towel around himself and walked back to the barber.

'Can I have my book?'

The barber laughed and stopped work. The barber took Claude's exercise book from a little table where he had set it and passed it back to Saul.

'What are the stories about? You can surely tell me that.'

Saul considered. There was no harm in that Saul decided.

'It's about the golem.'

'What's that?' the barber asked.

'It's a man made of clay. He can't talk much, well just a few words, but he has powers,' Saul said.

'You'd better get in line for the doctor.'

The barber pointed across the room to a table where a doctor sat with a nurse standing behind. In front of the table stood a line of dripping boys.

Saul moved off, heading for the back of the line.

'And don't lose that book,' the barber called.

When it was his turn the doctor examined Saul all over. The nurse took him away then and sprayed him with DDT. Then he went to another room where an elderly woman measured him brusquely and handed him a set of clothes and boots.

Later he was marched to a dining room. He was fed spaghetti with a watery meat sauce.

Later still, Saul and nineteen other boys were marched to a bunkhouse, number 36A. Inside the bunkhouse, Saul was assigned a lower tier bunk, number twelve.

Saul stood by his bunk motionless. He was aware of the other children around him. Some were talking, some were shouting, some were laughing, some were crying quietly. One or two were climbing onto their bunks and testing the mattresses for softness. Saul waited. He knew how to be patient. He let the hubbub grow and when he judged the other boys were all so involved in their activities they would not notice, he reached inside his shirt. In a single fluid movement he then pulled out his exercise book, lifted his mattress, laid his book face-down on the slats below and then dropped the mattress back in place. He felt a small surge of relief. First he found the exercise book in the forest. Then he managed to hold on to it. Now he had managed to hide it.

42

The interview

Some days later Saul found himself sitting in a small room in the camp office block. There was a battered filing cabinet with a grimy tin ashtray on top. The blackout paint on the windows was only partially scraped away.

'I'm going to ask you some questions,' said the man behind the desk. He had a prominent Adam's apple and it moved as he talked. His name was Frederic. 'You must tell me the truth. We won't be able to help you if you don't. You have to help us. You have to tell us everything. With that information we will then find your relatives or family members. Do you understand?'

Saul nodded. It was probably safe to talk to these people. He had come to this conclusion after watching the camp officials very carefully over the preceding days.

The man took the cap off his fountain pen and stuck it on the other end. He smoothed a piece of paper with the flat of his left hand. He wrote the date and time in the top left-hand corner of the sheet.

'Jewish?'

Saul nodded.

'Name?' he said.

'Saul.'

'What's your other name?'

'Roth.'

'Date of birth?'

Saul looked into the air. He had been told it. He did used to know this. But he'd forgotten. He shook his head.

'I don't know.'

'Don't worry. Hopefully we can find your records.'

'How old are you?'

Saul considered this. He was eleven.

'Eleven,' he said, cautiously, not quite certain where this was leading.

'So we can say the year of your birth was 1933?'

That number seemed correct.

'Yes,' said Saul.

'Place of birth? Do you know that?'

Saul felt a twinge of relief. He was on much firmer ground here.

'Nice.'

'Name of father?'

'Alphonse.'

'His place of birth?'

Saul shrugged. He thought his father was born in Alexandria, Egypt, but he wasn't quite certain.

'What's your mother's name?'

'Mina.'

'Place and date of birth?'

He knew she was from Nice. He tried to say Nice. It was what he wanted to say. But the word wouldn't come out. Instead, he got a sore feeling at the back of his throat and a trembling deep inside somewhere between his stomach and his spine. He knew those telltale feelings. Oh please don't let me cry, he thought, I don't want to cry.

Since he came to the camp he had kept all thoughts of his parents at bay. Every time a memory threatened to enter his mind, he had pushed it ruthlessly away. He hadn't cried once. But now everything he had kept out was about to get in.

He made his fists into balls and closed his eyes. It was pointless. The space behind his lids was suddenly flooded with salty water. Drops forced their way out and dribbled down his face and over his lips. A great sob ran through him. He realised it was now possible to say the word he was unable to say before.

'Nice,' he said.

He put his wrists against his eyelids and pressed them backwards, to stem the flow. It was pointless. The tears continued to force their way out. They wet his wrists and the backs of his hands as well as pouring down his face. He wiped the arm of his jersey over his face. This was pointless too. All he managed was to redistribute the wet from the front to the side of his head. He swallowed and dropped his arm to his lap. He let the tears flow on but kept his eyes closed. This way, at least he would not feel the shame of crying in front of a stranger.

As the tears flowed and his face burned, the man went on asking questions and Saul went on answering. He gave the names and rough ages of his brothers Robert and Francis, and his sister Nelly. He gave the names and rough ages of his Uncle Hugo and his Aunt Ida and his cousins, their children, Marcel, Rozette and Leon. He gave his family's last address in Nice. He gave his uncle's last address. He gave the names of his uncle's theatres. He gave the name of his family dentist and the name of his kindergarten. He was less successful with Claude and Agatha; he could only manage their first names. He described his last day, his escape, and the discovery of the bodies.

'This English woman, Agatha you say her name is, you didn't see her body?' asked the man.

Saul opened his eyes and looked over at him. He shook his head. That was right. He hadn't seen her body. It suddenly occurred to him that Agatha was still alive. A feeling of bitter rage welled up. Why should she be the one to live? Couldn't it have been his mother or his father or anyone else but her?

He got up and saw the ashtray on top of the filing cabinet. He picked it up and hurled it at the opposite wall. It bounced off the plaster and hit the floor with a bang.

'You stupid boy,' the man shouted. 'Sit down.' He slapped Saul, once, across the face.

Saul sat on his seat, put his arms on the desk and then buried his face in the crook of his elbow.

'You're not going to get anywhere by throwing things around,' said Frederic sternly. 'The only way we're going to be able to help you is if you tell us what you know. Everything you know. Then we can try to find somebody who knows you. This Agatha may be the only person left who knows you. And maybe she is even trying to find you now.'

'Nah – nah – nah – nah,' Saul chanted. He would blot out the words of the man with the bobbing Adam's apple. He should have stuck to what his father always said. He would tell this man nothing in future.

After this initial interview, Frederic attempted

several more conversations. Saul refused to speak at these. This made Frederic angry. He called Saul stupid and selfish and unhelpful. He told Saul he would spend the rest of his life in an orphanage.

43

Looking for Agatha

Saul woke and lay quite still, his eyes closed. Where was he? He asked this same question every morning on waking now.

He was in bunk number twelve, he told himself, in his bunkhouse which was 36A. He sniffed his sheet and blanket where they touched his nose. His sheet smelt of soap. His blanket smelt of a chemical that he had been told was called camphor. The bedding also smelt of DDT. It was a common smell in the camp. The auxiliaries spent their every waking hour, or so it seemed to Saul, spraying DDT everywhere in order to stop infestation. Despite these efforts the nurse, when combing Saul's hair, had found lice three times since he arrived.

He opened his eyes. He looked up at the underside of the bunk above. It was made of rough pine planks. There were French names and dates scored everywhere. He went to school now every day. His reading was coming along. He could read what was

written. Immediately above his face there was a
heart with an arrow through the middle, the name
Colette at the top and Michel below along with the
date, April 1941.

Now the war was over, this was a camp for
displaced children and minors. But during the war, it
was a camp for conscripted labourers. This was where
they were held before they were sent to Germany to
work. Michel, Saul guessed, like everyone else who
had scrawled their name on the bottom of the bunk,
was one of these.

The boards creaked and bowed as the boy in the
bunk above turned. This was Tobias, a twelve year old
from Bordeaux. Like Saul his family were dead, and
like Saul the authorities were trying to discover
someone from his family who was still alive and would
be prepared to take him.

Tobias settled in a new position and began to
breathe in the quiet constant way typical of a sleeper.
Saul listened to Tobias's breath as it slowly went in and
then out. A memory flitted into his thoughts . . .

It was a morning, in the cave, at the start of the
summer just gone, the one that was supposed to bring
liberation. He had woken early. The flour sacks and the
old coat under which he lay were slightly damp with
dew. He heard his mother and his father breathing

quietly in the cave. Then he realised he needed to pee. He got out of his cot quietly and slipped out of the mouth of the cave. The sun outside was hot and strong. He blinked and was then greatly surprised to see Agatha. She was just skirting the Cube rock. She came up to him, breathing heavily, her huge belly sticking out through her cotton dress.

'Look at these,' she said. She held up a bunch of wild flowers with short stems. He noticed red, blue and yellow petals.

'The early bird gets the worm,' she said. 'Well, in this case, the early bird got the flowers.'

She went into the cave and he headed off across the forest . . .

Saul turned on his side and looked across at the window. On the other side of the dirty glass grey light glimmered faintly. It was a little before dawn he guessed. He thought of Agatha again – not in a specific but in a general way. Frederic of the bobbing Adam's apple had mentioned her only the day before. His manner had been surprisingly pleasant, and even very slightly excited on this occasion, even though, as usual, Saul said nothing. As the number of English women called Agatha who had spent the war in the south of France was so small, the man assured Saul there was a very good chance of finding her.

Saul now considered this information. They were looking for Agatha. They thought they would find her. Did this mean he would live with Agatha? He decided that yes, this was probably what that did mean.

His thoughts drifted on. He wondered what this would be like? It was true that Agatha was irritating. She cried a lot in the cave and she was sad much of the time but the day of the golem story she had been so happy.

On the other hand, he remembered, she would have had her baby by now. He hoped it was a boy and not a girl. That way, if he did end up with Agatha, and he guessed it was probably the case that he would, he could be sure of having someone to play with. When the baby was older of course. But what age would that be? He tried to work this out but gave up.

He tuned in the breathing sounds made by all the other boys in the bunkhouse. He never tired of this noise. It had given him pleasure in the cave, that morning he woke early and before he went out and met Agatha with the flowers. And it gave him pleasure now. It was such a gentle comforting sound. What was more, or so it seemed to Saul, they were all breathing in and then out more or less in unison. But that's what always happened, wasn't it? At night, when people slept together, they always fell into step.

44

The collaborators

As Saul sat eating a piece of bread and cheese, a soldier came into the dining room. He wore a great coat and a steel helmet. He looked extremely young.

The soldier clapped his hands and told the children to be quiet.

'There are no classes this afternoon,' he shouted. 'As soon as you have finished eating, you are all to proceed to the square at the front of the camp. Do you understand?'

'Why, are we going to the seaside?' a child shouted out.

'No, you are not,' replied the soldier. He smirked and shook his head. 'It's October,' he continued. 'Why would you be going to the seaside now?'

There was silence while the children considered this.

'No,' continued the soldier, 'you're going to see justice this afternoon.' Then he turned and walked out of the dining hall.

When Saul got to the square he found there were

already several hundred adults standing in a circle under a clear blue sky. The crowd was talking in low voices. He did not like or entirely trust the atmosphere he sensed.

There was something of interest in the middle of the circle so he slipped through the adults. When he got to the front he found a table with a couple of officials sitting at it. Beside the table were a barber's chair and the barber, the one who had shaved his head. The barber was smoking.

From the road came the sound of a lorry. The crowd closest to the road fell back. A flat-bed lorry pulled up. There were soldiers in the back along with a number of women. Several members of the crowd began to shout and jeer. From the crowd a stone arched through the air and hit a woman on the arm. A soldier in the back of the lorry lifted his arm and shouted, 'Quiet.' The crowd fell quiet but Saul could tell their mood was ugly and resentful.

Two soldiers brought a woman down from the lorry, through the crowd and up to the table. One of the officials asked the woman her name.

The woman whispered her reply.

'You weren't always so behind when it came to talking to Germans,' someone in the crowd shouted. There was nasty laughter.

The other official picked up a piece of paper and began to read out the statement typed up on it. The language was far too complex for Saul to understand but he noticed the words 'fraternisation' and 'collaboration' were repeated several times. It was the woman's reaction to the statement that really impressed Saul. As the official read the woman shook her head and began to cry. Every now and again the official stopped reading and told her to be quiet. This made no impression on the woman whatsoever.

When he finished the official asked the woman if she had anything to say. She suddenly lunged sideways, as if she was about to run, but the soldiers were too quick for her. They caught her by the arms.

'Hang her,' someone shouted.

The official who had read the statement raised his hand, to indicate silence, and nodded at the soldiers. They led the woman away, not towards the lorry but in the other direction, towards the closest bunkhouse. They pulled her up the steps and disappeared inside. The door slammed.

There was silence and a great feeling of expectancy. Whatever was happening in the bunkhouse, Saul had no doubt it was ugly.

The bunkhouse door banged open. There was the woman again with the two soldiers. She was wearing her coat, the one she had been wearing before, and she was holding the coat tightly at the neck.

The soldiers brought the woman back through the crowd and pushed her into the barber's chair. The crowd whistled and clapped. The woman's feet, Saul noticed, were bare. Her shoes and stockings were gone. The barber put his hand into the pocket of his overall and took out a pair of scissors. Then he grasped a clump of the woman's hair. It was brown and long. He cut the clump at the bottom and dropped it on the gravel. There was a round of applause.

The barber cut off the rest of the woman's hair. He didn't cut it neatly. When he finished, though her hair was shorn, little tufts stuck up here and there from her scalp. To Saul, these tufts looked like feathers on a bird's head.

The official, the one who read the statement, said something. The soldiers lifted her by her arms and began to march her back towards the flat-bed lorry. The gravel hurt her feet and mixed now with her tears of shame were little cries of pain.

The crowd parted to let her through. There was jeering and catcalling. A young girl in a black dress – she was about Nelly's age Saul guessed – suddenly lifted the woman's coat from behind. The woman was naked underneath and at the sight of her bare white bottom the crowd roared again.

A few moments later a second woman was brought. The process was repeated all over again. It was then repeated twelve more times, for there were fourteen women in all up before the tribunal.

When justice had been dispensed the flat-bed lorry drove away with the women and the crowd began to disperse. Frederic appeared in a long black coat and a hat.

'You're to go back to the bunkhouse, Saul,' he said. 'Everyone's to go back to his or her bunkhouse. You're to wait there until you hear the call for the evening meal.'

45

The story begins again

Saul walked back across the camp. Dusk was coming and the electric lights had gone on in several buildings and showed through the windows. While standing and watching the dispensation of justice, Saul hadn't noticed the temperature. But now he did. He was cold, he realised, and what was more, it was cold. He could see his breath as he exhaled.

He reached 36A. He climbed the two steps, opened the door and went in. The electric lights were on in here as well, but the bulbs only produced a feeble yellow light. The interior was dark and gloomy but there was enough light for Saul to be able to see. He noticed the empty bunks first. These had belonged to boys who had been collected by relatives. If he had allowed himself to think about them and the life they now enjoyed which was surely better than his – he would have been envious and resentful. But he didn't let himself think about them. He could control his thoughts when he had to. He had a talent for that.

So bunkhouse 36A was a little less crowded than when he arrived, but there were still plenty of boys living in there and of these he saw several now. They were lying on their bunks with their faces to the walls. These included Tobias, the boy in the bunk above his. They were depressed, he guessed, and despondent. He felt the same way himself.

He walked to his own bunk and threw himself down. The mattress was lumpy and hard. He lay still for a moment. Then the idea came to him. His reading had improved. He was certain he could pull it off and what he couldn't read he could supply from memory.

He jumped up, lifted his mattress back and grabbed hold of the exercise book. He shook Tobias by the shoulder.

'Do you want to hear something?'

'What?'

'A story.'

'Why?'

Saul thought about this. It was a question he didn't know how to answer. All he had to hold on to was the conviction that this was absolutely the right thing to do.

He opened the exercise book and bent it back. He saw Claude's small neat words written in pencil, running across the first page from left to right. He made out the heading and then the first sentence below. Yes, there would be no difficulty. He could manage this. He coughed and then, in a flat trembling voice, he began to read.

By the end of the week Saul was reading to the entire bunkhouse. Word of this event trickled back to Frederic and one evening he slipped in to listen himself. The next day he wrote a short description of Saul Roth and the story he had heard him reading and he added that the only known living contact of the child was an English woman, called Agatha, who had lived in the Saint-Marie area throughout the war.

Frederic's appeal went off. It went to various agencies in France that were connected with displaced people. Among these was the hospital where Agatha was recuperating. An official read Frederic's circular and asked a nurse to pass a copy on to Agatha.

46

The end

Saul and Frederic walked down a corridor. They stopped at a door. Frederic grasped the handle.

'When you get in there,' said Frederic, 'will you try and smile?'

Saul said nothing.

Frederic turned the handle and threw the door open. Saul stepped forward and found himself in a small office with curtains on the window. The door closed behind. In front of him sat a woman on a chair. It was Agatha of course. But she didn't look like the woman he remembered as Agatha. She didn't have a bump at the front. She was slim. She was clean. She wore make up and a grey dress with a grey jacket.

'Hello, Saul,' she said.

Oh but it was Agatha, there was no doubt about it. That was her voice he was hearing all right.

Suddenly she jumped up so abruptly her chair fell back and hit the wooden floor. Then she ran two steps forward and put her arms around him. She kissed the top of his head and around his ears. She said his name over and over again. As she hugged and kissed him, she shook. He remained quite still.

Later, while Agatha smoked, he asked, 'What happened to my parents and everyone else?'

'Must you know?' asked Agatha.

He nodded. 'No one's said. I wasn't there. I'd run. You were there, though. Tell me what happened?'

'The policeman, Henri, you remember, the one who sent us things down in the basket?'

Saul nodded.

'He had a wife and, well, she didn't like me. She thought, after Liberation, it would be bad to have me running around. She thought it would be good if I was dead. Do you understand?'

Although he wasn't quite clear he understood exactly what he was being told, he knew better than to interrupt at this point.

'She had nothing against you or your family, or your uncle and his family or Claude. It was me she wanted done away with. So she waited until the Allies had landed, then she told the Germans where we were hiding. She thought, with the Allies being so close, you and your family would be rounded up and sent to a camp in the north but that they'd shoot me or something because they'd think I was a spy. I only found this all out much later, you understand. Are you following?'

He nodded.

'So they came. Your father told you to run. We all tried to flee in different directions. We all got caught. They came so quickly. And then what happened was the reverse of what Henri's wife hoped. They shot everyone else but they kept me alive. The officer in charge, he knew I would be extremely useful when he surrendered, as he knew he would have to. He would be able to say, "Look! Here's an English woman I saved from being shot".'

'And two days later this officer surrendered with me. He told the soldiers he'd saved me. I told them he hadn't and he'd had all these people shot. He was taken away. I heard later that he gave them a lot of intelligence information.'

She paused. She was quite close to the stub of the cigarette she was smoking. Saul watched as she took a fresh cigarette from the packet lying on the table, lit it with the stub and then threw the stub on the floor and trod it down. Careful as always, she lifted her foot away and checked that it was extinguished. Saul glanced down. The dead stub was like a flat white worm with a black head, he thought.

'Did you have your baby?' Saul asked quietly.

'Two days after I was liberated, I was in a tent and the baby started to come . . .'

'Did he have a name?'

'No,' she said, 'he didn't get a name. He didn't live that long. And I was too ill to even think what I would have called him. Of course I had some names before, but you don't know if a name's absolutely right until you see the baby, and I didn't. Well, I was told I held him but I don't remember that part, I was so very sick, which was why I had to stay in hospital for months afterwards.'

She stopped.

'If I had seen him,' she continued, 'I might have chosen Saul. I've always thought it was a lovely name. Like Paul, but at the same time not like Paul.'

Saul absorbed this piece of information without comment. He sensed something huge was about to be said. He guessed, as well, what it was. She wanted to take him with her, back to Eltham or wherever it was that she came from.

He stared at Agatha's face. It was long and quite bony. She'd been smoking so resolutely, the lipstick at the corners of her mouth had worn away while in the middle of her lips there was still plenty of it. Her eyes were dark and kind.

She was staring at him. He guessed she was trying

to read his expression. She was smiling, too. She wasn't family but at least he knew what she was like. On balance, all things considered, what else did he have other than the offer she was about to make?

The sources

Golem, the word, comes from the Hebrew *golem*, meaning shapeless mass. According to the complete Oxford English Dictionary, the golem, in Jewish legend, was 'a human figure made of clay, supernaturally brought to life'. It was Rabbi Loew of Prague, the entry explains, a real person, who 'blew the breath of life into the Golem of clay'. According to all the sources, this happened in February 1580.

Narrative accounts of the golem's creation and legendary deeds were carried first by word of mouth. Later, they were written down. In the writing of this novel I have mainly relied on two versions of the golem narrative that present the well-known outlines of the story in a direct and uncomplicated way.

The first is *The Golem or The Miraculous Deeds of Rabbi Liva*. This was published in 1909. The author was Yudl Rosenberg. This book was written in Yiddish but the author passed it off as a translation from Hebrew. It can be found in *The Great Works of Jewish Fantasy &*

Occult. Joachim Neugroschel, the compiler of this superb collection, was also the translator of *The Golem* into English.

Rosenberg's novel combines the old tradition of stories that celebrate great rabbis, with existing legends of the golem that are connected to Rabbi Loew of Prague, an historical figure.

As a read, Rosenberg's book is breezy, even racy. However, its apparent insouciance is designed to hide a deeply serious purpose. At the end of the nineteenth century, that is to say during the years immediately before Rosenberg published, the old idea that Jews murdered Christians and used their blood to make unleavened bread at Passover, an idea known in shorthand as the Blood Libel, had re-surfaced in Europe. In his novel, *The Golem*, Rosenberg sought to attack this idea by re-animating the ancient golem cycle that had been the literary response by Jews in the sixteenth century to this poisonous fantasy, as well as a compensatory narrative intended to buttress the self-esteem of a much put-upon community.

Rosenberg's novel inspired an episodic novel called *Golem: Legends of the Prague Ghetto* by Chayim Bloch.[1] This was originally published in German in 1919, and republished in English, in the USA, in 1923. Though

[1] And of course Leivick's play about the golem as well.

Bloch's work is duller and muddier than Rosenberg's is, I still found it useful.

As well as these two works, I also glanced at *The Golem*, by Gustav Meyrink first published in German in 1915. This disorientating work inspired both of Paul Wegener's films of the same name. (Only the second survives.) Meyrink's work was greatly admired by Jorge Luis Borges. It is superbly atmospheric but much less helpful with regards to narrative.

All additions to the golem cycle are of course my own.

The German Occupation of France in World War II

The German army invaded France in May 1940. The country was over-run in a couple of months. After signing separate armistices with Germany and Italy, the French National Assembly voted itself out of existence at Vichy on 10 July.

By the armistices France was divided into an occupied and an unoccupied zone (the latter being in the southern part of the country, with its capital at Vichy.) Thereafter, this part of France, the so-called Free Zone, was a totalitarian state. The Italian army occupied a small part of Vichy territory near the Italian border. This area amounted to eight departments, and included the city of Nice and part of the Côte d'Azur.

Vichy policy on the Jews was emphatically one of cooperation with the Germans. French Jews were rounded up and handed over. Italian policy was different to Vichy. The Italian authorities did not zealously round up and deport their Jews. As a result,

Jews living in Nice and on the Côte d'Azur survived. The area became a haven and several hundred Jewish refugees moved there.

On 11 November, 1942, on the pretext that an allied invasion was imminent, the German army occupied the Free Zone. Germans, with the exception of the Eight Departments occupied by the Italians, now controlled all of the territory of France.

On 8 September, 1943, Eisenhower, the American general, announced an armistice with Italy. This took Italy, which had been allied to Germany until this point, out of the war. The Germans immediately seized Italian trains and goods. Two days later, they moved into Nice. Unable to obtain lists of Jews in the possession of the Prefect of Nice, the Germans turned to more direct methods to find the Jews they knew were living in the town and Côte d'Azur. They raided hotels and boarding houses and they stripped men in the streets to see if they were circumcised. Those Jews caught during what was known as the 'human hunt', if they weren't shot on the spot, were shipped north to camps in Greater Germany.

A few Jews, however, managed to escape by going north. Here, they had two choices if they wanted to survive. They could either live semi-anonymously in villages and hope no one denounced them (Gabriel

Josipovici describes this course of action memorably in his remarkable memoir, *A Life*), or they could live rough in the countryside. Saul's family chooses the latter course.